Whatever his fate was, from now on, Dumont had the feeling it was decided and Colonel Zouak had only come to tell him.

After a moment Zouak said, 'I've brought you a woman.'

'You make it sound like a last cigarette, Colonel. Is that what you're offering me . . . a last woman before the firing squad?'

Zouak moved to the open window. He saw the flash of white as the woman came up the path. Then he turned to face Dumont, taking the prayer beads from his pocket.

They waited on in a silence broken only by the soft death-rattle of the beads, as they fell to and fro between his hands.

JOHN GILL

The Last Heroes

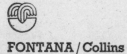

FONTANA / Collins

First published in 1973 by William Collins Sons & Co Ltd
First issued in Fontana Books 1976

© John Gill 1973

Made and printed in Great Britain by
William Collins Sons and Co Ltd Glasgow

For Pepi

It is not the courage of a man in the immediate past which explains his present prowess. . . . The connection between the self and its action is more like that between the hammer and its weight; the hammer is not the cause of the weight. But this removes the one remaining argument for determinism, and free-will seems to hold the field.

Encyclopædia Britannica

Brain research yields increasing evidence in favour of determinism, and against the concept of free-will.

New Scientist, 30 September, 1971

PROLOGUE

It was nearly three in the morning when Colonel Zouak decided to go and see the Englishman for the last time. Or the Frenchman. Or whatever else he was. Zouak wasn't quite sure because he still hadn't resolved the ambiguity of Dumont's nationality.

He opened the window of his small office but there was no trace of dawn in the sky – the sun was still far to the east beyond the *Haute Atlas*. He unhooked his mohair jacket from the louvred shutter where he'd hung it to air and put it on carefully. Then he took a flat half bottle of cognac and dropped it into a side pocket. It chinked faintly against his prayer beads but the incongruity didn't bother him.

It was a policeman's hour, he thought unhappily, when vitality was low and the life force was on the ebb. He smiled as he walked the bleak corridor towards the entrance, not altogether unconscious of the *banalité*. He wondered if Dumont would be awake. In a way he hoped not. So that he might let Dumont sleep on and show Dumont that he was capable of compassion.

He left by a side door in the building and stepped out into the hot aftermath of the night, which smelt faintly of musk and stale urine. An infant in a crumpled *djellabah* slept by the compound gate looking no bigger than a derelict newspaper. Zouak stepped carefully over him and went on down the row of cars until he came to the Citröen D.S.

He said softly, 'Wake up, Allal.'

As if he had jerked a string, Allal swayed upright behind the wheel. 'Colonel?'

'We are going to Béni Tanoute. Where is the woman?'.

Allal's finger pecked at the windscreen. 'She is there still . . . in the Peugeot.'

Colonel Zouak crossed the compound resetting his spectacles as he walked. They had dark, wrap-around lenses such as skiers wear, and they gave Zouak the bizarre appearance of an insect, as if they were some kind of antennae sensitive to other things than sight alone. As he came up to the coupé he noticed that it had yellow hire-car plates.

When he looked through the window Mrs Hoffman was curled in the reclining seat with her silk-trousered legs reaching up to the dashboard. Her hat and veil were perched on the steering wheel. Zouak rapped the glass with his talismanic ring.

He said clearly, 'Good morning, Mrs Hoffman. I am about to visit the Villa Menara now if you would like to follow me.'

She didn't speak but sat up carefully and lowered her face into her hands.

'Are you all right, Mrs Hoffman?'

The window lowered automatically as she pressed a button. 'Yes, I'm all right. What time is it?'

'About three o'clock.'

'Thank you for not forgetting me.'

'It is a policeman's misfortune not to be able to forget.'

For the second time that night he thought, Allah forgive me my *banalité*. 'Drive carefully when we leave the town . . . people will be coming into the markets by now.'

He walked back to his own car and as he climbed into the back seat the engine started and the lights came on. They followed the crumbling ochre-coloured wall to where the gate keeper was drawing the bolts on the compound door. As they swept out into the Boulevard Gouliman, the rear of the car was filled with a glare of light from the Peugeot behind.

They crossed Mohammed V Square with its crude neon signs and set off inland. Half-way down Avenue Barathon they had to stop for a string of donkeys crossing the road. There was a barrow on the corner selling mint tea and the kerosene lamp above it was black with insects.

The splendour of Casablanca's flowered avenues and the mansions and the institutional buildings gave place to trim villas, and eventually to the sad *bidonvilles* on the outskirts. When they reached the eucalyptus woods at last, Zouak leant forward to lower the window slightly. They had left the main highway and as they wound upward through the wood Zouak looked through the rear window again. The Peugeot was still there, its lamps dimmed by the dust pall, which looked lavender-coloured in the half-light.

After five kilometres they came suddenly to a tar-sealed surface again and shortly afterwards they forked right and began to climb amongst the unfinished villas of a small urbanisation. Where the road divided there was a modern older villa which, before independence, had been the home of a French *Colon*.

There were goatskin tents pitched below it and as the cars circled, the figures of the guard came doubling out. Up through the grove of mimosa and oleander, Colonel Zouak could see the orange square of light which told him that Dumont was awake. He ignored the guard and walked back to the Peugeot, where Mrs Hoffman already had the window down. 'I will send for you,' he said.

She nodded.

'If you are cold the guards have a charcoal fire. Shall I tell them to bring you tea?'

'No, thank you.'

Zouak turned and set off to the wrought-iron gates. As he passed the guard he waved vaguely. They were *chleuhs*, the tribe from the south, and one of them ran in front of him to open the gates.

As he walked on slowly up the path the *Mouddhin* began to chant from the mosque. '*Allah Akbar, Essehadou Muhamadu . . . Allah Akbar . . .*' The words were lost abruptly in the howling of a dozen dogs.

It was four o'clock.

The sentries standing in the shadow of the portico came silently to attention and one of them went forward to unlock the door for him. Zouak walked into the heavy antechamber, his shoes squeaking faintly on the stone floor. The door of the main room was open, throwing a shaft of light which sparkled on the metal inlay of the *terrazzo*. Zouak waited for a moment with hand in his pocket, clasping the prayer beads lightly.

Then from the shadow somewhere behind him Dumont said, 'Please go in. I heard the cars arrive.'

'You are awake, Captain Dumont.' Zouak walked on, hearing Dumont following. He crossed to the window and stood waiting. The chorus of dogs had died and the call of the *mouddhin* was audible again on the thin air. Zouak said, 'He is saying that it is better to pray than to sleep.'

'He can piss off.'

9

When Zouak turned, Dumont was lowering himself into a heavy empire chair. The supper tray beside him was untouched.

Dumont said, 'I'm sorry . . . that was unnecessarily offensive.'

His pitted, beefy face looked up steadily at Zouak and again Zouak was impressed with his indestructibility. Before independence Zouak had known other Frenchmen from that south-west region of France where Dumont's British passport said he had been born. Men had lived there in caves since the dawn of time. They had survived the beasts of prehistory and in modern times neither the Romans nor Richelieu nor the Third German Reich had been able to crush them. One could torture Dumont, hang him, burn him and stamp his dust into the desert but one could never reduce the memory of the way Dumont had once regarded one. In spite of the ski glasses, he felt compelled to turn away from him now, towards the window.

'In thousands of mosques the call is tape-recorded and broadcast through loudspeakers. They have forbidden it in Turkey . . . the Ministry of Religion there says that the hideous cacophony adds to environmental pollution.'

'You should have been a teacher, Colonel. You have a compulsion to inform. Isn't that a paradox in a policeman? A characteristic you should reverse?'

'I am not a policeman. I am head of the Internal Security Division.'

'It's a question of terms surely . . .'

Zouak put his hand into his pocket and brought out the flat half bottle of cognac. He carried it across and put it on the table. When he lifted the napkin from the supper tray he saw the small body of a bird untouched in the serving dish.

'You do not care for ortolans?'

'I wasn't hungry.'

'You permit . . .'

Dumont waved and unscrewed the small alloy cap from the brandy flask. Zouak speared the bird and stripped the limbs, sucking the bones one by one.

Dumont said, 'I read somewhere that Disraeli was very fond of ortolans.'

'Then they appealed to the Jewish sensualist surely. They would not appeal to the English sentimentalist. Actually I will tell you . . . these are corn buntings . . . someone has cheated the chef at the hotel.'

Dumont's food came three times daily in a 2 C.V. van from the hotel *Moulay Ismail*, down by the main road.

'The skylarks in this part of the world are delicious, and even more expensive than ortolans. But perhaps you are sentimental about them too.'

'*I'm* not sentimental, Colonel. It's merely that I wasn't hungry last night.' Dumont drank the cognac in a single swallow and screwed the top back on the bottle.

The *mouddhin* had finished and the eternal cicadas scraped on. The sky to the east had turned the colour of an unripened peach. Colonel Zouak twiddled the fingers of his right hand in the water bowl and dried them with the napkin. He moved away to the window again.

'Believe me, Captain Dumont, when I say I very much regret the fate which brought you here.'

'The circumstances were of my own choosing, Colonel. I don't really believe in fate. I go where I like.'

'Not really, Captain Dumont. We are like the earth, continually in orbit past the planets of our previous experience.'

Dumont was motionless in the chair. Whatever his fate was, from now on, he had the feeling it was decided and Colonel Zouak had only come to tell him.

He said idly, 'I daresay Islam has a saying about it.'

'We say that the leaf floating on a stream does not choose the direction it will go.'

'In a way that's rather my point. Nobody chooses for us.'

'Not really, Captain Dumont. The stream is Allah, don't you see, just as Allah is the sun around which we orbit. Excuse me,' he added abruptly and walked out into the anteroom again.

He crossed to the main door and rattled it, and when a soldier came he sent him off to the road to bring the girl.

Waiting in the chair, Dumont heard the brief, glottal exchange of Arabic and then the door close again. He had seen earlier the two sets of head-lamps sweeping up through the urbanisation and he had wondered who had been in the second car. It could have been bringing the members of a firing squad but surely the guard would have been adequate for such an occasion. He heard the faint squeak of soles as

Colonel Zouak came back, and then the sound of the door closing quietly.

After a moment, Zouak said, 'I've brought you a woman.'

'You make it sound like a last cigarette, Colonel.' And with a calmness he didn't feel Dumont added, 'Is that what you are offering me . . . a last woman before the firing squad?'

Colonel Zouak moved to the open window. He saw the flash of white trousers as the girl came up the powdery path between the oleanders. Then he turned to face Dumont again. Automatically he took the prayer beads from his pocket.

They waited on in a silence broken only by the soft death-rattle of the beads, as they fell to and fro between his hands.

PART ONE

CHAPTER ONE

It had been after midnight when the crews left the briefing tent and drifted out across the field towards the perimeter track.

Matches flared and there was a sudden release of conversation in half a dozen languages. Not the relief from tension, Dumont thought, more the relief from boredom. The briefing officer, an East European expert in air traffic control, had been long-winded and pedantic.

Turning his head, Dumont saw that Major Hausmann had followed them and was standing next to him. Then, unexpectedly, Hausmann was shaking his hand.

'I hope my instructions were clear, Captain?'

'Oh, yes, perfectly clear.'

Major Hausmann smelt faintly of cigars. He wore the blue beret and a rather faded United Nations brassard. Somewhere at the far end of the field an engine whined, coughed, and then ran steadily. One after another the other three started. Dumont knew it was the Air France Breguet which had drawn the first take-off.

Dumont's departure time was nearly an hour later, at 0417 hours. The jets, which could only use Dakar airport, wouldn't be going before dawn.

Dumont shook his head as the German took out a thin cigar case. 'I won't if you don't mind. Well . . .' He was on the point of moving but Hausmann touched his arm.

'This is better than war for us. You and I are old enough to remember that, Captain.'

'Yes.'

'Internationalism is better than nationalism!' The cigar crackled faintly as he drew on it and the smoke spiralled up as Major Hausmann's thoughts spiralled down into the *Geistesdunkel*, the darkness of the Teutonic soul. 'It is better that we unite against the elements than fight each other. You were an aviator then?'

'Yes I was, as a matter of fact.' As if apologizing for it Dumont added, 'One had to do something.' He tucked the chart and clipboard under his arm and stared briefly at the luminous sky. 'Well, we shan't have a weather problem.' Even as the words left his mouth he realized that, just as Hausmann's conversation typified the Germanic obsession with the soul, he had made a conventional English response when he mentioned the weather.

The racket increased as the Air Force captain started running up his engines. Hausmann said, 'There is, don't you think, a kind of . . . a divine balance about these things.' The tip of his cheroot moved in small tentative circles. 'One is compensating now for the beastliness we all did then. We are collecting life instead of killing it. No, that is not right . . .'

'I think I know what you mean.' Then Dumont said hurriedly, 'Well, I'd better be going . . . pre-flight checks and so on . . . perhaps we'll meet on the way back.'

'Perhaps we will,' Hausmann said. Then to Dumont's intense embarrassment, his heels clicked and his hand rose to his beret in a meticulous salute. Dumont waved vaguely back as he set off towards the planes.

The French government had thrown a cordon of troops around that part of Bordeaux airport which was being used as a staging post, and a young soldier with a rifle put a boot on the single wire fence when Dumont came up.

'*Bon courage,*' he said, smiling.

'Goodnight,' said Dumont, though he had been born less than a hundred miles to the east and could have as easily replied in French.

A moment later he reached the firmness of the steel peri-track which the French had used to extend the perimeter. No lights had been wired in yet and instead there were butane flares every twenty or thirty paces. Dumont's shadow kept circling ahead of him as he passed them. The huge darkened shapes of transport aircraft squatted in untidy groups and here and there crew with torches were moving around beneath them. Somewhere on the other side of the circuit Dumont could hear a trailer pump rattling away like a road drill.

G-ANCH was parked close to the track, close enough for the flares to show the Eurofreight insignia on her flat fuselage as he came up to it. He left the mesh and walked quietly across the grass. Someone lay curled in a bed-roll near the hatch but he couldn't see whether it was Scott or Forbes.

14

He stood there for a moment, hesitating.

They were down wind from the flares and the fumes were heavy and suffocating. From farther along the lines he heard a burst of laughter and a series of soft chords on a guitar. Someone was running along the track and a moment later the steps swerved off towards him.

It was John Forbes. He said, 'Hello, Skipper . . . I thought I saw you. Someone said we're near the top.'

'That's right. We're the fourth one out.'

'How long?'

'0417. We've got nearly an hour.'

John Forbes had shoulder-deep hair and innocent eyes which the world was constantly surprising. He said now, with amazement, 'There's a complete crew of women over there . . . six of them. They're Rumanians I think. They're with that bloody great Antonov that came in behind us.'

'Did you get off?'

'Hardly. They were all pretty butch.' He smiled. 'Christ knows how they'd want it.'

Dumont turned away. Several voices were singing to the guitar now, a dreary kind of song that sounded like a national anthem.

John Forbes said, 'Shall I wake Scotty?'

'Perhaps you'd better.'

Dumont started to climb the ladder. He knew he was a disappointment to John, that what John wanted was leadership and initiative. John had flown for eighteen months with K.L.M., where the command structure was more formalized. With Dumont he had to initiate his own orders, 'Shall I wake Scotty?' 'Shall I call A.T.C.?' 'Shall I take her down?' and Dumont's authority could only be expressed in responses. 'Perhaps you'd better . . .' 'If you'd like to.' Over the years since the war he had outgrown the habit of command.

Dumont entered the cabin. He passed the main bulkhead and felt for and closed the circuit breakers. The lights came on in the cabin and the flight deck. Dumont dropped his cap and the clipboard on to Scotty's seat and went back to the freight cabin. The Red Cross stores had been loaded during the afternoon by French army squads and Dumont swung himself along between the cases and the fuselage to test the tautness of the webbing and the fore and aft tie-downs.

He could hear Scotty and John moving around below,

then their feet were clattering up the aluminium ladder. Scotty came first with his bed-roll and started stowing it in a locker in the rest room. When John came to look for him Dumont said, 'Did you sign for all this?'

'Yes . . . twenty-three packages. There's a copy of the manifest on your seat. I also signed for the gas, six thousand gallons. I didn't use the Company stamp.'

Dumont moved along to the next bay. He knew he was irritating John, who had checked them already. He said quietly, 'One can't be too careful.'

'No, of course not. Are we coming back here?'

'That hasn't been decided yet. It depends on the turn-around time and the number of planes available. Actually the briefing was a bit of a shambles. There weren't enough interpreters . . . and no one seemed to have any up-to-date gen on the Mukuba strip. Both Freetown and Conakry are out and if we have to divert we go to a place called Yengema in the eastern province.'

Scotty came a little way in and leant against one of the slotted uprights. He looked thin and troubled in the feeble light. He said, 'Did they say how long we're going to be?'

Dumont shook his head. 'No.'

Scotty's lips were pressed. Dumont checked the last shackles and led the way forward into the cockpit. He said, 'Leave the door open . . .' and wound open a cockpit window. The air smelt faintly of herbs and the sounds of the airport were a distant murmur. He loosened the papers on his clipboard and held it where they could both see it.

'The flight plan is nearly the same as usual . . . we climb out over the bay on 198°, a direct course for Sierra Leone, Bordeaux control pass us straight down the line. Madrid . . . Rabat . . . Dakar. A.T.C. Freetown is non-existent, all this coastal strip is under water still. We come back this way and refuel at Dakar. The eventual idea is that we'll shuttle between here and Dakar International and the Caribous and helicopters will short haul it into Sierra Leone. And there's the weather picture . . . fairly stable with a north-westerly wind.'

Scotty said, 'Did they take an hour and a half explaining that?'

'It could have been longer. Believe it or not some fool from one of the relief agencies tried to lead us in prayer.'

Dumont looked at his watch. 'It's time we started. I'll have a pee before you stow the ladder.'

John said, 'Me too.'

The guitar had stopped and the shrill sound of cicadas was audible outside, and from somewhere in the trees beyond the perimeter Dumont heard the pulsating call of a tawny owl. In the same way as certain mammals mark out the limit of their territory by urinating, Dumont always peed against one of the huge tyres of the undercarriage. In a sense everything which the undercarriage supported was his territory. Afterwards from long habit he walked vaguely out to look up at the ailerons and the engines, then he circled the tail, looking at the elevators and rudder. Away to the east he could see the lights of Bordeaux refracted by the undercast and on his neck he could feel the coolness of the wind off the Bay of Biscay.

John came back and started up the ladder and Dumont was just following him when the glare of a searchlight swept from somewhere behind and stopped on the tail-plane. As it moved slowly along the fuselage Dumont clapped a hand to his eyes automatically.

'*Enculé!*' he said. 'Bloody hell . . .' and waved his other hand above his head.

The searchlight flicked off and he heard the sound of the marshal's jeep coming slowly along the track. Dumont waited as it came on with dipped headlights and stopped, level with the Britannia.

He could see the spotlight mounted on the back and a man standing with a hand on the windscreen. Then he heard Hausmann's deafening voice distorted by a loud-hailer. 'I shall lead you out, Captain.'

'There's twenty minutes yet.'

'All right . . . in twenty minutes.' As the jeep turned off he saw it was towing the external power unit and there were overalled figures riding in the back.

Dumont ran up the steps.

'Okay,' he said as he passed John. He went forward into the cockpit, where Scotty was already in the engineer's seat. Through the open panel he could see the jeep's crew unhitching the E.P.U.

He and Scotty began to go quietly through their routine. He checked the hydraulics and brake pressure and set the

17

trims and waited while Scotty checked the booster pumps, and opened the fuel line valves to number three engine. Then as they clipped themselves into their safety harness John came forward to join them.

. . . Numbers three four and two started up and ran smoothly but number one took longer and Scotty had to fiddle with the fuel control. When the torques and temperatures had been checked at full power Dumont throttled back and signalled the power unit away.

They had seven minutes to take-off. He looked at John, who winked and then pulled his headset loosely around his neck. He flicked on the landing lights and waited. After a moment the jeep came into sight below them, turning right on to the perimeter track.

Dumont pushed the two inner throttles forward and released the brakes. They lurched along the track with the jeep darting ahead framed in their landing light. The ground crew who were wearing steel helmets looked back at them occasionally with crinkled eyes and Hausmann, still standing at the windscreen, made ostentatious gestures every time there was a slight change of direction.

When they passed the last parked aircraft the jeep slowed. As they rolled out on to the concrete hard-standing, Hausmann was flapping both arms slowly like a great bird. Dumont corrected slightly to align himself and began closing the throttles. The jeep swung away suddenly and came back past the port wing. In the crepuscular light he could see Hausmann's hand at the salute again. He flicked the landing lights once before turning them off.

A Lilliputian voice called from the headset. 'Britannia Charlie Hotel. You are cleared for take-off. Wind easterly at five.'

John said, 'Roger Charlie Hotel cleared for take-off.'

Dumont released the brakes and took his hand off the throttles as Scotty reached for them and suddenly they were screaming down the flarepath.

John began to call the speeds in his sing-song voice. 'Vee-one, Vee R . . .'

They came unstuck long before the terminal lights and Dumont turned away, climbing slowly until the compass showed 198°. When they reached the cruising altitude of 19,000 feet, he plugged in the autopilot and said to John,

'Make some coffee before you kip down.'

John nodded and went back to the galley. Scotty was writing up the log and reading off the fuel meters.

In an hour it would be sunrise.

No disaster is acceptable but in a sense the disaster at Sierra Leone was more acceptable than most.

The Congo, Biafra, Bangladesh, had all been political disasters, the inhumanity of man. The disaster on the African coast was entirely God's responsibility. The first warnings had come two weeks before, somewhere in the Gulf of Guinea, when an oceanic survey ship had steamed north from Cape Town. It had just begun to report disturbances in the seismic belt which ran up the mid-Atlantic ridge when the tragedy struck.

Nothing more was known but it was thought that the major fracture zone on the line of the equator had suddenly extended itself eastwards and that the resultant upheaval had caused the biggest tidal wave since the Japanese disaster in 1906. A wall of water had been flung like a punch at the chin of Africa, of which Sierra Leone was the point.

The coastal plain of the eastern province had been flooded and all habitation had vanished in the fifty miles of lowlands below Freetown. The horrific extent of the disaster had taken some time to reveal itself, but now the relief agencies had moved in and member governments of the U.N. had provided emergency stores and transport facilities.

Army units and W.H.O. teams were already operating around the airstrip at Mukuba and although supplies were allowed to be flown in, no one yet was allowed to be flown out because of a cholera outbreak. In a cowardly way Dumont was relieved. He remembered a nightmare flight on another continent with a child in his lap no bigger than a foetus. Since then he had had an almost pathological dread of refugees and he was glad they would only be seeing officialdom at Mukuba.

It would be like the war. Flying on to a sky marker, the bombs falling away through cloud cover, and flying home again without having to face the consequences of one's actions. The guilt had come later and was still with him and Hausmann had pressed on the nerve tonight. But in spite of what Hausmann had said he wasn't seeking redemp-

19

tion by flying humanitarian missions now. The brutal truth
was that he had been flying the South American route
through Rabat already and that even if he hadn't been he
still would have been detailed, that he was an old pilot
flying an old plane and he was the one who was always
shaken out in an emergency, the one the company could
most easily do without. Normally he flew summer tours to
the nearer, less romantic places and in the off season it was
freight, flowers from Nice, tomatoes from Guernsey, Dutch
vegetables everywhere. Dumont didn't know how long it
would go on. At the last check his blood pressure had been
borderline but Louis Cave, the Australian doctor, had
stretched the rules a fraction.

Scotty tapped his arm lightly. Dumont turned his head and
Scotty was pointing away to starboard. Dumont banked for
a gentle turn and when he looked down he saw a flight of
six Westland helicopters about ten thousand feet below. They
had their tails up and were flying a course that looked as if
it was taking them to Gibraltar. They were most likely on
their way to Sierra Leone as well. Dumont brought the plane
slowly back on course, conscious of John Forbes asleep in
the hammock behind. It was almost day and in a few minutes
they would be crossing the Spanish coast. The brief sighting
of the R.A.F. helicopters had triggered off memories of the
war again.

Dumont knew that he was being less than fair to himself,
that the guilt really belonged to everybody. In fact he had
been a brave and efficient officer. When France had fallen
he and his crew had flown their old Potez bomber to England
only to be shot down in error as they were about to land.
He had joined the R.A.F. and the British had awarded him a
D.S.O. and two D.F.C.s before he was twenty-two. He had
also married Deirdre, but after the war she'd refused to go
back to France with him. So he'd stayed on in the R.A.F.

He was no good at the paper war that followed the real
one and after a while he'd gone back to flying, first with
B.O.A.C. and after that with Eurofreight, a British-Dutch
consortium. If his post-war career hadn't been brilliant at
least it had been honourable. There had been no real upsets,
no hard decisions, no Damascus Road. It had been a series of
long sensible hops without incident. Except for his marriage.

Dumont blamed himself for the failure of his marriage.

While he accepted that his wife had been unfaithful and extravagant he also told himself it was because she was temperamentally unsuited to the loneliness of being an airline pilot's wife. Since he was the one who subjected her to this loneliness then he was the one who was to blame. The fact that there were happily married air crew had nothing to do with it. He had married Deirdre.

It was almost as though he sought a kind of guilt in everything. As though, whatever happened, the buck must stop with him.

The plane dropped suddenly and then was lifted by clear air turbulence. Dumont glanced out of the side panel and saw that the straits had disappeared and that the desert far below was sepia in the dawn light.

When the plane pitched again in an up-draught he looked sideways at Scotty, who grinned, then he felt around in the nav bag by the side of his seat for a bar of chocolate. Amongst his personal gear he felt his writing case and he remembered that it was near the end of the month, the time when he always tried to write to his son Nigel, who was at Woodbridge School in Suffolk. He would write later, sitting in one of the bucket seats behind, when John Forbes relieved him. Nigel was fifteen and again, with him, in his pitiless moments of self-analysis, Dumont knew that he hadn't been much of a parent. That he had been called Nigel at all had been a snobbish little victory for his wife, and as he had given way over that he had also given way over subsequent things. His wife's argument had always been that she was in the front line of parenthood while he was only an occasional visitor. She had to live with Nigel where *he* didn't, therefore she must know best what was right. In the event she had got tired of having Nigel at home and he had been packed off to Woodbridge School.

Dumont visited him there as often as he could and during the summer holidays he always tried to manage a week at the cottage in Thames Ditton, during which Nigel stayed with him. Once he had taken him on a flight to Malta, but it hadn't been a success. Nigel had sat pale-faced and silent at the back of the flight deck and Dumont had felt embarrassed in front of the crew. In fact, embarrassment was the emotion which he associated most with being a father.

He had been embarrassed last Sunday while they were walking the meres above the Woodbridge tide mill. After a week's nervous resolution he had started to talk about sex.

'I'd rather you didn't,' Nigel said.

'You ought to know.'

'Oh, I know most of it . . . everyone does, and what I don't know is easy enough to find out. It's just I'd rather *you* didn't tell me.'

He'd walked on ahead quickly then and Dumont had seen that the back of his neck was scarlet. A pair of mallard got up and climbed steeply away through the crack willows and a moment later they were followed by half a dozen others. Then Dumont, with his head bent, heard Nigel say, 'Sorry, Daddy.'

It was as if taking the blame was an inherited characteristic. He said, 'It doesn't matter.'

'You can tell me about the war though . . . about your time with 911 Squadron.'

'You know I hate to talk about the war.'

'I don't see why. You did better than any of the other fathers at school.'

Dumont realized his failing. In the competitive heroics of the Upper Fifth he was denying Nigel his pride of place, but he still couldn't speak about it. 'I'm sorry.' It had been his turn again. The guilt was back with him. In a sense, as they walked on, he felt as if they had returned to the status quo.

The white ridge of the Atlas mountains was visible to port and far off in the Atlantic haze he could just see the Canary Islands. Dumont had stripped the silver paper from the dark chocolate and given a piece to Scotty. It was already limp in the heat of the African morning. Scotty was bent forward fiddling with one of the pitch controls when the incident began.

Two fighters suddenly dropped past them in a flashing dive at less than two hundred yards. Dumont barely saw them before they were gone, then they were hit by the jet blast and the Brit pitched to starboard.

CHAPTER TWO

Dumont punched out the automatic pilot and because of the load he let the plane go a little before starting to ease her back.

Scotty said, 'Jesus! That was close!'

Dumont peered sideways searching for them. 'Fighters . . . probably a training flight . . .'

'Where from?'

'Christ knows.'

The bulkhead door was flung open behind them and Dumont looked back briefly at John Forbes. 'Some show-off bastards buzzing us.' He looked down to port again. 'I think they've cleared off now.'

Scotty said, 'Not yet. They're at two o'clock.'

Dumont picked them up immediately, peeled in a tight turn about five miles out. He said, 'Are they Mystères?' and started to turn instinctively towards them.

John said, 'I don't know . . .'

They were coming down again, this time in a head-on pass that made identification impossible. Dumont continued his right turn and the jets flashed just below the port wing.

He said, 'I'm almost sure they're Mystères. I'll report them for this. Bloody fools!'

'Algerian or Moroccan,' John said. He was dashing over the pages of the identification manual.

'If they do it again try and get their squadron letters.'

'They're Moroccan, I think . . .'

Dumont noticed that his voice was fractured slightly with the excitement. 'What else does it say?'

'Well, they must have been Mystère IVas or IVbs . . . or F5s. That's all the service aircraft they have.'

Scotty had opened the log on his thigh and was making notes. Dumont said, 'They'll deny it, of course. They always do.' He remembered the instinct that had made him turn into the attack. They were old-fashioned tactics, he realized, and would have availed him nothing against modern rockets. He brought the aircraft back on course.

Scotty said, 'What's our position? We're not even over Moroccan territory, are we?'

'See if you can raise Rabat and get a bearing. Anyway it doesn't matter a bugger if we are. They said at the briefing we were cleared for over-flight all the way.'

John was murmuring into his headset and Dumont strained forward to search the sky on the port side. He was just turning away when the first Mystère appeared, almost touching his wing tip.

He said, 'Christ!'

The squadron signs on the fuselage and tail were in Arabic. The pilot had his face shield up and he stared urgently at Dumont and pointed earthwards.

Dumont shook his fist. 'Fuck off! *Je t'emmerde!*' he shouted. Then he remembered the emergency V.H.F. and flicked the switch. The air was full of Arabic. 'This is Britannia Golf Alpha November Charlie Hotel. We have clearance for Sierra Leone. Please get out of my way!' But when he released the transmitter button the hysterical Arabic shouting was unabated.

When he looked out again the leader had peeled away and the wingman was hanging in his place. The wingman, surprisingly, had long blond hair which was hanging below the edge of his helmet, and he repeated his leader's gesture, stabbing his finger at the desert below, before peeling away.

John said, 'I copied his marking as near as I could.'

Dumont had his head turned still looking at John when the next attack came, so that his first warning was the look of sudden fright on John's face. As he turned back he saw the rocket fire passing close over the cockpit and falling away ahead of them. The stream of tracer swept away to starboard and a moment later was followed by one of the Mystères in a screaming pass.

Until that moment, Dumont often thought afterwards, he had not been even faintly concerned. He had thought of two young fighter pilots, a bit screwed up, practising passes on an elderly freighter. Then suddenly he realized it was all very serious and he remembered the jet attack on King Hassan's plane and, more recently, the Libyan Airline Boeing forced down in the Sinai peninsula. As he checked course again the second Mystère came floating past on full flaps and the blond pilot was waving Dumont downwards. As he drew ahead slowly he flicked on his navigation lights and dropped his undercarriage. Dumont let him get half a mile ahead and started to follow.

He eased the throttles forward slightly to try to maintain his position. 'Did you raise A.T.C.?'

John said, 'I couldn't get Rabat but I think I got Gib . . . or maybe it was Dakar.'

'Call Rabat again and if you *can* get them give them our approximate position. Say we've been intercepted by the Moroccan Air Force and ordered to land.'

'Bastards!' he added with feeling. They were down to eight thousand feet flying parallel with a long escarpment. There were some kind of diggings at one end of it which looked like worm casts.

John said quickly, 'Nothing doing . . . maybe we're too low. Why don't we just put on power and head back. They wouldn't dare do anything.'

'One can't really do that, I'm afraid, John.'

From John Forbes's silence, Dumont knew he had disappointed him the way he disappointed Nigel. He said clearly, 'There are several things to consider . . . not only our own safety. Keep trying A.T.C. will you?'

The heat in the cockpit was suddenly stifling as they hit the lower air and the sweat formed as heavy as glycerine on his face. They were at five thousand feet and the Mystère ahead was banking slowly around to the west again. Dumont cut the corner and managed to close on him a bit. He was conscious of Scotty staring at him, and when he turned his head Scotty smiled.

'Fun and games,' Scotty said. 'The book doesn't say there's any strip in these parts that I recall. They can't expect us to put down here.'

'It looks like it.'

John said, 'But what if we . . .'

'Don't worry,' Dumont said curtly. 'If it's not on I won't do it.' The altimeter read two thousand, the Mystère was still sinking.

'Where's his mate gone?' Scotty said.

'Behind us, I expect. That's the usual drill.' Dumont pulled the edge of his hand tightly down his face and wiped it across his thigh. The glare of the desert below was stinging his eyes and he felt in the tray for his sun-glasses.

Scotty said, 'One thousand. It looks less.'

'It always does in the desert.'

The Mystère ahead eased up gently and they saw a series of scrub-covered wadis running from north to south. Then he was rocking his wings and turning gently to starboard. Dumont cut the corner again and closed to about half a mile.

Scotty said, 'Five hundred feet.' He and John peered out of the side windows.

'What's the going like?'

'It looks okay,' John said. 'No drifting sand. Just a few rocks here and there.'

They seemed to be in a slight depression that was three or four miles wide. Through the haze Dumont could see distant escarpments. The jet ahead was throttled right back and scarcely two hundred feet above the ground. Dumont wondered if, in fact, it was going to put down in front of him. But suddenly the pilot must have given it full boost because it stood on its tail and started climbing away to the right with its undercarriage retracting. Dumont kept on, holding altitude at five hundred feet.

'There's his mate,' John pointed away and Dumont saw the other jet coming in across their front. The pilot waved invitingly towards the floor of the wadi.

Dumont said, 'I'll go round again and have a close look. Have a smoke cartridge ready, will you.' He turned in a wide circle and flew slowly back along the track. When they had gone three quarters of a mile he wiped his face, which was streaming again.

'All right . . . fire off the smoke.'

Scotty fired the pistol through the sextant valve and the sound of the shot was deafening in the cabin. Dumont banked the plane and they saw the flare fall away in a trail of black smoke.

Dumont said casually, 'Get me a towel, will you, Scotty. I'm sweating so much I can hardly see.'

When Scotty had gone he said to John, 'Whatever they want it must be official . . . Something at Government level. I intend to make the biggest bloody stink of all time over this!'

Scotty came back and gave him the towel and he wiped his face briefly with it.

They passed over the still-burning smoke cartridge again and John said, 'The wind's about north-east . . . light, maybe seven knots.'

'They said north-west at the briefing so we may have drifted a few miles off course. Nevertheless, there's no question of an infringement. The briefing officer said we were cleared with traffic control centres all along the coast. Give me 15° flap will you . . .'

John said, 'The Mystères are still with us.'

'Never mind them. I'm going to fly a mile downwind from the smoke while you and I look at the ground. Boulders or soft patches are the danger.'

'Right.'

John said, 'You're at four hundred feet now . . speed one-five-oh.'

'Right.'

The sun was still low in the east but it cast no shadows on the hard unvarying surface. Dumont banked in a slow circle. 'Well, it looks okay, but you never know. Lower the gear.'

When the undercarriage light came on, he said, 'All right, here we go. You can give me 30° now.'

He lined up on the distant skein of smoke and heard John say, 'Speed one forty . . .'

The plane bumped slightly on an up current and then steadied.

'Three hundred feet,' John said.

'Full flap.' Dumont used left rudder to correct slightly. 'Here we go,' he said.

The wheels struck, rose a fraction and then settled in a steady rumble. Scotty's hands were busy closing the throttles and fuel cocks.

Dumont said loudly, 'Bags of room. We'll have no trouble getting out.' He let her run almost up to the flare before he started to brake.

'Piece of cake.' Even as the words left his mouth Dumont realized they sounded more trite than usual. It was ritualistic, really, a sort of euphemism for a prayer.

John said, 'What happens now?'

'Christ only knows, but I hope it happens quickly. See what you can raise on H.F.'

Dumont unclipped his harness and went back into the fuselage where the heat was already building up. As he rubbed his head vigorously with the towel he saw Scotty watching him. He said, 'Better open the forward door and the cockpit windows.'

Beyond in the cockpit, John's voice was calling monotonously. 'Britannia Charlie Hotel calling Rabat tower. How do you read?'

Dumont spread the damp towel over the top of one of the crates. Scotty opened the forward door and the next moment the aircraft seemed full of white heat. Blinking in the glare he heard John call, 'I think someone repeated our call sign but it sounds like a barnyard out there.'

Dumont went back to the cockpit. 'Forget it now and shut everything down.' Then they heard the jets coming from somewhere and only a second later they flashed over at no more than fifty feet. The leader veered outwards and rolled the Mystère once to starboard.

Scotty said, 'Silly bastard.'

Scorching air was coming through the windows. 'I think it'll be cooler outside,' Dumont said. 'Have we any beer in the galley?'

John Forbes had just started to say, 'A dozen cans . . .' when they heard the jets again.

As Dumont leant forward the racket of gunfire began and he saw a burst of cannon shell pass down the port side. A pall of sand was flung as high as the flight deck and it hung there before starting to disperse. In the sudden, ensuing quiet John said, 'It'll be healthier outside, too. They could be stupid enough to blow the bloody thing up, like those Palestine bods.' He turned and went back to the cargo bay.

'Don't forget the beer,' Dumont called after him. He saw John turn.

Then John Forbes wiped the hair away from his forehead characteristically. 'No, of course not,' he said.

'Just in case they do something silly we'll take our personal gear with us.' He stopped to look round at Scotty, 'You don't suppose some war or other has broken out and nobody's told us? Something like the Suez "do"?'

'It's hardly likely. There's been nothing in the news.'

Dumont picked up his nav bag. He called to John. 'You *are* quite sure you had someone on the blower?'

'Quite sure. They acknowledged in English.'

Dumont zipped up his nav bag and picked up the duffel bag with his personal gear. He took his sun-glasses off the tray and looked around. There were sweat drops on his nose. 'I think that's everything.' And then he added, 'I hope they don't shoot the old girl up.' There was a flash of light far out in the desert as the sun caught the Perspex of a turning fighter.

Dumont said, 'After you, Scotty.'

Scotty stepped through, slapping the bulkhead as he went. Dumont took his cap from the basket rack and followed. John already had the ladder in place. The two flight bags were at his feet.

Dumont said, 'You'd better be properly dressed. Caps anyway.' He tried to sound less pompous as he added, 'We might be waiting in the sun for some time.'

John said, 'Right, I'll get them.' He went down to the locker.

When he came back, Dumont said, 'Lead on.'

He watched them both to the bottom of the ladder and then followed. The air was heavy with fumes and the fuselage cracked as it expanded in the heat. Scotty was walking around the wheels.

'Tracks aren't very deep,' he said.

The smoke float had burnt itself out. John said, 'I noticed a bit of scrub about five hundred yards back on the left. There may be some shade there.'

'All right, let's try it.' As Dumont hooked his bag on his shoulder and led the way, the two jets came down the wadi in another low pass. They were only about a hundred feet up and the blast seemed to make the ground shake. Dumont saw the leader quite clearly. His shield was still up and he touched it with a finger in a salute.

Dumont said, 'I wish the bastard would fly into the ground.' Then as he always did he immediately denied it. 'I don't mean that.' While they walked on, the jets went into a long circuit over the distant escarpment.

The scrub was no more than desert thorn and the shade it gave was minimal. Dumont said, 'Well, there's nowhere else,' and sat down with his elbows on his knees. 'Let's drink the beer before it gets any warmer.'

And while John was unpacking it he said, 'Whatever these

bloody fools are up to I hope they are not going to take all day about it. I don't fancy trying to get into the Mukuba strip after dark. They said it was right in the bush.'

John had a can in his hand and was looking at him. 'No opener.'

Scotty said, 'I'll go.'

'No, it's my fault,' John stood up and after walking away for a few yards he broke into a trot.

'Don't run,' Dumont called. 'There's no hurry.'

John slowed to a walk and looked back at them grinning. Scotty said to him, 'What do you think they want?'

'God knows.' Dumont moved the cans one by one under the shade of the flight bag. As he heard the jets behind him he said, 'Not again.'

John had heard them, too, and was looking back. Dumont could see the flash of his teeth as he waved briefly upwards and then he stuck up two fingers in a derisive gesture.

The next thing happened with heart-stopping suddenness.

His body seemed to be picked up and slammed backward. Then it seemed to hang in the air for minutes before falling, to disappear in the dust. When he thought about it afterwards there only seemed to be one shot, one short burst from the cannon.

He was on his feet before Scotty and as Scotty moved he said sharply, 'Don't come. We mustn't all get killed.' Then he was running.

Ahead the sand slowly drifted and sank and he could see John's body propped somehow on head and knees. The jets were banking steeply beyond and almost standing on their wing tips. He was heaving for breath when he got there and as he stood staring, quite suddenly tears came, and just as suddenly stopped. In spite of the heat they felt warm on his cheeks.

John's right buttock and right foot were missing. Dumont said, 'John?' hopelessly and dropped on his knees.

From the lower elevation he saw that half the rib cage was also gone. He remembered a mid-upper gunner from the war with identical wounds. A Yorkshire boy . . . but now he couldn't even remember his name. He looked around and the planes were small black specks at the head of the wadi again.

As they turned in to start another run he hesitated, looking briefly back at Scotty. He said, 'No!' out loud and bent quickly to slide his arms under John's body.

He rose, first on one knee and then the other and as he straightened a trough of blood was released from the lungs and ran in a hot wave down his forearms.

He started walking unsteadily back to where Scotty was standing. John's head rolled against his chest and looking down he could see the lashes of one eye pleated with blood. When he looked up the Mystères were only a thousand yards off, coming directly at him.

CHAPTER THREE

Dumont stopped, facing them, a short bloody figure in an almost featureless landscape.

'Connard! Fausse-couche de putain!' he screamed. 'Dirty sodding bastards!' His eyes were fastened on the blackened muzzles of the thirty millimetre cannon.

'Connard!' he screamed again and again.

It wasn't a firing pass but he didn't even flinch as they swept just above his head. For a moment the heat of the jet stream scorched his face. He turned towards Scotty and struggled on again, breathing with difficulty.

Scotty came a little way to meet him, and stopped. He looked pale and was breathing through his mouth. He said stupidly, 'He was only going for an opener . . .'

'And I told him not to run. Perhaps if he had run they wouldn't have got him.' Then Dumont bent to lay the body beside the thorn bush.

Before he had straightened even, flies had appeared from nowhere and were clustered on John's face. Dumont flicked his hand at them but only one moved and quickly resettled. He turned away and when he looked down at himself he looked like a butcher. He wiped his dripping face with the part of his wrist that was free of blood.

Scotty stood with his face averted. 'We should bury him.'

'What with?' Dumont said harshly, and he moved away scattering the beer cans with a foot. The blood was as stiff as glue on his arms. He walked twenty paces away from

Scotty and sat down facing the other way.

The Mystères came sweeping down the valley again but Dumont didn't look up. His hand waved intermittently at flies. In a way he was glad of the flies. They existed, they were *there,* helping to convince him of the reality of what had happened. He didn't have to look back at the body in the sand.

The helicopters, when they came, came quietly. They slid over the escarpment and circled the Britannia at about one hundred feet. Then one of them came to hover briefly above them. Dumont looked up and saw the shadows of people watching him through the plexiglass. They were Alouettes, those ubiquitous French maids of all work and they had the same markings as the jets. Dumont watched as they settled slowly on cushions of dust one at each end of the plane.

Scotty started to move curiously but he hadn't gone more than ten paces when Dumont saw him and shouted. 'Don't go over. Let the bastards come to us.'

His hands were shaking slightly, not with fright but the way they had shaken before with the aftermath of action. He clenched them slowly and closed his eyes for a moment. He opened them again to see a squad of swarthy men in army fatigues milling about the aircraft. In the centre of the cargo hatch a man was standing looking across at them. He was tall, well over six feet, and he wore a white tropic suit and sunglasses with shields at the side. As Dumont watched, he flicked a fly whisk delicately across his front. Somehow it was a camp gesture, remote and unrelated to the man himself. He came down the ladder to speak to a soldier, his face still turned towards Dumont. Dumont looked away. The hum of flies behind him was audible as the sound of a beehive. He could feel them on his own arms, wet over the dried blood. Even if he went back to John Forbes's body there was nothing he could cover it with.

Scotty came to stand near Dumont. 'What do they expect to find?'

'I've no idea.'

'I suppose in a moment they're going to apologize and say we can go on our way.'

The man with the fly whisk left the shade of the plane and began to walk towards them. When he was about ten yards

32

off Dumont stood up and faced him. The man stopped. He said, 'My name is Zouak,' and after a long pause, 'I'm a colonel in the Security Division of the Moroccan Army.'

'Then what the hell is going on!'

'I'm sorry about your friend,' Colonel Zouak said quietly.

'It's a bit late for that . . . now you've bloody well murdered him.'

Zouak's hand moved and the whisk jerked in that strange seemingly non-volitional gesture. 'It was not intended,' he said. 'Captain Sayid thought he was going to destroy the evidence.'

'What evidence?'

The colonel had turned his back and was speaking rapidly in Arabic. A soldier came two or three paces to answer and then doubled away to the nearest helicopter.

'What evidence?' shouted Dumont.

Colonel Zouak turned again. He moved loose sand away with the edge of his suède boot as though to uncover an answer, then he looked steadily at Dumont. 'I'm sorry, Captain Dumont,' he said.

'How do you know my name?' There was no alarm in Dumont's voice, only curiosity.

Two men were coming with a stretcher loaded with equipment. As they arrived Colonel Zouak flicked the whisk carelessly at John Forbes's body. Turning away he said, 'His body can be returned to your country or he can be buried at the cemetery in Casablanca. There are Catholic and Protestant cemeteries there. I have a friend buried in the Protestant cemetery.'

The men had lowered the stretcher and were unpacking polythene and plastic tubing.

'I should bring your belongings, Captain. The smell in a moment will not be very pleasant.'

Scotty said, 'I'll get them.' He went away and picked up everything except the beer. When he came back Dumont took his duffel bag.

Scotty said, 'What are they doing?'

'The body is sealed in the plastic bag with formaldehyde gas,' Colonel Zouak said. 'It is less satisfactory than the aqueous solution but it is invaluable here where they putrefy quickly. All our desert patrols carry the equipment.'

The colonel moved a pace ahead of them back towards

the plane. Two men were sitting in the hatch with their legs dangling, the rest had gone back to the helicopters. Dumont stopped suddenly and put out a hand to stop Scotty. He said quietly, 'We'll try and stick with the plane.'

Scotty nodded. His unshaven face still looked pale.

'Come on then.'

As Dumont moved away towards the steps, Zouak spoke quietly in Arabic and the two men in the hatch scrambled to their feet. Then in English he said, 'I must ask you to accompany me in the helicopter, Captain Dumont.'

'Where to?'

'To Casablanca.' He spoke without turning. 'I'm sorry. First the helicopter will take us to Agadir.' The whisk rose and fell as though the thought was as troublesome as a fly.

'I'm afraid I can't leave my aircraft. For one thing if it is going to stand for any length of time the cargo . . .'

'Don't worry about that. There is a relief crew on the way. We operate three Britannias on our internal air services.'

Dumont still waited. In the silence the motor of the distant helicopter coughed once and caught. It didn't rise. Dumont said, 'You really must tell us what we're being charged with.'

Zouak turned and walked back to face him. Dumont stared at his twin reflections in the plastic lenses. Zouak said calmly, 'But you are not under arrest, Captain Dumont. At the moment I am detaining you while we complete our inquiries. It's quite lawful.'

Behind him, Dumont heard the stretcher party start marching back.

Lowering his voice Zouak went on, 'If you refuse to come with me you will only embarrass us both. I shall have to ask the men to put you aboard forcibly. Nothing will have been gained but a great deal will have been lost.' Then Colonel Zouak said, 'Please *help* me.'

The stretcher party trudged heavily by, going towards the second helicopter. The plastic bag was as tight as a balloon. Dumont could see the faint shape of John's body at the bottom of it, an embryo in a giant transparent uterus.

He said quietly, 'All right. But believe me when I say you are making a bloody fool of yourself. We're on charter to the International Red Cross to take relief supplies into Sierra Leone and we're briefed to over-fly your borders.'

'Then no doubt that will emerge at the inquiry,' Zouak

34

turned and set off again.

Dumont looked at Scotty, who shrugged and then went ahead. Dumont looked up at the plane where the two guards were sitting with their legs swinging again. One of them smiled down at him. Dumont followed Scotty.

The helicopter cabin was like an oven. Colonel Zouak sat opposite them. He had laid aside the fly whisk and taken a string of amber prayer beads from his pocket instead. They clacked in his lap as he moved them apologetically. 'It is better than smoking,' he said.

The motor wound up slowly and exploded into life. As the Britannia fell away below them Dumont thought she looked old and fat, sitting there in an alien landscape. Like most planes he had known intimately, she had become almost an extension of his personality. He hoped to hell the relief crew knew what they were about.

As he turned away Colonel Zouak smiled. 'It's cooler up here,' he said.

'You speak excellent English.'

'I received my higher education in England.' He lifted his full face to Dumont and the polished amber of his brow almost matched the prayer beads in his hand. 'At Manchester University. One had to endure much bad weather there.' Then the mouth below the dark glasses smiled again. 'Come, Captain Dumont . . . you are still alive. A prophet has said that a small calamity sometimes saves us from a greater one. You might have crashed into the *Haute Atlas*!'

The villa was on the edge of an urbanization to the east of Casablanca. It looked out on terraces where the vines, unattended for seasons, had grown as rife as blackberries in an English hedgerow. From the living-room windows on the ground floor it was possible to see the two army tents near the gate which were used as a guardroom.

They had flown from Agadir to Casablanca on the normal jet service without any guards being in evidence and a staff car had brought them to the villa in the late evening.

Colonel Zouak had walked ahead of them, flinging open doors. 'You see it is not a prison, Captain.'

As well as the ceiling fans turning slowly there were new American air-conditioners built in below every window. In the living-room a portrait of King Mohammed V hung above an empty fireplace.

'Your food will be brought from the hotel we passed on the main road, and drink, too, of course, if you require it. They have beer . . . whisky, anything you want.'

'Can we go there?'

'I'm sorry.' Zouak lifted a hand, still with the beads entwined. 'There are tourists there . . . until we have cleared this matter up we would prefer it not to be discussed in public.' He turned. 'But you have the freedom of this house. I hope you can be patient for a little while.' Then he added dryly, 'You are really no worse off than the rest of us. A man without restraint makes his own prison.'

Dumont said, 'I don't find Mohammed much comfort.'

'Not Mohammed . . . Only his poor prophet Zouak. If there is anything you want or you have any particular complaint talk to the guard commander and he will get in touch with me immediately. His name is Lieutenant Ibrahim. Can you remember that?'

'Yes, I think so.' Dumont added, 'You won't forget our families . . . We're several hours overdue at Sierra Leone already. It's possible they've been told we're missing.'

Zouak laid his hand on his breast pocket where the notebook was. 'I have the addresses. I shall see to the matter personally. I don't expect we'll have to keep you here long . . . it's just a precaution.'

Afterwards Dumont had walked out to the gates with him, where the staff car waited with its flag limp in the after-heat of the day. The sweetness of jasmine just failed to conceal the inefficiency of the sewage system.

Zouak said, 'You are permitted the terrace and the garden, but no farther, and at night the ground floor doors and windows will be locked. It has been explained to Lieutenant Ibrahim.'

Zouak had held out his hand then for the first time. It was not open forward in the western manner, merely an extension of his fingers in front of his body.

Dumont blinked and turned away. When he looked back, Zouak was on his way to the staff car. Before he entered it, his hand fluttered in the dusk. 'I shall see you tomorrow, Captain Dumont.'

As Dumont walked back up the path Scotty came on to the terrace to meet him. 'What do you reckon?'

'Oh, he'll let them know, I think.'

Scotty had a young wife who worked in an antique shop in Weybridge. They had bought a cottage in the country nearby which they were doing up themselves. Scotty worked there in his off-duty periods. He was always reading books with unlikely titles like *'Teach Yourself Modern Drainage.'* Dumont thought fleetingly that if they were here long enough he could probably explain what had gone wrong with the villa's drains.

Out among the shrubs a match scraped and they could see the silhouette of a young soldier as he lit a cigarette. The end of it glowed steadily like an approach marker from five thousand feet. As nearby sounds gradually ceased, only the cicadas were left and Dumont could hear the steady racing of motorway traffic somewhere towards the coast.

He said, 'In all probability our people will know now, anyway. The Press will have got it from the air traffic control people at Dakar. But even if they didn't we would have been overdue at Mukuba for several hours and they would have been bound to have started some sort of search procedure.'

'John said he heard someone acknowledge . . .'

'Then we have nothing to worry about really. I wonder if there's anything to read in this dump . . .' Two soldiers came to lock up the ground floor rooms about ten minutes later and Dumont decided to go to bed. He knew after three broken nights he could sleep twelve hours without difficulty. But when he closed his eyes they felt suddenly hot.

It seemed as if grief had been waiting in ambush throughout the day. He was unable to stop the picture of John Forbes that formed in his mind. His careless way of walking, his hair sitting on his shoulders, the endless surprise in his blue eyes.

He would have to go and see his parents. Dumont moved restively in the narrow bed. Once he had known the sort of litany that went with that kind of visit. Once it had been a part of his life explaining death to other people. Forgotten phrases came to his mind.

They had always been killed instantly, and there was never any pain, and if possible the manner of their death had been instrumental in saving the rest of the crew. There was always an element of self-sacrifice. John's parents lived in Bristol.

He remembered that it had always been better with parents. Parents were able to prop each other up . . . there was something left. Wives had always to be left alone, frozen and huddled, as though they were already abandoned to attitudes of death themselves.

Eventually he slept.

It seemed only minutes later that he was woken by a stream of shouted words and the revving of an engine. Then the glare of lights swept across the ceiling. Dumont was groping his way from under the net when the bedroom light came on.

Scotty faced him, standing by the switch. 'Now what?' he said.

'I'll tell you.' Dumont reached for his underclothes. 'I bet you a month's pay that they've discovered their stupid bloody mistake and we are about to be transferred to the Casablanca Hilton and suitably compensated.'

They were both almost dressed when someone knocked at the door. Dumont crossed and opened it. In the feeble light of the staircase, Colonel Zouak was leant against the newel post on the landing.

He carried neither the fly whisk nor his prayer beads and he showed Dumont his open palms as though to prove it. 'I'm sorry.'

'We're leaving?'

'Not yet. I wish you to accompany me, Captain Dumont, by yourself.'

'Where to?'

'A little way up the road.'

'Just a moment, will you . . .' Dumont stepped back into the room and faced Scotty. He pushed the door slightly.

Scotty said, 'I heard.'

'Well, I haven't any alternative.' He looked away frowning. 'They wouldn't dare do anything silly . . .'

He realized that he was putting responsibility on Scotty and felt embarrassed. He said hurriedly, 'Right. I'll be off,' and opened the door again.

He'd gone past Zouak and was halfway down the first flight of steps when he heard Scotty call, 'Good luck, Skipper!' When he looked back Scotty had this thumb up. He smiled briefly. Why was it that when life imitated art it was always the art of the B film?

He didn't wait for Zouak but walked deliberately ahead, leading the way across the terrace and down the path to the waiting car. A soldier held the gate for him. As Colonel Zouak took the seat beside him, he noticed that the air was faintly cachou-scented. They followed the private road of the urbanization, and Zouak said, 'I want you to know there is no need for alarm. I was not using a . . . a figure of speech when I said I was taking you for a ride.'

'I'm not in the least alarmed.' Dumont was aware of Zouak's head turned close to his ear.

'I also want you to know that I am your friend, Captain Dumont, and will try and deal with your fairly. I ask only that you remember that we do not exist alone. We are not free.'

'I'm sure Mohammed wouldn't approve of Jean Paul Sartre.'

But Zouak repeated it again. 'We are not free,' he said insistently as if the words were some sort of talisman that might protect them both.

They had not driven for more than about five minutes when the staff car slowed and turned off the road on to a narrow track. Dumont saw the headlight beams sweep across wasteland before coming to rest on a huge diesel army transport with a camouflaged canvas roof. The car slowed and stopped a few paces away and the headlights went off.

'Please come with me.'

Dumont followed him into the warm night. The hum of traffic from the by-pass was louder and there was a scent of wood smoke on the air. The tail-board of the truck was down and there were foot-holes cut in it. Colonel Zouak climbed up and then turned to offer Dumont a hand.

As Dumont went up under the flap, he saw a soldier holding a trouble light. In the centre of the floor was one of the Red Cross packing cases from the plane. Someone had broken the steel bands and prised the top boards loose.

Zouak said, 'The plane was flown out this afternoon. It's at Casablanca Main now. We off-loaded this earlier in the evening.'

Zouak held out a hand and a soldier passed him the light. He kept it just below his face. 'What do you think it contains, Captain Dumont?'

Dumont said irritably, 'Oh, guns of some sort. Probably

F.N. rifles. Possibly even a howitzer. It wouldn't surprise me. The world knows that half the relief planes into Biafra carried arms.' The silence was so complete that Dumont knew that he must be right or nearly so.

He was reminded of an altar piece, lit by candlelight. A soldier on either side of Zouak completed the triptych. He moved impatiently. 'For Christ's sake stop playing games . . .'

Zouak said sharply, 'You are wrong.'

'Well, why all the drama . . . Why bring me here in the middle of the night?'

'Please . . . I brought you here because the International News Service has already reported your misadventures and there are thirty or more journalists waiting at the Ministry in the Place Victor Hugo.'

Dumont said, 'What I meant was why are you playing these bloody childish games . . .'

'Because if you know what is in the crate then you would be an accessory.'

Dumont said, 'How could I bloody well know! The plane was loaded by the French Army like all the other planes. In any case I wasn't even there when they were doing it. I was at the pilots' briefing.'

There was a long pause before Zouak said, 'But it doesn't mean that you are not an accessory.'

Dumont put out his hands slowly and gripped the sides of the case, leaning his weight across it. 'I don't know what's in it,' he said in a quiet voice. 'Why don't you tell me?'

An owl hooted with unexpected clarity, from somewhere across the wasteland. It was a barn owl, Dumont knew, and it was on the wing. Zouak raised his open hands again, completing the illusion of an altar piece.

'All right,' he said, 'I will tell you. The case is full of raspberry jam.' While Dumont waited with his eyes closed, he added, 'Why don't you look?'

The nails squeaked as Dumont bent back the boards. Some tins were missing from the top row and he lifted one out. There was only a small utility label on it, with a border of coloured fruit. *Confiture de Framboise. Feuillet Frères, Marseilles.*

Dumont dropped it back. 'I wish you'd get to the point.'

'Long steps do not shorten the distance, Captain Dumont.'

'Nor does it make it any the less boring.' Dumont waited. The owl called again. It was far away, only just audible. There would be field mice, of course, in the wasteland.

Colonel Zouak said, 'There has been a mistake in the labelling. It isn't raspberry jam.'. He snapped his fingers downwards and the sergeant bent to pick up a tin from the floor. It had been roughly hacked open with a bayonet. Zouak took it and held it out to Dumont.

'Have some.'

Dumont took it. It was grey and glutinous. 'What is it?'

'R.D.X. It's a plastic explosive which is old-fashioned now but there is still sufficient here to derail a hundred trains or destroy twenty bridges or do something even worse.'

'What proof is there that it came from my plane?'

'On information received the cargo of your plane was examined by members of the security police.'

'But what proof is there?'

'Don't you see,' said Colonel Zouak wearily, 'that your question is pointless. What possible proof is there ever of contraband other than the evidence of law enforcement officers.' He moved around the packing case to the rear of the transport and Dumont smelt the sweetness of cachou again. 'Please . . . it's time I took you back.'

He held the canvas away from the tail-board and found the foot-holds. Dumont, watching him, said, 'But you must see it doesn't make any sense. We were flying the stuff into a strip administered by the Sierra Leone authorities.'

Colonel Zouak paused. In the half-light and not being able to see his face, Dumont found it difficult to read his expression. It seemed as if he was faintly amused but there was something else as well. He said, 'Quite.'

'And we couldn't have dropped it anywhere else because as you saw for yourself we weren't equipped for free-dropping.'

Colonel Zouak was still staring up at him, his lips slightly curled. He said, 'Quite,' again and Dumont suddenly realized that the something else in his expression was a mixture of pity and contempt, that Colonel Zouak was regarding him as a patient teacher who has been disappointed by a deliberately dishonest child.

It was on the way back to the villa that the colonel had told him he would arrange for someone from the British

Embassy to call at four on the following day.

When Scotty had met him in the hall he'd said, 'What have you done to your hand?'

They both looked down at Dumont's hand, but it wasn't blood. It wasn't raspberry jam either, Dumont thought wryly.

CHAPTER FOUR

At three Dumont found he could rest no longer.

He laid the mosquito net gently aside and stood silently. On the bed opposite, Scott didn't stir. Dumont drew on his clothes with care and went quietly down to the living-room. He had only been sitting there about fifteen minutes when he heard a commotion at the gate. A moment later an old Daimler came up the road very slowly in bottom gear. There was a small chrome flagstaff on each wing but no pennants. He went through to the hall and shouted up the stairs. 'He's here, Scotty.'

When he went back to the living-room again a thin grey figure had left the driving seat and was staring up at the villa. Then he reached into the back seat for a yellow briefcase. As he came up the path Dumont went into the hallway to meet him.

The man stopped when he saw Dumont and held out an attenuated hand briefly. 'Dumont? I'm Philip Anderson. I'm second secretary at the Embassy.' He was already looking into the room beyond Dumont as if there wasn't much time. 'In here?' he said.

Dumont nodded and waited for him to pass. He was about to follow when a door closed above and Scotty came hurriedly down the stairs. Dumont pointed wordlessly to the living-room door before going in.

Anderson was looking around. 'Well, they've made you quite comfortable.'

'This is Mr Scott, my engineer. Mr Anderson is from the Embassy, Scotty.'

Anderson shook hands and then sat on the edge of his chair with his case on his knees. His thin grey hair was long at the back, ending in a drake's tail. Dumont said, 'I hope

42

you can get us out of here today.'

Anderson was silent. He opened his case, thumbing the catches carefully. Dumont knew something was wrong. 'I don't want to mislead you about our role,' Anderson said, 'but the truth of the matter is that there isn't a great deal that H.M.G. can do for you. People have got rather bored with hijacked planes. If you'd had passengers . . . perhaps someone of importance . . .'

Scotty said, 'But . . .' and stopped when he caught Dumont's eye.

Dumont said calmly, 'We can't really accept that, you know. They forced us to land and they murdered my co-pilot. Now for Christ's sake . . .'

'I don't think it's going to help if we get emotional about it,' Anderson said. 'I'm going to take down a full statement from you in a minute but you must see that H.M.G. can't pre-judge the issue. As a matter of fact we have reason to believe that Mr Scott is going to be released and that bail in your case is going to be fixed at about twenty-five thousand pounds.'

'But I'm going to be brought to trial?'

'That would seem to be their intention.'

'And they still execute people here.'

Anderson's hand moved in a vaguely deprecating way.

Dumont moved abruptly and went down to stand at the window. He closed his eyes. For better for worse he had to deal with Anderson. Behind him Anderson was saying, 'In a statement put out this morning the Moroccan Government are claiming that you were flying explosives to insurgency forces. They claim also that they killed a member of the crew when he tried to blow up the plane and destroy the evidence.'

'You must know that's rubbish. Whatever insurgents there are in Sierra Leone can't be very active at the moment. The airports . . .'

'Who's talking about Sierra Leone?'

Dumont turned slowly. Anderson was still hunched over the document case watching him. 'The statement says that you were going to off-load at some remote spot in French Equatorial Africa.'

Dumont understood then the curious look Colonel Zouak had given him in the truck the night before. The pity and the contempt were for his innocence.

He said, 'I see.' He looked at Scotty. He suddenly felt inadequate to the situation.

He started to think about John suddenly, and for no reason, while Anderson's voice went on from beyond the edge of consciousness. 'You've had quite a good Press at home. Public opinion is certainly on your side. I saw yesterday evening's in the club at lunchtime. D.S.O. fights back was the sort of thing. And the dead hero treatment for young Forbes. They're handing over the body, of course, and H.M.G. has authorized transport back to U.K. We don't know whether they'll release the plane later in the week but we've been in touch with your company H.Q. in London.'

'But there is absolutely no truth in the charges,' Dumont said patiently. 'We were flying relief stores which came from Switzerland, and were loaded by the French Army at Bordeaux airport. They showed me a cargo of explosives last night but it hadn't come from our plane. The Red Cross marking could only have been painted on yesterday. I had wet paint on my hands when I got back. Scotty here saw it.'

Anderson cleared his throat. 'Well, that is certainly something in your favour.' His voice lacked conviction.

'I don't suppose H.M.G. would lend me twenty-five thousand pounds?'

'Not really . . . because that would be, *de facto*, an admission of your guilt. And it would be associating H.M.G. with the charge that has been made against you personally.'

'I don't know why you bothered to come.'

'Well, you are a British national if only a comparatively recent one. And believe it or not there are some things we *can* do. Diplomacy is not like justice . . . It doesn't have to be seen to be done.' The phrase seemed to be worn smooth from constant repetition. 'You'd be surprised what H.E. can do with a case of Scotch here and there. I think what I'd better do first is take down from you a statement of exactly what happened, then we'll just have to try and find out what it is they want.'

'I should have thought that's obvious.'

'Well, not really. It could be they just want the Britannia for spare parts . . . they operate two or three on their internal routes. Or they might want to exchange with us for some new area of the Sahara and want to stop over-flying in that particular piece of air space. That's why it really doesn't matter whether you had red paint on your hand or not. Whatever actually happened there's a protocol in dealing with these matters which has nothing to do with reality.

'But you mustn't get too depressed. You are being kept here in reasonable comfort and as soon as we know what the game is we'll play it. But it would upset the apple-cart completely if we paid the fine, and no one else is likely to, which they are perfectly well aware of. One of the newspaper reports said that the British Airline Pilots' Association had discussed the matter but had reached no conclusion.'

Anderson opened a small pocket diary and pressed it flat against his knee. Then he looked up at Scott. 'You needn't stay, Mr Scott. In fact, you can pack your things and put them in the car if you want to.'

Scotty looked at Dumont. 'All right, Skipper?' It was almost a reflex habit and Anderson's pencil began to tap irritably.

'You may as well, Scotty.' Dumont said evenly.

When Scotty had gone Anderson said, 'Now we can get down to it.'

He glanced at his watch before starting to write.

At the end, before he went, Scotty had wanted to stay. Anderson had waited patiently by the car while they argued.

It was a situation which didn't occur in protocol. Dumont had prevailed but after the car had driven off he had stood for a long time, listening until the sound of its engine was lost in the murmur from the by-pass. As he turned away, a sentry by the gate waved cheerfully to him. It was a gesture that confirmed him in his isolation. In the scheme of things he had no more control of his destiny than the sentry at the gate. He was another pawn in the conventional game that H.E. and Anderson would play with their counterparts.

'Fucking hell,' he said in quiet desperation, as the dust settled.

He resolved not to think about it. He went through into the kitchen and took two bottles of Stella beer from the fridge. It had been Scotty's idea making them fill it up the night before. He carried them back, with a glass, to the terrace.

He would desensitize himself, he decided.

He was still sitting there long after midnight, the empty bottles accumulating with the hours. He saw the reflection of the headlight beams far off in the desert before the cars themselves appeared. It was then that Dumont wondered whether they were coming to shoot him.

He knew, of course, that it couldn't really be so, that it was only a thought born of alcoholic despair.

When Colonel Zouak opened the door for her Dumont was struck both by her chic and her authority. He couldn't see her face because she was veiled in the Edwardian manner as if motoring was still a hazard to the appearance.

Zouak came behind her, the whisk resting against his shoulder, his face expressionless.

She said, 'They have given me permission to speak to you. My name is Mrs Hoffman.'

'Good morning.'

She put the tips of her fingers together as though in prayer and bent her head. And then as if to put him at his ease she said, 'Have you any more beer? I'm dying of thirst.'

'Of course.' Dumont looked at Colonel Zouak, who showed the palm of his hand in refusal. Dumont brought another glass and bottles from the fridge. When he came back, Mrs Hoffman had removed her hat and veil and laid them aside. She was about thirty, Dumont guessed, and there was certainly nothing else Edwardian about her. Her hair had been bleached ash grey and had the outline of a bell. Behind executive spectacles her eyes were dark and almond-shaped.

As she took the glass she said, 'This wind dries me up.' Her accent was slight but noticeable. She said, 'Cheers' and leant back in her seat looking up at Zouak. 'You promised me I'd be able to talk to him alone . . . to explain how the situation has come about . . .'

Zouak was looking at Dumont. He said, 'Good tidings do not need an army of heralds.'

Dumont smiled but the colonel did not smile back. The whisk touched his forehead in salute before he turned away. From the picture window Dumont watched him go down the path and reach in the back of the police car for a document case. In the faint light he opened it on the bonnet.

Mrs Hoffman said, 'In a sense, Mr Dumont, you and I were uniquely created for each other. I don't mean in any personal sense . . .'

Dumont held the cold glass in his hand. He thought it was

just possible he was being freed. They were the only good tidings he could really expect. He said calmly, 'I'd rather like to know whatever it is you've come to tell me . . .'

'Well, I hope you'll be free in an hour. But it does require a little co-operation on your part.'

Dumont let his breath go slowly and stood up. He walked to the edge of the terrace and stared down. Colonel Zouak had a foolscap file open on the bonnet. He must have been aware of Dumont's shadow because he looked up slowly.

Without turning Dumont said, 'I think you'd better explain . . .'

'I'm a lawyer, Mr Dumont. In fact, I'm a specialist in international law and I'm consulted by several companies and organizations in that capacity. One of these is the International Veterans' Trust with its head office in Geneva. It is probably one of the most inefficient and unproductive charities in the world in that it is top heavy with capital and spends only a fractional part of the annual interest on the purpose for which it was founded. The statutes that set it up are so formulated that they can't at present be changed. Situations such as the one you are in aren't very common and they are very welcome to me because they give me the opportunity of earning a fee.'

'I gather the Trust is going to bail me out.'

'In a word, yes.' She made a small oriental sweep with her hands. 'This used to be a Roman province and their law derives from Roman law. In this case we have applied for your release under a writ of *multa prae judicum postulata,* which means you are fined before judgement. It was a kind of bail used to avoid imprisoning people before a trial which might be delayed. Of course, they got it back in the end if they were innocent.'

He went back to his seat. Mrs Hoffman watched him critically as if she was still assessing his legal requirements. 'I'll tell you about the trust as briefly as I can. Like a great number of very rich men, Mr Ingram, the founder, is very eccentric. Mr Ingram's particular fixation is with physical courage. The reasons are fairly simple. His father was a hero in the Second World War, where he served with the American Fifth Army in Italy. He was awarded the Medal of Honour on the Anzio beach-head. Apparently he destroyed a troop of tanks single-handed and was badly wounded in the process. He died five years later of alcoholism and the only thing he

47

left his son was the medal. It was the only thing he wouldn't pawn to buy drink with.'

She stopped for a moment. 'I'm not telling it very well.' She looked away. In the dawn light the colonel was refolding papers on the car bonnet. 'It's not entirely original. In France they used to have an association of war veterans who had received citations for bravery called the *Croix de Feu*. And there was a similar one in Germany called *Der Stalhelm*. What's new about I.V.T. is that it's multi-national.

'Anyway, you get the general idea,' she said vaguely. 'Mr Ingram believed that his father died from neglect by the society on behalf of which he had offered his life. And the irony of it was that this same society eventually made his son a millionaire. So about three years ago when he read about an American who had been caught smuggling in Paris, a boy who had been a much decorated marine flier in Korea, Mr Ingram set up this foundation. I went to Paris with him, arranged for the best defence, and after he had served his sentence, which wasn't long, we met him at the prison gates and spared no expense in his rehabilitation.'

Mrs Hoffman recrossed her legs. 'The trouble with the idea is that it is created for a class of citizens who doesn't very often need charity. Heroes as a group don't seem particularly disaster prone. I've only had about two assignments a year since then and usually one of *them* is phoney. Now you know why your adversity is so welcome to me. You were five times decorated in World War Two and you are in real trouble.'

'I'm afraid I'm not a criminal though.' She smiled faintly and Dumont added, 'I'm sorry to disappoint you.'

'They were going to make you one whether you liked it or not. In fact, it's taken me a lot of talking to obtain your release at all. They know the British government won't involve themselves so we have rather upset things. Colonel Zouak is not happy.'

'And what would happen to me?'

'The International Veterans' Trust will accept full responsibility for you. We have a *gentilhommière,* a kind of small château, in the hills behind Cannes. Naturally you can stay there for as long as you like and there are endless funds available for you to set yourself up in any occupation of your choosing.'

the necessary arrangements about your car. Then I shall take you both to the airport. You will accompany Mrs Hoffman, Captain Dumont.' Zouak turned and went back to the police car where Allal was already holding the door.

Dumont, settling in the car with the aura of Mrs Hoffman's scent, was unwillingly conscious of new casual factors at work.

He was like a coin travelling from hand to hand, engaged in a kind of endless, spiritual kinesis.

They waited in the car at Casablanca airport a few hundred yards from the embarkation pad.

'A precaution against the Press,' Zouak had said, although most of them had departed after a Moroccan Government release saying that Dumont was being freed and only the plane's cargo impounded.

'They have gone to Spain on the midnight flight,' Zouak said now. 'Apparently a plane-load of British tourists have been given inferior accommodation.' And he added quietly, 'The world is holding its breath.'

An official came to the window of the car and received guttural instructions from Zouak. Afterwards he got Mrs Hoffman's suitcase from the boot. He took it away, together with their passports, to the administration building. Zouak was sitting opposite Dumont in the back of the car, his prayer beads trailing from his hand. In the confined space, the scent of cachous was overpowering.

Dumont could not be sure whether Zouak was watching him or not, and he could no longer stare fully into Zouak's face. He wondered fleetingly if Zouak was married and if, when he made love to his wife, his trachomatous eye was also shielded. Or whether perhaps she had learned to endure the sight of it along with all the other harsh disciplines of Islam.

The beads clacked as Zouak stirred and wound down the window, letting in the glare. The official was coming back and he passed the forms in one by one to Zouak, who nodded before handing them on to Mrs Hoffman. He wound up the window while the official was still talking.

The car moved away up to a barrier in the fence which was lifted clear, plank by plank, by two sweating soldiers. They rolled along, passing the mobile fuel pumps and fire tenders until they came to an Air France Boeing 707. The gang plank was in position and a stewardess stood in the open hatch. The

51

driver opened the door of the car.

From close by came the tinny sound of military music being played over the Tannoy system. Mrs Hoffman left the car first and looked in again briefly. 'Goodbye, Colonel Zouak,' she said. 'And thank you for being so helpful.'

Zouak waved vaguely and she moved away to the gang plank.

Dumont said, 'I don't suppose we'll meet again but I shall remember you, Colonel.' He put out his hand and Zouak touched his fingers lightly.

'And I shall remember you, Captain Dumont. Quite often, I expect. As the prophet says, for a journey of the mind a baggage train is not necessary.' Dumont smiled but Zouak had already turned his head.

The crew of a white Land-Rover were fixing a tow rope to the gangway as he followed Mrs Hoffman up the steps. The stewardess said, 'Welcome aboard,' with a sugary accent and led them the length of the plane to a first-class compartment just behind the flight deck.

When Dumont looked down from the window the car had turned and was speeding towards the gap in the barrier. He leant back and again he had the feeling of being out of control. Perhaps his moral resistance had been lowered by the death of John Forbes, and his arrest, so that he had surrendered the will to determine his own course of action. And there was something else he felt, that whatever was planned for him wasn't finished yet. What had happened so far was only a microcosm of something yet to come. A rehearsal in time . . .

He looked across at Mrs Hoffman and her dark eyes were as compelling as the eyes of a medium.

PART TWO

CHAPTER ONE

They were up at about thirty thousand feet, Dumont supposed, and somewhere over Spain.

His hands moved restlessly. Despite the fact that he was conscious of it he couldn't stop them for very long. It was a Pavlovian response to his surroundings. He looked at the engine pods swaying slowly against the misty blue and tried to remember the control layout. The company had sent him to a conversion course on big jets about three years ago.

He smiled slightly as Mrs Hoffman's hand rested lightly on his knee. 'You are looking very unhappy,' she said.

'I'm not really.' He leant back looking at her. 'I'd like to know something more about this place near Cannes.'

Her eyes considered him. 'What sort of thing . . .' It was a lawyer's answer which gave them both time to think.

'Well . . . what do I do?'

She transferred her weight slightly in the seat and he noticed how incredibly thin her waist was.

When he looked up she was watching him as seriously as usual. 'You do your own thing. You have this apartment which is very luxurious and you may have your family to stay with you there.'

'My son's at boarding school and I don't live with my wife now.'

'How long have you been separated?'

'Oh . . . several years, I suppose.'

The rot had started when he was flying Constellations to the Far East. He'd hardly ever been home more than twice in a month, and then one day when he *did* come home it was to find a tall, pale, serious man waiting for him. He had, he said, insisted on seeing Dumont by himself. He had sent Deirdre to London for the day.

He had moved about anxiously avoiding Dumont's eyes until Dumont said bluntly, 'I suppose you want to marry her.'

'We're not sure about that. We've . . . both made a mistake already. We don't want to make another.'

They were still together and seemed to be content. Nigel

occasionally spoke of Gerald Hale, which was what his name was. He was kind, it seemed, and a great handy-man. He had put super new shelves in Nigel's room and done wonders in the garden. She had been attracted to a handy-man before they were married, he remembered. Like some women she demanded the patience of a craftsman. It was something he had never had. Twice in bed she had called him an impatient bastard and she had often complained that he hurt her.

Since then there had been other women, principally a stewardess called Molly, motherly before her time, whom he slept with as regularly as their schedules allowed. He never knew whether she slept with anyone else or not and he didn't care. He looked up and Mrs Hoffman's dark eyes were still on him.

'I'll ask Nigel if he would like to come down for a week during the Christmas holidays. He wouldn't be able to come for all of the time, of course.'

'You could take him ski-ing. The Trust has a continuous arrangement with a hotel in the Haute Savoie. It is quite near Chamonix.'

Dumont looked away through the window. He had felt the faintest drag a short while before when they'd started closing the throttles and he knew the long descent to the Nice circuit had begun. He looked back at her and then away out of the window again. 'I'm still not sure what the hell is going on.'

She brought the tips of her fingers together in that curious gesture of submission she was given to. 'We exist to help you and we have resources which you might describe as endless. Initially we're going to pay you an allowance equal to twice the salary you received as a Eurofreight captain. You will have your own apartment and access to all the other amenities of the Trust like the ski hotel about which I told you. You are free to come and go as you like. In other words what the Trust is offering you is a sabbatical period and if you want to develop any new interests then the Trust will subsidize any expenses which you might incur. Please don't try and ask me the reasons for it all again, or whether it's a good idea or not, or whether it's been a help to anyone yet. I don't know and I don't really want to know. I'm just the administrator. Mr Ingram is the person to explain the rather complicated philosophical ideas.'

They were descending through drifting cumulus. A shore

line was visible far below, milky where it touched the coast.

'Is there anyone there now . . . at the place in Cannes?'

'Oh yes . . . three or four, and there's a resident staff, of course. You don't have to do anything.'

'Who are the three or four?'

'Oh, there's a German there . . . and an American, Major Granger. I fetched him from New York about six months ago. He was decorated two or three times in Korea for his bravery in close combat patrols . . . he served with an infantry division and later with Kincaid's Raiders . . .'

'What happened to him?' And Dumont added dryly, 'Did he stoop as low as I did?'

'I think he had a drink problem. He was all right until one day when he had a letter from a sergeant who had been in his squad and who was dying from some stomach complaint in a small New Hampshire village. Granger went down there and the man was on the floor of a shack unconscious. Everyone in the town knew he was there but no one had been near him. Granger rushed him to a hospital and then went back to the town. Somehow he did ten thousand dollars' worth of damage and put seven men into hospital before he was arrested.

'We paid for the defence and got him off on appeal. We also took responsibility for the sick man but he died before the trial. In a way it was another case for which the I.V.T. was essentially created. Normally one would like to think that informed public opinion would have gone to the sergeant's aid but there was an anti-war mood prevailing at the time.'

Dumont could hear the crackle of radio voices from the flight deck and knew they must be talking to the tower at Nice. The sea below was close enough to see white caps as they circled the bay. The light came on over the cabin door and Dumont fastened his seat belt.

He watched her shifting around in her seat while she found the pieces of her belt and again he noticed how slim her waist was, and the sharpness of her breasts above it. She looked up again, too, and he realized suddenly that she had meant him to see. He was aware of the faint shock in his genitals, the first tremor of sexuality.

He looked away out of the window and tried to speak calmly. 'I've landed here quite a lot myself. It's always tricky in winter. The mistral blows from the north so you have to come in low from the sea, and if visibility is poor it can be damn' difficult.'

He looked at her briefly. Her head was resting on the seat-back and her eyes were closed. He'd been flying D.C.4s then. 'Every January we used to load up with mimosa and fly it to the markets in northern Europe. I always remember it because the cabin used to smell of flowers for weeks afterwards.'

He looked at her again but her eyes were still closed. He looked out at the sea as they swept over a fishing boat pulling at its anchor. The flaps were right down and the engine pods seemed about to meet the water, when suddenly the runway was beneath them and the wheels thumped. For a moment or two they rumbled and then the whole plane subsided.

They left by the forward door and as they walked across the hard standing towards the reception gates Dumont said, 'Will Mr Hoffman be here to meet us?'

She shook her head. As they reached the gates she said, 'Piet Hoffman is alive and well and living at home in Indonesia.'

She walked ahead of him into the immigration channel.

Outside in the morning glare an oyster-coloured Rolls-Royce was waiting with a liveried driver. As they settled in it, Dumont felt a kind of meaningless guilt, that he was being rewarded for an act of betrayal. Not the betrayal of others but of himself. He said, 'Besides the American, who else is there? Who is the German?'

'Max Sendelbeck. He's very amusing.'

'I don't suppose he was with the Luftwaffe . . .'

'No. He was a naval officer. He was one of the few U-boat commanders to survive. He has the Knight's Cross, of course. And there's an Englishman . . . a Mr Jameson. That's all.'

They were on the motorway, swinging inland to cut off Cap d'Antibes. There was hardly any traffic.

Mrs Hoffman said, 'Max is a very gay person.'

Dumont moved uncertainly. 'The nearer we get the less appealing it sounds. I'm not really a gregarious man . . .'

'Please . . . wait and see. If you like you can be by yourself there, you don't have to mix. If you don't want to stay the Trust can help you in other ways but in any case Mr Ingram will want to meet you first. He takes a personal interest in everything we do. And you must agree he has made a considerable investment in your life.'

'Where does he live?'

'Here in Antibes.'

They were passing to the north of it. A cluster of signs showed and the car swerved into an outer lane. A finger-post said Grasse. They followed the side road for half a dozen kilometres before turning off another side road, and entering the sudden silence of an olive grove.

After a few hundred metres, villas appeared scattered amongst the bleached silver of the olive trees. Beyond in the distance the Bay of Cannes was deep blue.

In the private suite which she showed him to, the shutters were opened by canvas straps fitted to the wall beside the window. She half-opened one and light seemed to explode into the room. There were some comfortable leather chairs and an open escritoire in a recess by the chimney breast.

She came back past him, walking slowly, and opened double doors into the next room. As he followed her into the darkness he cannoned lightly against her. She drew breath almost as sharply as if he'd hit her and he knew she'd stopped and was standing against the wall.

'I must have blinded myself opening the shutters,' she said quietly. 'I can't see a thing . . .'

He waited motionless beside her and in the coolness of the room he could feel the heat of her breath against his cheek. Dumont knew that he should move, that he should find his way to the faint glow which showed where the window was. But he remained standing there. He knew, perversely, that by doing nothing he was in fact committing himself to a course of action. They seemed to be rooted where they stood, preserved in some way by the chemistry of attraction.

Gradually in the quarter-light he became aware of the set of her head and of one dark tragic eye regarding him. He had seen the same look once before, in the eyes of a woman refugee, in another darkened room. It was a curious compound of entreaty and provocation. He opened his hands vaguely in a sort of half-gesture and in a flash she had reached for his head and drawn it swiftly down on her mouth. For almost a minute they were rigid against the wall. Dumont hadn't slept with Molly for more than a month and he realized that he had passed beyond restraint.

She must have felt the same, because when at last he slid

a hand inside her shirt he could feel her heart action as rapid as a drum roll.

Dumont always knew he was a clumsy lover.

With Deirdre, the coldness of the marriage eventually invaded the marriage bed and froze the lubricity of their lovemaking so that towards the end he had found it almost impossible to penetrate her. And because he was hopelessly aware of his own faults, Dumont blamed himself as usual. With Molly he had had a more complex relationship. She was a shrewd, ugly, sensual girl with a bitter sense of humour and they made love in hotel rooms all over Europe and the Orient. She always shook his hand when they met, like a man, and she always made the same inevitable remark: 'I'm only here for the orgasms.'

But often in the night when he woke it was to find that they were wrapped in each other's arms and he knew it wasn't only the orgasms that drew them together.

'Marnix?'

Somebody's hand thudded on the front door of the apartment. 'Marnix? Are you there?' It was a man's voice.

Neither of them moved or spoke. They were lying a foot apart on top of the bed. For an hour their bodies had been scything in the darkness and he was exhausted from a new range of experience.

She had only spoken once when she'd whispered, 'You are a rock, Dumont. You are my *granit rose* . . .'

He was a rock, he thought wryly, in the hands of an expert geologist. He heard movement beside him and when he put out a hand she had gone.

Somewhere in another darkened room beyond he heard taps running. Later when she'd made the bed they went back to the living-room. Dumont pulled the shutters to the top and she opened floor-deep windows on to a wrought-iron balcony. They could see the blue of the bay and the *Iles des Lérins* on the horizon.

'Do you know?' she said. 'It is where they kept the man in the iron mask . . .'

He was about to cover her hand on the railing with his own but some instinct seemed to warn her and she withdrew slightly. The melancholy eyes watched him calmly. 'Only in the dark, Dumont.'

'Yes, all right,' he said with regret. 'I don't suppose it'll happen again.'

He wasn't prepared for her sudden smile. 'Oh it'll happen again . . . here it happens all the time. It's almost the *raison d'être* for the bloody place.'

She walked back into the room before he fully realized what she'd said. While he stood there, somewhere around the side of the house he heard a man singing.

> *'Ihn hat es weggerissen*
> *Er liegt vor meinen Füssen,*
> *Als war's ein Stück von mir*
> *Als war's ein Stück von mir.'*

He turned and saw her seated on the end support of the settee, her hands folded in her lap. He said, 'I'm afraid I don't understand what you mean.'

She stared up at him and the sadness in her eyes was ironic. 'Why did you come with me?'

'I suppose because nobody else seemed to want to help me. It made me bloody angry. By the way, I'd like to make some phone calls . . . to England if I can.'

'You can do it downstairs.'

'I'd better tell my son where I am. And I daresay the company would like to know.'

'Christiane will help you, she is in charge of the office. Why don't you fly to England this weekend and see your son? She can arrange that, too.'

'Well then, I think I will.'

'You will like Christiane. Her name is very apropos because she is devoted to God. She is also a Lesbian. Mr Ingram believes that administrative efficiency will therefore be preserved on two counts. Mr Ingram greatly believes in contingency thinking . . . there is an alternative reason for everything.'

When he smiled wryly, she added, 'The two things aren't necessarily exclusive, Dumont. God is love . . . not sex. She has a different *raison d'être*, that's all.' She levered herself off the end of the settee and went towards the door, which Dumont opened for her. 'Of course, if you are going away, Mr Ingram would like to see you first. Can you come tomorrow?'

'Yes.'

'I'm afraid it will be rather boring.'

When they reached the cavernous hallway again they went towards the rear of the house where Marnix Hoffman opened double doors into a bright office. There was a large, polished centre table and along one wall a smaller desk with a type-writer and a manual switchboard. A girl in a swivel chair was reading a paperback and she plucked off square-lensed spectacles as they approached.

Marnix Hoffman said, 'Christiane . . . this is Mr Dumont,' and the girl put out a small dry hand.

She had blonde sprigs of hair curled on her temples. She smiled at Dumont and said, 'I don't speak English very well.'

'French is my native tongue.'

'*C'est bien.* Mr Jameson is trying to improve my English vocabulary.'

'Mr Jameson is the Englishman I told you about,' Marnix said.

'He says I am speaking much better now.'

'Christiane will show you all the amenities . . . and introduce you to the others. I must go now.'

Dumont walked back across the hallway with her. He wanted her to stop if only for a moment but she kept on walking. He had thought she might have touched him or made some other brief acknowledgement of the things that had happened in the bedroom.

But all she said was, 'Please don't come any farther. I expect we'll be in touch.'

'I don't know where you live . . .'

'Oh, I'm at the Villa Julian most of the time . . . Mr Ingram's villa.'

She went on away from him, her heels tap-tapping down the hall, and she didn't look back when she reached the portico.

Behind him, Christiane said, 'Would you like to come with me now?' She opened doors into a long salon that looked down towards Cannes. Dumont noticed for the first time the crucifix almost lost against the gold of her skin. They walked through the salon and out into a conservatory that gave in turn on to a cloistered passage.

She stopped under one of the archways and Dumont waited at her shoulder. The garden was a sort of classical mélange. Cypresses alternated with Michelangelo reproductions in an avenue that led eventually to a kind of tetrastyle Greek temple. The swimming pool was in the centre foreground where once a water garden must have been. The fountain remained in the middle of it, a scalloped basin in which garlanded water-nymphs reclined.

Two naked girls were swimming the length of the pool in lazy unison. The water was the unnatural blue of copper sulphate. To the right, two men and another girl were slumped in canvas chairs around a wheelbarrow bar with an awning over it. Below on one of the long terrace steps that went down to the level of the water a man was lying on an airbed with a beer can beside his head. He was about Dumont's age, with iron grey hair and a deeply tanned face.

Christiane said quietly, 'Mr Jameson is the younger man over there and that is Mr Granger with him. Here is Max Sendelbeck. I'll introduce you.'

She led the way out on to the terrace and Dumont trailed after her, feeling faintly embarrassed. As they turned to look up at him he felt he was being subjected to some sort of corporate judgement.

The two girls had stopped swimming and, treading water, were staring up. Jameson was standing. Christiane said, 'This is M. Dumont, who has come to join us.' Dumont went down two steps and waited, slightly hunched.

The German spoke first. He said. '*Wilkommen.*'

Dumont bent to shake hands and then went on to the other two. The girl sitting between them looked no more than sixteen. She went on smoothing cream into her legs without looking up. The American was tall and dark-skinned with a look of ugly integrity. As he shook hands he said, 'My name's Doggo Granger. This is Jamie Jameson.'

Jameson, who only looked about twenty-five, wore a blue-spotted head-band. His hair was as long as John Forbes's had been. He shook hands without smiling. 'You're the gun-runner.'

Dumont hesitated. 'That's what I was accused of.'

He waited awkwardly but nobody seemed to want to introduce the girls. He began to move away. 'Don't let me spoil your party . . .' Even as he said it he realized it sounded unutterably patronizing, as if he was giving them permission to carry on.

Jameson grinned without charm. 'Oh, don't worry. You can't spoil it. It goes on all the time.'

As Dumont went on back towards the house, Sendelbeck said, 'Would you like a beer?'

'Yes, I think I would.' He went up and sat on the step above Sendelbeck. Christiane had gone back along the cloistered passage.

Sendelbeck shouted, '*Bière!*'

One of the girls swam to the corner of the pool and climbed out. She walked to the barrow, jumping lightly to shed water. Sendelbeck said, 'It's quite cold, you know. There's a bottle gas fridge built into it.'

Max Sendelbeck rolled on to his stomach and drew up his knees in a way that reminded Dumont of a guard dog crouching. His hair was streaked with silver and his eyes were deepset and faded. It was as if the years were slowly bleaching him.

Watching Dumont, he said, 'But you are a flier, Dumont...'

Dumont nodded. The late sun was hot on his face and he started to take off his jacket. Sendelbeck said, 'A flier. Now that is very interesting.'

The girl came across with four cans of beer and put them neatly between them. She smiled at Dumont as she turned and his eyes dropped to the wisp of colourless hair that covered her pubic arch.

Sendelbeck said, 'That is Anne-Marie.' He leant forward to pick up a can and held it out to Dumont. 'They're not really trying to provoke us ... to be wanton or whatever you say. They must go around like that by order of the Veterans' Trust.'

'I'm afraid I don't understand ...'

'Then you are like the rest of us.' Sendelbeck opened another can and took several mouthfuls of beer from it. 'Nobody understands what's going on here ... but I can tell you one thing, the business is being managed by someone who's a bloody primitive! He thinks that heroism and virility must go together! That if we aren't fighting we must be fornicating.' Sendelbeck smiled. 'But I've been worried. I keep saying to myself, Max ... what else is this bugger up to?'

The deep-set eyes watched Dumont and he was unwilling to look away, as if it might be a signal for the guard dog to launch itself.

He said, 'I've only just arrived.'

'You don't find it curious, then, Dumont ... homes for heroes and all that sort of thing.'

'I can't say I've thought about it very much. When somebody throws you a rope you don't stop to see what it's made of. There are certainly crazier charities.'

'What kind of hero were you, Dumont?'

'I don't really regard myself as a hero . . . no more than a lot of others. And most of them are dead.'

Sendelbeck looked away at last. *'Ja, ja, ja,'* he said softly. 'They are all dead.'

There was a rush of water as the girls reached the end of the pool just below them and turned. Their naked bodies seemed sexless in the water, as innocent as amoebic tadpoles. Watching them, Sendelbeck said, 'At first I thought . . . here is some other crazy mixed-up monster who wants to produce a master race. So he gets some men who he considers heroes and a lot of beautiful girls and starts a sort of stud farm. Because that's what it's like, Dumont . . . even during the war we used to say that making love in the south of France was as common as shaking hands anywhere else.'

Dumont remembered her sudden smile on the balcony when she said, 'Here it happens all the time. It's almost the *raison d'être* for the bloody place.' He said quietly, 'That doesn't seem very likely to me.'

'No, you're right. It isn't that.' Max Sendelbeck's head swung slowly back to look at him. 'You were a hero of the air force, Dumont.'

'I suppose that's how some people regard it.'

'It is a terrible thing to have been a hero, Dumont. How many women and children did you have to incinerate first?'

'Oh, for Christ's sake . . .'

'But I mean it. I was a hero of the German Navy. I had to sink 200,000 tons of ships to get the diamonds to my Knight's Cross. Unarmed ships, Dumont . . .'

'It was a war . . .'

'Ja . . . it was a war. And now it is peace.' The water splashed lazily below them. Somewhere beyond the cypresses a lark was climbing slowly into the heart of the sky. The grey eyes came slowly back to him again. 'I have been a hero once and I don't want to be one again. Whatever this bugger wants I hope he doesn't ask me to be a hero again.'

Dumont turned away from the steady glare of his eyes. Whatever secret they were guarding he didn't want to share it. He said, 'I haven't met Ingram yet . . . I may be seeing him tomorrow. I'm afraid he might find me a disappointment. I'm not really the type for a stud farm.'

As he picked up the second can of beer Jameson came by with his arm around the bare midriff of the girl who'd been sitting with him. They went up the steps in a sort of three-legged race and when Dumont caught Jameson's eye he thought he saw faint contempt behind his curiosity.

Sendelbeck said, 'We have to stick together . . . you and I, Dumont.' He took a sea knife from his pocket with a black bone handle.

'Why do you have to have a theory about Ingram?' Dumont said. 'Why shouldn't he indulge himself . . . a lot of rich men set up charities. There's probably a tax advantage anyway.'

Max Sendelbeck raised the knife to his shoulder and held it there for a moment. Then it flashed downwards at the empty beer can. Again and again he struck, until the end of it was riddled. Then he took up Dumont's empty can and holed that, too, several times. Then he flung them far out across the pool, towards the centre, where they sank immediately.

The girls checked in mid-stroke and arched their bodies. For a moment their pale bottoms broke the water in unison before they went gliding down. They surfaced again, gasping for air, and put the empty cans on the edge of the pool.

Max Sendelbeck said, 'To begin with I used to do that because they exhibit themselves so charmingly. Or that's what I thought. Then I began to think it might be a hangover from the war, that I couldn't bear to see anything still floating. But lately I think it's because I'd like to go to the bottom myself, Dumont. That's where I'd like to be.'

Dumont drank more beer from his can. He heard Sendelbeck laugh suddenly, but it had a lethal quality and his eyes still had a look of steel. 'I'm a liar, Dumont,' he said.

'What do you mean?'

'I know what this bugger is up to.'

Dumont waited. Max Sendelbeck drained his can of beer and smiled again. 'He is up to no good, Dumont. As they say in English, he is up to no bloody good.'

He laughed again, without humour.

CHAPTER TWO

Later, when he went back upstairs, he passed an open door halfway down the corridor to his own. He had just gone by it when Jameson called his name. 'Dumont!'

He went back and looked in. Jameson was lying on a chaise in a short white towelling robe with his hands tucked under his armpits. An ashtray on the table beside him was spilling over. Out of the sunlight, Jameson's hair was sandy-coloured and Dumont could see he had flecked hazel eyes.

Dumont waited, looking at him, and at last Jameson said, 'I thought I'd better tell you, in case no one else does, that I'm no bloody hero like the rest. As a matter of fact I'm on the staff here.'

Dumont nodded. There didn't seem anything to say.

'I was in the army all right, with a Jock division. But there were no wars going at the time and anyway I was in vehicle recovery. I was stationed in Germany as a matter of fact and I was recovering a few private cars on the side until some bastard shopped me. Maybe I was lucky, after all I've got a cushy number here.'

Jameson's hand dropped mechanically to an open packet of Gitanes on the table. He lit a cigarette and exhaled smoke with voluptuous satisfaction. He waved a hand suddenly and said, 'Come in, come in.'

Dumont walked over to the window and looked down at the peeling bark of a eucalyptus tree. The bay was not visible. He noticed that Jameson had brought the smells of the army with him, a compound of unclean socks and blankets and endless cigarettes. He was one of those men who belonged to the armies of history, who for ever find themselves cushy numbers and hedge themselves around with minefields of complicity.

Dumont said, 'What did you want to tell me?'

'There's a rumour in the latrines which I think we ought to talk about.'

Like the smell, Jameson had brought the language of the army as well. Dumont said, 'What is it?'

'Someone said you've had it off with the head girl.'

Dumont's face didn't change. He said, 'Christ, how I hate that expression.'

Jameson exhaled noisily again and watched Dumont with a cheeky, knowing stare.

Then Dumont said, 'I shouldn't listen to rumours if I were you.'

'I just thought I'd let you know.'

It was part of the old army game, where knowledge of someone else was another mine to be laid against his own protection. Dumont moved away from the window. 'What do you do on the staff?'

'I do the lot, Dumont. You might say I'm the quarter-master to the Trust.' He rolled over to stub out his cigarette in the ashtray and turned back, still exhaling smoke. 'I've just come back from U.K. as a matter of fact, where the Trust has acquired another stately home. It's in Dorset.'

'I don't know that part.'

'It's a very nice county, Dumont. I've been getting the house organized and I built a beautiful coffin while I was over there . . . One of the most ingenious you've ever seen.'

Dumont turned to face him. 'What for?'

'I can't tell you, Dumont . . . Not yet, anyway.' He turned his head and smiled. 'Claudine!'

After a moment a door opened in the corner of the room and the young girl he'd seen earlier came in. She wore a short white robe similar to Jameson's. She smiled at Dumont with a kind of fixed unreality.

Dumont said, 'Well, I'll be on my way.'

'Sorry to turn you out, mate,' Jameson said, 'but it's time for my manipulation.' And as Dumont was going through the door, Jameson called, 'Watch out you don't end up in the coffin, Dumont! One of us is going to!'

Antibes was as quiet as an English village, and nothing moved in the long palm-lined street where the Rolls-Royce eventually stopped.

The villa was masked by a high wall and a screen of cypresses, and they waited for a small boy to draw the bolts of the heavy wrought-iron doors. They drove into a cool silent garden around a circular driveway which stopped in front of a long villa, draped in bougainvillaea. The stone beneath the creeper was yellow-coloured, that pale crystalline limestone which is deposited across Europe, and in the triangular pediment that was carried by the door columns, some battle scene from ancient Greece was taking place. Dumont left the car before the chauffeur could open the door for him.

The chauffeur said, 'Mr Ingram said you were to go straight in, *monsieur*.'

Dumont saw then that the door was half open. He walked into a hallway rather like a temple. There was a raised fountain in the centre and the spray from it thudded on the leaves of dark evergreens. The floor around it was inlaid with the signs of the zodiac.

Dumont walked around it vaguely and waited. Someone was shouting somewhere but the sharpness of the echo muffled the original words. He reached the entrance to a corridor, then another, then an enormous double door with a curved *trumeau* dividing it. The shouting seemed to come from somewhere beyond, and when Dumont stepped out, it was into a closed courtyard and he realized the caller was shouting his name. It was like a voice from the war, distorted by the intercom and fear.

'Dumont? Dumont?'

It was coming from a swimming pool at the far end.

Dumont walked on through the funereal greenness to the marbled edge of the empty pool.

'Oh, there you are . . . I thought I heard the car. I'm Ingram.' He appeared to be about thirty-five, and as thin and white as a peeled stick. He was standing at the deep end among the flotsam. There was a pedal boat there and various rings and beach balls. 'It's the butler's day off.'

Dumont didn't know whether he was making a joke or not.

'Come on down,' Ingram said, and he waited motionless while Dumont stepped carefully down the ladder. Dumont was unwillingly aware that he was being made to walk to Ingram, that somehow or other a pecking order was being established. Some obscure prestige was involved. He walked down nearly to Ingram but didn't shake hands. Close to, he saw that Ingram's face, like Dorian Gray's, was totally unmarked.

Dumont said, 'I'd like to say that I'm very grateful for what the Trust has done for me.'

'That's all right, Wing Commander.'

'Actually that was a wartime rank . . . I don't use it now.'

Ingram's eyes were mild and brown behind the spectacles and they examined Dumont closely without embarrassment. 'I'm very proud to know you, sir. A D.S.O. and the Croix de Guerre and how many D.F.C.s? They said . . .'

'To be quite honest one prefers to forget these things . . . the war's a long time over.'

'Maybe some people have forgotten . . . but not me.'

Ingram's suit was light and beautifully cut, and the fabric had a faint, reptilian glitter. He moved suddenly to slam one of the beach balls with his foot and it hit the wall a few yards beyond Dumont and shot away up the shallow end. Although he felt the wind of the ball against his leg, Dumont didn't blink. He had the feeling it had been deliberate and that Ingram was making some idiotic check on his reflexes. It was the sort of childish thought to go with his childish face.

'I've had the engineers in today. They say the walls aren't *imperméable,* so I have to have some fresh tiling done.'

He walked past Dumont towards the ball, which was trickling slowly back towards the deep end. He looked at Dumont for a second and smiled briefly. Then he slammed the ball again in another diagonal kick. His smile went as instantly as it came, as if what he was saying called for instant forgiveness. As the ball trickled back again he walked beside it keeping pace.

'By the way, did you speak to your boy yesterday?'

'Yes. I got through last night . . .'

Ingram turned for a moment and his smile came and went. 'Had he seen the newspapers?'

'Yes, he had.'

'We thought the best thing was to put out a statement straight away saying you were recovering from your ordeal in one of our hotels. I know how persistent newspapers are.'

He watched the ball with concentration before putting another long slanting kick up the shallow end, then he said, 'Have you been in touch with your company yet?'

'Not yet. I thought I'd call them later in the day.'

'You can call them from here.'

'There's no hurry.'

The ball came back towards Dumont but Ingram came to intercept it. He dribbled it to the wall and then slid his back down the tiles to sit on it. Through the wide spectacle lenses his eyes were innocently oblate.

'Why did you come here, Dumont?'

'Well, you arranged for it, didn't you?'

'I mean, why did you accept? Don't you think it was un-heroic? That you should have gritted your teeth and taken your punishment like a man? Don't you think that would have been more courageous?'

'No I don't, as a matter of fact.' Dumont moved away blinking. 'I think that would have been bloody silly. I came because I was innocent but I knew they'd find me guilty if it was politically expedient. Also I knew the British Consulate didn't give a damn about me. Courage doesn't really come into it, but if it did the essential part of courage is an ability to weigh up the factors and look after yourself. Quite a lot of heroes are the biggest bastards you could ever meet.'

Ingram flipped his fingers. 'You've said exactly what I wanted you to say. You've made me very happy.' When he looked up his smile lasted longer, almost as if he was rewarding Dumont.

Dumont said suddenly, 'I told you why I came . . . you haven't told me why you asked me.'

'I thought Mrs Hoffman explained it all.' Ingram pushed himself slowly up the wall again and put a foot on the ball to steady it.

'I'm afraid I didn't believe her.'

Ingram screwed the ball away in an angled kick and came up to Dumont. 'You were quite right,' he said seriously. 'She told you a load of shit. Far from being a hero, my old man ducked out of the war and instead of medals he left me six million dollars.' The ball trickled back past him down to the draining hole, circled a little and was still. Ingram turned away and walked towards the ladder.

The conversation, like the ball, had made its impact and was now at rest. Dumont started to follow.

'Don't get the idea that those girls up at the villa are scrubbers, Dumont. You may have noticed they all speak pretty good English and one of them was at Grenoble University before she came to work for us. Believe it or not she was a student of economics. Are you comfortable there?'

Ingram was standing at the end of the long salon, which overlooked the front gardens and the street beyond. Six or seven nineteenth-century windows gave on to a long wrought-iron balcony. Beside Ingram a small gate-leg table was set for luncheon and on the sideboard behind there were a dozen glass and silver serving dishes.

Dumont was still silent and after a moment Ingram said again, 'Do you like it up there? Are you fully accommodated?' The smile came and went but there was no innuendo in it. It was a constant, that added nothing to what either of them said.

'Yes, very comfortable.' Then Dumont added, 'In one sense . . .'

'What's wrong, Dumont?'

'I'd rather like to know what's going on here . . . Why you should have bailed me out. I'm grateful, of course . . .'

'I hope it's only a down payment. I hope you may stay on. Like the others . . .'

'I'm afraid that won't be possible. You see, I have a service contract with Eurofreight. They'll want me back after a reasonable time.'

'Surely.'

'So if it's not really a home for heroes, I'd rather like you to tell me what's going on.'

Ingram walked away, troubled. 'I don't really mind telling you . . . the only thing is I feel we have a real communications problem. Your character and background haven't really equipped you to understand what I'm going to say.'

'I shouldn't count on that. I've listened to illegal propositions before.'

'Well, you could say it's an illegal proposition, I suppose.' Dumont smiled.

'I mean it. A fairly remarkable criminal enterprise I would call it. The planning, which is quite simple, has already been completed. The only factor that can fault it is the human factor, which is why I'm spending a great deal of time and money in getting hold of the right characters. Crime is much too important to be left to professional criminals.'

'So you're collecting heroes.'

'That's right.'

Dumont laughed shortly and stopped. Somewhere in another room a clock began to chime softly and sanely. Then Dumont said, 'Max told me you were round the twist.'

'Did Max say that? He's a great character. Did you know

he sank over two hundred thousand tons of allied shipping and had his Knight's Cross with Diamonds personally from Adolf Hitler? As a matter of fact you and he have a lot in common. You both represent the kind of heroes I'm interested in. I don't want one-timers who led the Charge of the Light Brigade, but guys who went back time and again. Men who evaluated danger and lived with it. You said it back at the pool . . . that the essential part of courage is weighing up the factors.'

Dumont laughed again. 'You know I can't really believe you're serious.'

'I'm trying not to be dramatic, Dumont, but I *am* serious.'

'Then I'm sorry to disappoint you. I am afraid I don't have any criminal tendencies. If I had to choose, I'd be on the side of law and order.'

'Well, you're a free man. You *can* choose.'

'Then I'm sorry, Ingram. I hope you won't be too disappointed.'

Ingram laughed and moved over to the laden sideboard. Very carefully he picked up a bottle of claret with the cork drawn, and turned back. He raised it slowly. He looked like a priest before the high altar, displaying the Host, and offering Dumont absolution and eternal peace.

'Come and get it, Dumont,' he called, and as Dumont moved forward he said, 'I'll tell you something else. Philanthropists who bail people out of trouble can be bastards, too. Just like heroes.'

Afterwards they sat in swing seats under a mimosa tree at the back of the house.

In a street near by children were chanting, and once Dumont thought he saw the figure of a woman at an upstairs window. He wondered whether it was Marnix Hoffman. He closed his eyes and put his head back listening to Ingram talking. Ingram's voice had a casual authority about it.

'You know, I've thought about this thing a lot and you reacted just the way I figured you would . . . in fact, in the way some of the others did. So I tried to reason out a formula that would get a normal, well-adjusted person like you interested in my venture, and I came up with certain basics. To bend Von Clausewitz a little, I believe crime to be a natural extension of normal business trading. It's a rotten world,

Dumont . . . right now we're worried about ecology and the environment but nobody gives a damn about the moral ecology. Democracy is only freedom to con your neighbour, like Humphrey Bogart said, one half of the world is squirrels and the other half is nuts. It's not actually legal to gun people down yet but you're allowed to promote the sale of cigarettes and unsafe cars, which are the biggest killers of our time. And the rot goes all the way up . . . there've been seventeen alleged cases of corruption within the U.S. administration this year and the French Government isn't doing much better. This is my first *big* point, Dumont. What we're going to do won't hurt anybody, won't cause any suffering. In fact, it's going to help a lot of people who are less fortunate than we are. It's a clean operation without any fallout.

'I thought about the hopelessness of people in other places whose living standards and life expectancy are way below our own and I decided that fifty per cent of the take we get should go to the agencies who are trying to do something about it. In other words, we're giving it a Robin Hood twist, where we take it from some faceless institution and give it to those in need. Hey, are you awake, Dumont?'

Dumont opened his eyes to look across at Ingram but Ingram's eyes were closed. Dumont said, 'Yes, I'm awake.'

'The second big thing that you have to be convinced about is that I really do have a brilliant, analytical mind capable of planning initiatives which are absolutely foolproof. I have the resources, mental and financial, to crack anything in the world. You must come to believe in me, Dumont . . . *and* my ideas which are workable and complete. Nobody will have to look over his shoulder afterwards. What do you think, Dumont?'

'Do you want to be a hero?' Dumont said.

There was a long silence before Ingram said, 'You were right to ask. The only kind of neurosis I might have is that I want to do my own thing and not my father's thing. But I need heroes and you people up the hill are all from the vintage years. It's difficult to make it any more . . . in Vietnam one side had all the hardware and World War Three is going to be a nuclear wipe-out. You are one of the last *real* heroes, Dumont.'

'All the same isn't it a needlessly elaborate method of recruiting? And expensive . . . because I'm afraid you've wasted

72

your money on *me*.'

Ingram shrugged, opened his pale hands. 'Considering what's involved it's only peanuts. In fact, it's because there's so much involved that nothing must be left to·chance. Particularly the human factor. I have to have characters of *proven* reliability in crisis. There's no simulation test for coolness . . . you have to be put in the crucible to find out. Well, you've been through the fire several times, Dumont, and you didn't crack. Picking up heroes in trouble may sound to you like going all the way round Barney's pig but believe me it's paid off. Why don't you go away and think about it for a while. That's what the others did and in the end they stayed.'

When Dumont opened his eyes again it was in time to see Ingram smile. It came and went as usual, like a door opening and closing on an empty cupboard.

CHAPTER THREE

Somewhere up the hill behind the villa there was a bonfire burning. Whatever it was wasn't very combustible because the smoke that blew across the gardens was heavy and yellow. Dumont thought it smelt faintly of tar.

The Rolls had gone and as he crossed the hallway he heard a shutter ticking steadily on the switchboard in the office. He went on up the stairs, thinking that he would ring Eurofreight later that same day. When he fitted the key in his door he found that the latch had already been pegged back.

He opened it and went in.

Marnix Hoffman must have heard his key because she was coming along the passage from the bedroom. She was wearing a black one-piece swimsuit and her hair was damp at the ends. She held him and kissed him, without smiling, and afterwards stayed leaning against his body.

'We were all given the day off in your honour . . . including me. He wanted nothing to disturb him while he was talking to you.'

'I thought I saw a woman at the window. I thought it might be you.'

'No. It wasn't me. I came out here at lunchtime.'

Dumont gripped her buttocks lightly and pulled her upwards against him, clear of the floor. As he started to walk with her she said, 'That's a very unscientific way to lift a person, Dumont. You could damage a disc.' Her elbows rested lightly on his shoulders.

As they went into the bedroom she added, 'The others are having a picnic up in the wood. Max organized it. He calls it a land party.' Dumont put her down beside the bed and she peeled the straps of her swimsuit down.

'I thought I heard someone calling à while ago. Then I could hear Max singing up in the woods.' She knelt naked on the covers. 'I haven't got long.'

Dumont began tossing his clothes across the seat of a farthingale chair. He walked back in his underpants, powerless to shed them any more than he could have shed the rather old-fashioned inhibition that made him keep them on.

Like a bullfighter, Deirdre had once said to him a long time ago, hiding the sword in the *muleta*.

When she said goodbye, less than an hour later, she added, 'Until the next time, Dumont. And always remember that I lack for nothing in between.'

There were voices calling somewhere up on the hills behind and from farther away there was the sound of a rifle shot.

'What's wrong, Dumont . . .'

'Can't we meet away from here?'

'What do you mean. In a hotel room?'

'No, not that . . . I mean away from here and everything.' Then, unsmiling, he added, 'Away from the old *raison d'être*.'

'That doesn't fit into my scheme of things, Dumont.' She had started to dress.

Dumont kept his eyes closed. 'You've spoilt this place for me . . .'

'Are you going away?'

'I think so.'

He'd watched the car drive away, and showered, and was standing at the window when the picnickers came back, struggling across the lawns between the sprinklers. Max walked alone at the rear, carrying a sea bag.

Dumont was assailed by a sudden loneliness. He hadn't the temperament of Marnix Hoffman, who could isolate the

74

sexual act and had now gone back to whatever sufficiency she found at the Villa Julian. He felt the urgent need of other relief. He decided to telephone Nigel again and perhaps now that he knew what his plans were he would call the Euro-freight office. As he went down the wide staircase he saw, through the branches of the heavy empire chandelier, the door of the office open beyond. Christiane was sitting there with her head bent over the typewriter.

When he walked in she looked at him calmly. She was wearing a loose sweater and knee-length jeans and the crucifix swung in its usual place.

She said, 'You're back.'

He nodded.

'The others went to a picnic.' She pronounced it in the French way.

Dumont said, 'I saw them coming back.' And without knowing why he added, 'Did you go?'

'I'm not allowed.' Her voice was serious. 'I'm on duty.'

'Yes, of course.'

She took the paper from the machine and pushed it away. 'Was there something you want, Mr Dumont?'

'Well, I thought it was about time I got in touch with my employers, and I'd rather like to ring my son again.'

She put the headset around her neck and opened a pad. 'I have your son's number . . . Woodbridge, England 02839.'

'And the other one's in London. It's 01-349 7284.'

'Which shall I call first?'

'I don't mind, really . . . London perhaps . . .'

'I'll call you.'

Dumont walked across into the long room. He could hear splashing in the swimming pool but no voices. He picked up a copy of *Nice-Matin* at the centre table and walked on towards the french windows. As the room opened out he suddenly saw Max stretched on one of the quaint embroidered settees.

Max must have heard him because his eyes opened. 'Dumont.'

Dumont stopped, not wanting to be unfriendly but uncertain of what to say. 'How are you, Max?'

'I am played out. Is that correct?'

Dumont nodded.

Max's English was littered with rather charming expressions

75

from the pre-war schoolroom. 'I am played out with women, Dumont.' When he looked up again, Dumont saw that one of the dog's eyes had a ruptured artery in the corner. 'We have a *Landpartie* in the woods, a picnic.'

'I thought I heard you singing once.'

'I'm always singing.' Max closed his eyes again.

The splashing in the pool had stopped and a distant murmur of voices began. Dumont was about to move away, out into the sunlight when Max said, 'We have an old German proverb, *"Raubvögel singen nicht."* It means birds of prey do not sing. That's why I am singing all the time, Dumont.'

He swung his legs away suddenly and pulled himself into a sitting position. 'Why don't we drink some beer together? . . .'

Dumont hesitated. 'All right,' he said at last. 'I'll get some.'

'Let the girls bring it!'

'No, I'll go.'

When Max stared at him he knew he was letting down the Officer Corps, that group of men who commanded and were obeyed.

As he moved, Max said, 'Kronenbourg Export. None of that table beer.'

The kitchen was empty. Dumont rummaged in the deep freeze until he found a frosted carton of Kronenbourg. He found glasses on the Provençal dresser. Beside it was an earthenware crock full of black olives, and Dumont scooped a handful on to a dish and took it back with the other things.

When he went in, Max was standing in the doorway to the courtyard, rubbing his wet head with a towel. 'That's better,' he said. 'That's much better.' He slumped down on to the settee, still rubbing at his huge, shaggy head.

Dumont opened the beer and poured it. He sat opposite Max with half his mind on the hallway from where Christiane would call him to the phone. Max said, 'You should have let one of the girls do it, that's what they're paid for.'

'Are they paid?'

'Not much . . . At St Tropez they're cheap at the end of the summer.'

He swallowed several mouthfuls of beer. He kept his glass in his hand, resting it lightly against the slight shelf of his belly. 'You have talked to Ingram?'

'Yes, I saw him today.'

'Are you staying with us?'

Dumont walked to one of the open windows and threw some olive stones out into the garden. 'I don't think so . . . I haven't fully made up my mind.'

'We need you, Dumont.'

'Come off it, Max.' Then he said quietly, 'You must admit it's a strain on one's powers of belief. I thought this sort of a thing went out with Edgar Wallace.'

'But if he wasn't serious, why should he spend all his money?'

Behind Max's back, Granger came into the doorway from the courtyard. 'How did you get on? Are you on the team yet?'

Dumont didn't answer and Max shook his head.

Doggo Granger said, 'What's wrong with it, Dumont?'

Dumont shrugged, 'Nothing, I daresay. I just happen to have a job already.'

Granger said, 'For how long and what do you expect to do afterwards at your age?'

Dumont turned his back. 'I daresay I'll find something else . . .'

'Selling encyclopaedias? Oh, grow up.'

Max said, 'He's right, Dumont,' and closed his eyes. 'For less than a week's work we're being offered nearly three million francs each. Enough to keep us for as long as we need. But then, of course, you may be rich already . . .'

'I'm not rich. In any case one would have to know a great deal more about it before deciding.'

Beyond someone dived into the pool and the splash echoed flatly. After a long time someone gasped.

Granger said, 'Did you ever know about the assassins, Dumont?'

'The assassins? . . .'

At that moment the double doors opened wider and Christiane said, 'I have your call to Woodbridge, Suffolk. They're getting your son now . . .'

'Oh, thank you.' As he followed her back across the hall he was still thinking of Ingram and Ingram telling him that nobody was going to be killed, so why was Granger talking about assassins? He went into the phone booth, picked up the receiver and waited.

The line was silent but Dumont could hear someone picking at a typewriter nearby and after a moment a door slammed and there was the sound of footsteps.

'Dad?'

'Hello, Nigel.'

'Is anything wrong?'

'No. Why?'

'You rang yesterday. Are you still in the South of France?'

'Yes, still here.'

'How super. We're doing *The Merchant of Venice* at the end of term. I'm a magnifico.'

'What's that?'

Nigel couldn't have heard because he said, 'We're rehearsing in the gym now as a matter of fact.'

'Then I mustn't keep you.'

'Five minutes won't matter. Why did you ring?'

'I thought I might come over this weekend. Can you get an exeat on Sunday?'

Nigel hesitated before saying, 'Well, I've got one already, as a matter of fact. There's a fair on in Fen Meadow. Hayter's parents were going to take me.'

Dumont waited a moment. 'Well, if you've got it all laid on . . .'

'I daresay you could come as well.' Nigel's voice lacked conviction.

'No. I'll leave it, I think, and come a bit later on. I'll write next week.'

'Okay. 'Bye, Dad.'

He heard the click before he could reply. He put the receiver back carefully and waited before going out. He couldn't remember whether he'd met Hayter's parents or not. He'd met quite a lot of people at prize-giving and on sports day. Nigel had sounded happy, he had to admit that. He pushed the door open at last and went out.

As he crossed the hall Christiane called, 'I'm still trying London . . .'

Dumont waved vaguely. He walked on past Max and picked up his glass again.

Doggo Granger said, 'Well?'

'What did you mean when you mentioned assassins? I thought that no one was going to get hurt.'

'I didn't mean that . . .' Granger opened his hands. 'I meant *this,* Dumont . . . the set-up *here.* I read somewhere how the original assassins were drugged and brought to a place like

78

this where they had all the wine and women they wanted. They were kidded they were in paradise. This is what motivated them later. Their courage was based on the fact that they wanted to be killed so they could get back to the kind of goodies they had in the so-called vision. That's all I meant, boy.'

Dumont picked up his glass and went to sit opposite Max. 'Why did you join, Max? What happens if it's a cock-up? If they put you away?'

'The world's a cock-up already, Dumont . . . There isn't really very much to lose.'

Max drank his beer and tore the tab from another can. 'Perhaps you're right to stay out, Dumont. You have a conscience which is very obvious. During the war neither of us had a conscience but you have grown one since.'

'You talk an awful lot of crap, Max.'

Dumont knew they were both watching him, measuring him, and he could feel a sense of challenge. He opened another can of beer for himself and poured it slowly. 'I have a conscience but it's got fuck-all to do with what we're talking about.' As he put the glass down it rattled slightly.

The door opened suddenly again and Christiane said, 'I've got them. I've got London.'

When he picked up the receiver, Birkett's voice sounded faint and somehow out of pitch. 'We have your cable and everybody is happy you're safe.'

'How do I get back?'

'You'll be pleased to know that things have been moving and we're in touch with the Moroccan representatives here. They're releasing the plane and we're flying in a relief crew tomorrow. Scotty's going with them.'

'How's Scotty?'

'This line isn't very good. I can't hear you very well.'

Dumont said slowly, 'When do you want me back there?'

'There's no hurry on that. I've had a memo from the top office . . .'

'I'm quite fit, you know, Birky!'

'You may think so, but after what you've been through the company doesn't want to rush things. They want you to have a thorough medical when you get back here before you are reassigned.'

Dumont was silent for so long that Birkett said, 'Can you

hear me, Dumont?'

'I'm quite fit. There's no problem . . .'

'It's an I.A.T.A. regulation and we have a new doctor now who's very regulation-orientated.'

'Where's Louis?'

'Gone back to Australia. He wasn't reappointed at the last staff review. They seem to think he was a bit easy-going. there've been some other changes at the top in the last month . . .'

'I'd like to get back as soon as possible,' Dumont said. 'Is there anything going through Nice these days?'

'Not regularly, but I'll let you know later on.' Birkett hesitated again, and when he said something else the puppet's voice was so indistinct that Dumont couldn't hear it.

'I'm sorry,' he said. 'You're fading, Birky . . .'

'I said you've no need to worry. There's a note on your file to say you're to be taken care of.'

'What do you mean?'

'Well, there's a ground manager's job at Gatwick coming up in the spring. You'd have the first refusal. Believe me, it's a great feeling getting your feet on solid ground.'

'First refusal.' Dumont repeated it mechanically.

Birky went on talking but his voice had begun to fade again.

Dumont remembered that Bumpy Birkett had been a pilot until five years ago. In fact, he had got his nickname because of his memorable landings. And then Birkett's voice came surging back again.

'I've sent off a lot of bumph to the address you gave. There are forms you have to fill in . . . statements required about the crash.'

'It wasn't a crash,' snapped Dumont, but again Birkett didn't seem to hear.

Birkett was saying, 'Well, keep in touch . . .'

'Goodbye, Bumpy.'

'Goodbye and don't forget . . .' Dumont put the receiver back and stood there with his eyes unregistered. It wasn't quite like the old Bumpy, he thought, not like the Bumpy of the old days, bouncing and fish-tailing along the runways of Europe. Now it was a Bumpy that went with the puppet's voice, a dummy that had taken the place of the real Bumpy behind a desk. There was a small vanity mirror fixed over the phone and Dumont was suddenly aware of the middle-aged man who stared back at him. He stepped out of the box and walked towards the open front door.

He swung out across the lawn, walking towards the late sun. Far to the north he could see a big jet descending, just visible against the evening sky. It was probably in the landing circuit for Nice.

He went striding on down, through sweet-smelling eucalyptus trees. He would refuse the office job, of course, purely on the grounds that it wasn't logical. A retiring judge doesn't become a law court messenger, an architect doesn't become a bricklayer.

Whatever he did next would have to be something different. He picked up a slender branch, stripped the aromatic leaves from it and strode on swinging it as if he was trying to keep some thought at bay. He came suddenly on the terraced gardens of another villa. A nurse was pushing someone very old, in a panama hat, along a path. He veered away into the trees again, heading north. Even if Louis had been there it was unlikely he would have been passed fit again, and with the new man there would be no chance at all. He walked up through the thinning wood and saw the house now lying back on his right. The last of the sun was making the windows glare and on one of the balconies a girl was hanging out her underwear to dry.

Of course he would have to ask Ingram more about it and then when he knew all the answers he would have to weigh them up and decide. Money wasn't entirely a factor, as long as he could pay the school fees. There were swifts skimming the lawn in search of a late supper and from the village up on the road a church bell had begun to toll slowly. He wondered if Ingram was planning for him to fly something and if so what it was. He wouldn't have anything to do with drugs, he was quite certain about that. He threw the stick away and walked more slowly, not wanting to reach the house before a decision had been made.

Gatwick, if it happened, could only be a temporary solution. He could never grow old on the edge of an airfield. On the other hand, if Ingram's project was really watertight and if all the other things he said were true, he would be able to grow old wherever he wanted. It was an opportunity to buy his freedom by investing what Ingram called his courage, the same way that another man might invest his life's savings in an annuity. But this so-called courage was the only asset he had left. He was walking on gravel now, under an arch of Zephirine Drouhin, the thornless French rose and the most sweetly scented in the world. The sun was down and lights had come on at some of the windows.

Max was standing in one of them, downstairs in the lounge. Seeing him there, secure against the warmth of the room, increased the sense of isolation that Dumont was already feeling. He put a foot on the low-terraced wall and vaulted over, making for the front door again. When he went into the hall the office door was closed and Doggo Granger was sitting on the stairs with a glass of whisky and a newspaper. He looked at Dumont coming in and then bent his head to the paper again. Dumont had a sudden sense of revelation, that he wasn't after all taking the decision alone.

In a way he might be deciding for all of them.

The door of the phone booth was open and the light was on. He could just smell the staleness of cigarette smoke that came from it. He walked half-way towards it, then suddenly he was striding out and making for the stairs. He took them three at a time and walked along the corridor to his room. On one of the doors there was a notice hanging 'Ne pas déranger' and beyond in the room he could hear a girl singing. He went into his own room and closed the door. He decided to shave before dining and thought that he might drive down to the Mont Fleury above Cannes. He would ask Max to join him.

He stripped off his sweater and went into the bathroom and stopped. In a corner of the mirror with her silver lipstick she had printed 'Mon roc! Mon granit rose!' He turned away from it and spun the taps.

Then he looked back at it again, trying to read into the words a first sign of tenderness.

Ingram followed Marnix Hoffman with his eyes as she brought the cigar box from the humidor in the corner, and opened it on his lap. He said, 'I have a feeling of oppression. Do you have a feeling of oppression tonight?'

'Yes I do.'

'I thought you might have. You often have one when you've been to see a movie. What was it, by the way?'

'Oh, it was a revival of an old Sacha Guitry film. From

ages ago . . . the thirties, I think. I don't know why I hadn't seen it before. Arletty was in it . . . and Raimu.'

He picked up the table lighter and singed the end of the cigar with care and concentration. It was a Reine de Cabana open at both ends, like a cheroot. 'How did it end?'

'How did it end?'

'How did the film end? What were the closing scenes? That's how I can tell whether I've seen it or not. I never forget the closing scenes of a movie.'

She took the lighter from his hand and laid it down. 'I don't know how it ended . . . I got bored with it, and someone behind me kept coughing. I was afraid he would give me his virus. I left early and walked along the *plage.*'

Ingram laid his cigar on the ashtray and his smile came and went like a camera shutter. 'Come and sit here.'

His eyes followed her as she came around the low table towards the chesterfield. He said, 'Right here,' and opened his hand. The cigar smoke wavered as she slid down beside him. He let his head go back against the upright.

'I think we'll have an early night,' he said. 'Something must happen soon.'

She rested lightly against his stomach and picked up his hand. It was small and pale and clean. She brought it to her face and held it lightly against her lips. His fingers stayed flaccid and she moved them slowly to and fro across her lips. Ingram said, 'You love my hand, don't you, Marnix?'

'Yes, I love your hand.'

'I know you do.' Just for a moment his fingers contracted against her own. A twitch that came and went as quickly as his smile.

From the table the telephone bell began to throb. As she lowered his hand and straightened he said, 'I'll take it,' but he didn't move. 'I'm superstitious . . . let it ring a little.'

When he picked it up finally, someone began speaking hurriedly. After half a minute Ingram said, 'Okay, Dumont. I'll call you tomorrow.' He put the receiver back and turned to look at her.

His face was blank with an intensity of thought.

Marnix said, 'I only hope he *is* the right man . . . after all that trouble.'

'We didn't *want* an international incident, Honey . . . all we wanted was an aircraft stopped and the pilot held for a simple inquiry which is what would have happened if Dumont had been making his scheduled stop at Rabat on the South American route. What screwed things up was the disaster . . . we had to act quickly or we might have lost him.'

Ingram stood up. The smile flickered and was gone. He said, 'And it's not just a question of Dumont being the "right" man . . . he's the *only* man, which is why we've been seven weeks checking him out. No one else flying regularly within Zouak's reach had the capability we need *and* the personal circumstances.'

Dumont left the phone booth and crossed the hall into the living-room. He wanted a drink badly and someone to drink with.

'Max,' he called as he went through the door.

The lights were on and Anne-Marie was sitting in one of the wheelback chairs by the window with a book on her knees. Perhaps she was the graduate from Grenoble, thought Dumont, reading her Laski or Keynes, or whatever they read nowadays.

She looked up at Dumont but kept a finger on a line. 'He is asleep,' she said.

Dumont walked on until he could see the blanketed figure lying in the big settee. Dumont said, 'Max,' softly and moved the blanket away from his face. Max's eyes were closed and his jaw had dropped as if in death. As he laid the blanket back Dumont felt like a relative visiting a morgue.

Behind him the girl said, 'Don't worry, I'll look after him . . .' Without irony, she added, 'It's less than I am paid to do.'

Dumont went out into the kitchen and got whisky and a bottle of cold Vichy water from the fridge. Going up the stairs his mind still retained the memory of Max's face.

She took Ingram's arm as they went upstairs, leaving the lights for the Spanish servants.

As they reached the top landing he said, 'We'll write to Zouak in the morning . . . he'll be pleased everything turned out the way we hoped.' And as they passed into the bedroom he said, 'I remember that movie now . . . Raimu played the part of Napoleon.'

He was watching her face in the long cheval glass. She said, 'No. Jean-Louis Barrault was Napoleon.'

'That's right. I meant Jean-Louis Barrault.'

Dumont sat on the balcony with the whisky glass in his lap but after the first sip he couldn't drink any more. It tasted like caramel in his mouth. The long hops were over, something had happened at last, but he'd never thought he'd end up as a sort of Doctor Faustus.

But at least, he thought, he'd made up his own bloody mind about it.

PART THREE

CHAPTER ONE

Ingram said, 'They're doing something about the heating. There are a couple of men up from Weymouth working on it now.'

He was standing in front of a fireplace of white Carrara marble. The hobs had brass inlays of two different coats-of-arms and there was a brass trivet in front of it, with a shallow pan. The parquet floor at his feet was splashed with a dozen brilliant colours where the sunlight was refracting from a case of antique glass paper-weights which stood by the window. It was the smaller salon of the two, on the east side of the house.

Beyond the windows steps led down from a brick terrace to a mile-long vista of parkland laid out by some contemporary of Lancelot Brown, the eighteenth-century architect. There was a lake at the end of it, and half-way along, the crumbling ruin of a temple of French worthies. The statues had been carved from soft Bath stone and only Descartes, with his back to the prevailing wind, had stood the ravages of time. Beyond the lake a herd of sedate Friesian cows grazed the soft Dorset landscape. Ingram had told them the house was rented for three months and he had brought his Spanish servants with him, from the villa in Antibes.

Dumont waited with the others. They stood awkwardly in depth, like the depleted figures in an end game. Even Ingram must have been aware of it because as he walked through them he said, 'Why don't we get all the seats into a kind of circle . . . and make ourselves comfortable.' There was an air of expectancy in the room as on a first day at school, or in the army. Ingram had enhanced the classroom atmosphere by putting up a new-looking blackboard and easel, just to one side of the fireplace.

Dumont nearly yawned. The trip had been longer than expected with a stopover in Switzerland to open bank accounts. From Geneva airport Dumont had driven a hired car thirty miles to Lausanne and had deposited a cheque for his advance in a numbered account at the Banque Nationale de Suisse. It was for ten thousand pounds.

Marnix Hoffman was at a long table by the window, arrang-
ing papers in neat piles, counter-rolling maps and plans to
flatten them. Dumont tried to catch her eye as he and Max
lifted a sofa nearer the fire but she was intent on what she
was doing. The others lifted lyreback chairs until they were
all in a semi-circle. Nobody smoked or talked and the air of
expectancy increased.

Ingram walked outside the circle, to and fro behind them.
He said, 'We're pretty secure. The Spaniards are sticking to
the kitchens during the day and they go down to the east
lodge at the back entrance of the property for the night. We
represent a kind of do-it-yourself international study group
examining English social customs in the present day. In the
unlikely event you ever have to explain yourself that is what
you say. This house is costing a great deal of money, as did
the villas in France, *and* your deposits in Switzerland, but by
putting up a lot of seed money towards what we are going to
do, I hope to show you how confident I am that we are going
to succeed in what is a well-thought-out operation. We're
going to spend today discussing the detailed plan and tomorrow we carry out phase one. Altogether it's a nine-day
hitch.'

Doggo said, 'Put us out of our misery.'

Ingram's smile flashed on and off. 'I'm trying to be calm
about it. Everything has to be well rehearsed and there mustn't
be any dramatics or hairy behaviour. That's why I had to
have seasoned, courageous people. Briefly, what we are
going to do is to remove eleven million dollars' worth of nineteenth-century art from the Turner Gallery in London. It's
the third biggest in the country. That's not as much as it
sounds . . . On today's valuation, in fact, we only need to
remove six pictures.' Ingram stopped for a moment but nobody
broke the silence.

'What we are operating is really a very simple idea which
won't be dangerous for us or the authorities involved. And
the follow-up is just as simple. When we have the pictures
safe out of the country we negotiate their return to the gallery
at a written down price. And about half of that goes to
charities. It's the kind of deal they'll leap at and in the end
it won't cost them a cent because the insurance companies will
have to pay up. Let's have the gallery plan now . . .'

Marnix brought it and there was a delay while the thumb

tacks wouldn't go in and she had to fetch tape instead.

Dumont knew that Max was looking at him. Without turning his head he said quietly, 'What do you think of *that*, Max?'

Max shrugged.

'I'll show you the problem first,' Ingram said. 'Just the way I came to it. The security at the Turner is much the same as at any other of the world's leading galleries, that is the system designed by Karl Steinitz in 1948, and it is supposedly foolproof. In a gallery of the cubic footage of the Turner you'd require a pretty big night staff to guarantee security. This introduces a very high running cost but as well as that it introduces the element of human corruption. The basic Steinitz system is a unique combination of pressure and contact switches together with vibrator switches and infra-red beams. During closing hours there's a complete canopy around the outside of the gallery which is impenetrable, in fact if you so much as breathe on a window the change of temperature would be enough to set off the alarm. The alarms are wired direct to Scotland Yard and the New King's Road Police Station, so within a few minutes of them being set off every pool car that's available would be around the gallery. For that reason you need a minimum night staff. Two men who stay behind and activate the system. It's dual-circuited, has two other power supply systems available in case of electricity failure. Nobody has yet faulted it. There has been no single case of a night theft from a gallery during the hours of closure since the Steinitz systems were introduced. Several attempts have been made, mostly by people trying to find a by-pass either through the roof or the cellars. There isn't any by-pass. There's this multiple system of switches and beams which covers every inch.

'It's a great problem and they made it even tougher about fifteen months ago when Steinitz installed Jezebel switches all through. They're a new type of ball switch which is only sensitive to high frequency sound.'

Ingram walked a slow semi-circle near them, as though wanting them to feel the weight of it for themselves.

Dumont thought first of bribing one of the guards inside, and second of concealing someone inside the gallery during the hours when it was open. Then all you would have to do ...

'The obvious thing you will all have thought first is of introducing someone into the gallery and concealing them while the place is open, but that isn't possible for a variety of reasons. The surveillance system during opening times is as near perfect as you can get. Of course, there's closed circuit television coverage of all the main halls but as well as that there are two men on duty in every room in the building and an attendant in each washroom. For obvious reasons there's no place where a potential thief could be alone. Even if all that surveillance fails, there is another check which makes it totally impossible to infiltrate. That is a body count in and out at the entrance hall. Two to be exact, one manual and one electronic, so there's no chance of a slip up.' Ingram stopped again and this time walked around outside them.

Standing somewhere behind Dumont he said, 'You have to admit it's an intellectual challenge.'

His footsteps moved away. He was picking something off the table. Dumont was visited by a sudden feeling of detachment. He was not really sitting there in a manor house in Dorset, listening to an American explaining how they were going to remove half a dozen Impressionists from the Turner. He closed his eyes against the reality and waited. He heard a sudden click, quite close.

When his eyes opened Ingram was holding a flick knife. The dark gunmetal blade travelled slowly around them like the second-hand of a clock. Then Dumont said calmly, 'You told me that no one was going to be killed.'

The room remained silent and Dumont looked at Doggo, then at Max, then at Jamie. He had the feeling that they had been briefed before, that they already knew. He felt suddenly like an outsider.

If it *was* the first day of school then he was very much the new boy.

Ingram drove them to Yeovil in a dark green delivery van.

Although Marnix was sitting next to him in the passenger seat he made small talk with Dumont most of the way, speaking over his shoulder. 'It's convenient the Impressionists are all together. Are you an art buff, Dumont?'

'Not really.'

'There are three Renoirs from his vintage period in the

nineties. All of Gabrielle at the bakery . . . the Gauguin is the Paimpol fisherman, one of his greatest. And none of them cost the gallery a cent, they were part of a bequest after World War One. The Van Gogh and the Cézanne are terrific too. Actually the current valuation runs at just over eleven million dollars but we'll give them back for seven million.'

Dumont said, 'That's a million dollars more than your father left you.'

The van slowed and for a long time there was silence. Then Ingram said, without turning his head, 'That's right. But he spent a lifetime making his.'

They didn't speak again.

It was a crisp October morning and the hedgerows were full of blackberries and rose hips and the feathered seeds of traveller's joy. Twice Dumont saw a stoat cross the road ahead of them. As they ran through Ashfield, a small thatched village, Ingram turned again to say, 'Don't worry because you only have a bit part today. You really have the star part later on. You'll have to start getting ready as soon as we get back.'

'Yes, I daresay.'

As they left the lanes and came out on to the main Dorchester road the telegraph lines were alive with long strings of swallows waiting to emigrate.

They reached Yeovil with ten minutes to spare before the train. Ingram took the wrong turn at a roundabout and they circled briefly before coming in on the Ilchester road, past the Pickett Witch House.

'Damn it . . .' Ingram said, 'One day I'll stop and ask the good people there what in hell that name means.'

After they had parked in the station yard Marnix waited in the van because she was getting a train later on. Ingram walked as far as the platform with them, still talking in a low, serious voice.

'The thing is, nobody should *worry*. The whole scene has been tested already. Just do it the way we walked it through at the manor house. If your part isn't finished by six o'clock tonight, Dumont, don't forget to call Drivehire and arrange to keep the car for another day. And the day after that, if necessary, but my guess is you will be done today or by to-morrow midday at the latest.'

The train came in, dull green, the same colour as the van that had brought them. Steam covered the windows like cobwebs, and when it stopped the brakes relaxed with a giant sigh. Doggo opened the door of a first-class compartment and Dumont followed. Max stood aside for a middle-aged woman, then followed her. As Max closed the door and opened the window, Ingram called something, but it was lost in the melancholy sound of the hooter and the train jerked. Ingram's smile came and went. The misty window distorted him for a moment, then he was gone. When Dumont turned he saw Doggo stepping into a compartment farther along the corridor. Max was still beside him.

'Do you think he's crazy, Max?'

'Maybe he is.'

'We could take off now, of course . . .'

'Why take off, Dumont? It's going to be a *Landpartie* . . . a picnic.' Max put a hand on the window rail and looked back. His dog's eyes were full of suspicious anger. 'You would be letting the rest of us down, Dumont.'

'That's one of the things he's taken into account, no doubt.' And while Max still stared at him, he added, 'Don't worry, Max . . . it's just that the whole situation is so totally improbable.'

When they arrived at Paddington Dumont left the others and walked on out of the terminal building and down the steps to where a line of taxi-cabs waited. He took the first available.

'Grosvenor Street,' he said. 'The Drivehire place.'

As they ground away in the traffic stream the driver opened his window. 'They always meet you, you know, sir, if you just ring them. You just have to ring them.'

'Thanks,' Dumont said. 'I'll remember next time.'

The window closed and the driver's eyes smiled at him in the rear view mirror. Although he was quite young, he wore the traditional cap and choker. Dumont tried to relax. He thought of Marnix, who would be getting the train about now. At least they would have the journey back together, perhaps the night together. He felt a kind of half-formulated hunger for her, only hunger was not quite the right word. He needed not so much her body as her persona and everything else. In the short time they had been together he had had a glimpse of a previous happiness which had lasted such a short time with Deirdre, when you lived with someone for their approval and they for yours. He thought longingly of a white house in the Perigord Noir with a small vineyard on the slopes below and the sort of life they could make together. It was the first time in many years that he had been visited by a dream of peace that was entirely radical. Always before dreams of peace had been associated with the status quo. The senior captain of an airline with a pleasant cottage somewhere in the Home Counties.

The dream receded as the taxi took a sharp U turn and stopped in the forecourt of the Drivehire garage. Dumont paid off the driver and went into the office. The man who attended to him was as Victorian as the cab driver, with his hair licked across a pale forehead, and a wing collar.

Dumont showed his driving licence and signed the contract and they walked out to a row of Minis. He got into the first one, started it up and ran it backwards and forwards against the brakes.

As he slipped back the window the hire clerk came up. 'Right, sir? Have a good day then.' He slapped the bonnet of the Mini lightly as though he was slapping the flank of a horse in some Victorian livery stable.

Dumont drove out to Oxford Street and straight on up the Bayswater Road. When he glanced at his watch it was ten-fifty and there was no time to go joy-riding. He kept on till the end of the park and then turned south towards Kensington High Street. He drove on through Earls Court and Fulham, making for the river.

After he'd crossed King's Road, he parked the car and walked back. He found a newsagent's shop in the first block and bought a street map of London. As he returned to the car he was conscious of a feeling of exhilaration.

He sat in the car and refolded the map to show that section of the river where the Turner gallery was and then drove on again. When he reached Chelsea Creek and the dock he turned up-river, and a moment later he could see the curious flat dome perched on its elongated drum that was only partly concealed by the tall terraces of Victorian houses surrounding it.

It had been built a hundred years ago, twenty years after the painter's death and the embankment road now carried industrial traffic where once the original river bank had been. Dumont had to wait before turning right into the short approach road that led to the square. As he came up to the stained yellow front with its plain Tuscan columns he noted automatically the police box standing on a corner of the square.

There was a continuous flow of traffic around the square, and on the northern side there was a special parking area where two coaches were nosed against the pavement. Dumont drove around slowly and saw the high wall at the back and the door which gave entrance to the courtyard. He went round a second time and found a place to park at the back of the gallery.

He left the car and locked it, and as he walked back towards the front of the gallery he could smell the sourness of the mudbanks from the river where the tide was out. He went up the steps and saw Doggo walking ahead of him with a newspaper under his arm.

Dumont went through the turnstile door and into the cavernous entrance hall. He bought a catalogue at the desk. Two or three commissionaires were circulating and ahead of him he could see Doggo crossing a gallery that was lit by the huge lunettes in the dome above.

He walked a little way in, casually leafing through the catalogue. There were doors leading off to other galleries, and at the entrance of each there was a notice on a small mahogany easel and a uniformed man.

Dumont looked at his watch. It was 11.55. He was absolutely dead on time for his station.

He hesitated near a middle gallery where the notice said, 'English Paintings of the Eighteenth Century,' and then walked back past some dark varnished portraits to the gallery immediately to the left of the main entrance.

The card said, 'Expressionist Painting 1902-1968,' and the man beside it was rising and falling gently on his heels. Dumont went in. It was another long room with a vaulted ceiling. Twenty or thirty people were there. Down the centre there were heavy pieces of nineteenth-century furniture back to back and at the far end another attendant stood by a segmental arch leading into a further gallery.

Dumont turned into a slight recess on the left where six small pictures were hung. Two young priests in soutanes were standing in front of one of them. They whispered continuously as if they had brought the confessional with them.

'*Tu n'as payé l'autobus que pour aller seulement . . . nous sommes revenus à pied, tu te rappelles, au bord de la rivière.*'

'*Ca ne fait rien. Les tickets que voici ont coûté moins que je n'ai payé hier.*'

'*Non. Dès maintenant je voudrais que nous payions chacun sa part . . . alors nous n'aurons plus cette confusion. Que chacun paie pour lui seul.*'

Dumont looked around vaguely and saw Max step into the archway at the other end and turn to stop in front of a huge, livid oil painting.

Dumont looked at his watch, it was one minute to twelve. Doggo must have been delayed. Then suddenly he saw Doggo seated half-way down the room on one of the long sofas. An old lady beside him was re-packing a shopping basket.

The priests had caught him up and Dumont stepped back to let them go by. After they'd passed him they fell silent and crossed to the other side of the room. Dumont moved to look at a picture which was hanging on the east wall of the recess. With his head half-turned he could now see Doggo again. The middle-aged woman had picked up her bag and gone and Doggo had spread half the paper beside him.

It was the signal for Dumont to ask the attendant at his end about Sunday opening, but as he turned to go back he saw the man had his back turned already and was talking to the other attendant in the main hall.

Dumont waited.

A party of blond Scandinavians, hung with cameras, worked their way by him and when he turned his head again he saw that Doggo had gone. The newspaper still lay there, spread across the seat.

It was all over, Dumont thought dryly, except the shouting.

The shouting began about twenty minutes later. Max had left for another part of the gallery and Dumont, who had been making notes in a pocket diary, had reached the far end near the arch. He was looking at a monolithic painting by Cassou in which the bodies of dead people hung from the window sills and piled up on the pavements around a high-rise block. Dumont didn't hear the first exchanges but suddenly there were two new attendants arriving through the door with a spectacled administrator following them.

They stood around the sofa, which had been slashed to ribbons, and Dumont could just hear their conversation, which ranged from violence to pained resignation.

'Bloody hooligans . . .'

'It wouldn't happen if we kept the long hairs out, sir!'

'Unfortunately that would mean a lot of artists . . . anyway, take the usual steps, try and get it arranged today.' The administrator was leaving.

He turned to look around the room briefly and his eyes crossed those of Dumont, who moved on towards the arch. As he went through it, the two men started to trundle the sofa towards the main gallery.

Dumont walked out into the square and along the approach way to the embankment. Max and Doggo were leaning on the river wall. Beyond them a string of barges were punching through the smoky London light. When Dumont joined them they turned their heads to look at him. 'It didn't take long,' he said. 'About twenty minutes, I think. An old lady discovered it, actually.'

Doggo said, 'Did they take it?'

'They were just moving it when I left.'

Doggo took the flick knife from his sleeve and threw it far out into the mud. 'That's my bit of heroism over,' he said. A large grey rat was questing unhurriedly along the bank below.

With obvious enjoyment Doggo said, 'It's the turn of the *Kapitänleutnant* next. Then yours, Dumont. We'll find out whether you're worth all that fruit salad they pinned on your chest.'

Dumont said, 'If the bloody thing works . . .'

'It'll work, Dumont, the way it worked today.'

'You may be wrong.'

'I *can't* be wrong, Dumont. We did the rehearsals only four months ago but that time we emptied a bottle of ink over a seat in another part of the gallery. Unfortunately we couldn't rehearse Max's part . . .'

'Never mind,' said Max quietly, and only a little louder he said, 'You are a man who lives on *Schadenfreude,* Doggo. Malice is the plasma that keeps you alive.'

'Relax, Max.' Doggo laughed. 'The strain hasn't started yet.'

Dumont went to get the car. Afterwards he drove them over Wandsworth Bridge to the underground station. When Doggo went ahead to get the tickets Max came back to offer

Dumont his hand. Dumont said, 'Don't worry, Max. Doggo isn't the only one with the wind up.'

Afterwards he drove back a different way, almost to the King's Road before turning in to approach the gallery from the rear. He drove slowly along tatty streets lined with grey-stone houses and eventually found his way to the rear of the gallery again. He stopped a long way off in the street behind where he could just see into the square and the huge double doors that gave into the courtyard. He settled more comfort-ably in his seat to wait. After a while a small boy of about twelve came to stand by the railings and watch him. He wore a beautiful grey suit and a striped school tie which somehow looked incongruous in that neighbourhood. Dumont noticed that his eyes were troubled, as if he found Dumont incongru-ous, too. They stared on in silence as the shadows lengthened over the river and the afternoon grew cooler.

At twenty minutes past four the Harrods van arrived and the rear gates were opened at last.

It was inside for about five minutes and when it came out again it came straight down the road towards him. Dumont let it go by, then did a U turn and followed it. In the rear view mirror he saw the gates of the gallery close again.

Nearer at hand the boy had left the railings and was crossing the road listlessly.

'They went straight to the warehouse . . . off the Fulham Road near the Brompton Oratory. That's what you expected wasn't it?'

'Yes.' She had opened her overnight case on the bed, and was taking out a leather toilet case. She carried it into the bathroom, walking slowly as if she was thinking of something else.

When he'd first arrived they hadn't embraced as he'd expected. Instead she'd said, almost with mockery, 'It's a pity to waste the bed . . . You can catch a train at eight.'

She came back now carrying two small glasses, which she set out on the dressing table. 'It's after five,' he said. 'Hadn't you better ring them?'

'They don't close until five-thirty. It's better to leave it till the last minute.'

She went back to the bed and lifted a flat half bottle of whisky from her case and put it beside the glasses, then she

96

took the carafe of water that was on the locker beside the bed and took it into the bathroom. He heard the water gurgle away before she refilled it. She brought it back to the dresser and put it down. She then made a drink, fussing about it like a priest at the communion table. The act of love was becoming as ritualised as the Mass.

When she brought him his drink he noticed that the front of her dress was already unbuttoned. He stayed deliberately in the chair and said, 'I thought we might go somewhere in the car. Have you ever been to Kew Gardens?'

The question hung stupidly in the air until she said, 'There isn't time.'

'No. I suppose not.'

She slipped off her wrist watch and laid it beside the bed. 'I'll ring now,' she said. She took off the receiver and asked for an outside line, then she opened a notebook on her lap. After she'd dialled, Dumont went over to stand beside her and she tilted the ear-piece for him to hear.

A girl said, 'Harrods warehouse.'

'Can I speak to the furniture repair shop . . .'

'One moment, please.' There was clicking for nearly half a minute before a man came on the line.

'Workshop . . . Denis speaking.'

'This is the Turner gallery, Mr Hezeltine's secretary . . .'

'Oh yes, love. Proper carve-up they've made of your seat. It'll take a bit of time.'

'That's why I'm ringing,' Marnix said. 'Mr Hezeltine wants to redecorate that part of the gallery and he may change the colour scheme. In that case we'll want it covered differently. Can you keep it until we decide?'

'Okay, love. We'd be glad to. We're pushed already. Just let us know.'

'You'll be getting our usual letter but just ignore it. Goodbye.'

Marnix pushed the phone away and picked up her glass. Dumont said, 'What happens next?'

'Next we make love, Dumont.' She stood up and dropped her dress and kicked off her shoes. 'It's cold,' she said as she opened the bed and rolled into it.

Dumont took her glass and went back to the dresser and poured them both another whisky. 'We could have dinner together, at any rate.'

She sat up to take the glass from him. 'There won't be time for that either. I have plans for keeping you amused.'

'What are you bloody well frightened of . . .' He turned away. After a moment he started to shed his clothes.

'Come to bed, Dumont,' he heard her whisper. 'Come to bed and be thankful for what we have.'

Dumont drew the curtains before he got into the bed. Afterwards he didn't know why he'd done it except that it seemed to be part of making love to her.

If they'd been going to Kew Gardens together or if they'd been going to have dinner together later, he thought, perhaps he wouldn't have drawn them at all.

'You are my *granit rose*, Dumont. The world would break itself on you.'

He didn't speak.

'I mean it, Dumont.'

'Oh, for Christ's sake . . . what do we know about each other if we never get off the bed!'

'That's all I want to know. Nobody ever tells you anything, do they, Dumont.'

'What do you mean?'

'I mean I could never go away with you because my husband wouldn't like it.'

'He'd hardly know about it. You said he was in Indonesia.'

'I said Piet Hoffman was in Indonesia. I've been married again since then . . . I'm just keeping my name till this business is over.'

Dumont lay still for a long time, conscious only of the smell of bleach from the sheets. At last he said, 'What are you doing here? . . .'

'I've told you before, Dumont . . . sex and love are different things. Sex is like a meal . . . something else the body needs. You can have it alone or with anybody you like.'

He was never quite certain of the moment that he started to make love to her again, just that he was doing so. At the same time he was telling her in a savage whisper what an immoral bitch she was and how she had debased them both. As he strained and swore, her head rolled and the tears came and he could see a pulse racing in her neck. When she cried out suddenly he didn't know whether it was pain or whether she'd reached her climax.

He left her immediately and went into the bathroom, slamming the door. As he spun the taps he saw, almost with disgust, his naked reflection in the mirror over the bath. Then the steam spread upwards, mercifully obliterating it.

He wished it could go on spreading until it filled his mind.

CHAPTER TWO

He dined on the train as it tore westwards through the Hampshire night.

She hadn't spoken until he was dressed and about to leave the room when from the shadow of the bed she'd whispered, 'I'm sorry . . . Please don't desert me, Dumont . . .'

And while he stood there hesitating she added, 'I didn't mind . . . I didn't mind your hurting me . . . Does that mean I'm kinky, Dumont?'

Looking back at her he said sadly, 'I'd rather you felt that than nothing at all.'

He'd left then and almost run through the airless corridors and out into the harsh night air.

The only wine they had was from Cyprus and it was well shaken by the motion of the train. Nevertheless, the waiter gravely poured a mouthful into his glass and Dumont sipped.

'Excellent,' he said, without smiling, and he thought miserably of a previous ritual. When he left the train at Yeovil, the platform was empty. Then Ingram moved forward jerkily to stand under a weak light.

As Dumont came up to him the jagged smile came and went. 'Max wanted to meet you but I thought it was a good opportunity for you and I to talk over some details.'

Dumont followed him out into the station yard. The air was misty. They climbed into a beaten-looking Land-Rover.

Ingram said, 'I've driven a jeep many times but not one of these. They're kind of heavy.' As he turned out of the yard he added, 'You're quiet. Nothing's wrong?'

'I'm tired, Ingram. It's been a long day.'

'It surely has.' They turned south towards the coast, lumbering at about forty.

Once Ingram shouted, 'She's kind of low geared,' but for

the rest of the time they drove with the noise of the engine. When they got to Ashfield again Ingram slowed down and pulled up under the inn sign of a pub. In the sudden silence he said, 'We may as well talk in comfort.' He led the way past the tap room to a door farther on. They went into a small, slightly cold room which had an open hatch into the other bar. 'What will it be, Dumont?'

'I'd like a pint of bitter.'

Ingram went to the hatch and ordered it. He ordered orange juice for himself, making the girl bring the bottle so he could check on the vitamins or something. When he came back to the table with the drinks the girl opened the half-door under the hatch and followed him. She went down to the outer door and turned the key in the lock.

As she came back past them he said, 'Thank you very much, Elsie. I greatly appreciate it.'

Elsie smiled and went back into the bar, closing the half-door behind her. Ingram spread himself out across an old wooden settle. 'I checked this place out on the way over. I wanted to talk to you on your own.'

'The same way you checked me out.'

'The way I check everything and everybody out. Several times over if necessary.' He sipped his orange and looked at the glass critically. 'As a matter of fact what you did today was pretty simple and not very spectacular. It's the sort of thing some of these teenage slobs do every day. But we had to have it exactly right. I was very relieved to get the call saying it was okay. The whole shebang depended on it.'

Then he said, almost sharply, 'Let's not waste time, Dumont. We have you with us for a very specific reason. You are driving, so to speak, the get-away car. What I mean is this, we have to remove the loot, when we've got it, to another country. There are various reasons why, one of which is that this island is over-populated. Sooner or later people get around to taking a close look at you. The train robbers' farmhouse wasn't a secret for long, neither was the place where those two characters cut up a newspaper owner's wife a year or two back. So how do you do it, Dumont?'

'I suppose you buy a plane. And if there are clearance problems you fly it out from an improvised airstrip.'

'No dice. We'll have to have a big four-engined ship which is pricey and the sort of purchase which would attract attention. The reason is, we need a range of over two thousand miles plus, and the reason for that is that we can't risk flying in European air space. Someone is bound to pick us up.'

'Well, I suppose you could hijack something.'

'No. You can't really disappear in a hijacked plane. Besides, the security is getting too hot. Go on, *think,* Dumont . . . It's an intellectual exercise like the gallery.'

'It's been a long day. Why don't you tell me?'

'Okay, I will.'

Ingram picked up his orange juice and examined it again before swallowing the last mouthful.

'There are two solutions. The first one I checked out was the Meteorological Air Service. They have their own base at Polryn, about a hundred miles west of here in Cornwall. They fly Shackletons . . .'

'Shackletons!'

'That's right, Dumont. A variation on the original Lancaster. To be precise they fly M.R. mark 3s. They do routine flights out across the Atlantic collecting high altitude weather data, which they re-broadcast on the single side band. I had Jameson monitor the transmissions for two months. We fed it into our own teletype machine. They have a very low security profile at Polryn, and I figured that if we could snatch a plane and keep the crew out of circulation we could make up a tape from the recordings. We could then play it back over their waveband at the correct times so that they wouldn't know for eight hours that the plane was missing.

'But there were problems. The thing that couldn't be matched up was the weather. You'd have to have some approximation to the prevailing weather pattern. So *that* was out.'

'Where am I supposed to fly to?'

'At the moment that is classified information.'

Dumont smiled and said, 'Somewhere in Scandinavia.'

'Why do you say that?'

'There's plenty of private coastline and plenty of places to put down where no one would ever know.' Dumont stood up. 'Would you like some more of that?'

'No, I'm fine, thanks. You go ahead, though.'

Dumont went up to the hatch and waited while Elsie refilled his tankard from the stillion. In the other bar old men talked quietly in settles around the fire, and Dumont could hear the clack of dominoes.

When he took his pint back he said, 'It's rather important I should know what sort of aircraft I'm going to fly.'

'Oh, it'll be a Lancaster type, Dumont.'

'You can't be serious. There aren't any now.'

'You're wrong. There are four left in the world. One of them is in Canada. And two of them are just up the road not twelve miles from here.' Ingram leant forward and put his hands preacher-fashion on the table between them. 'That's how I came up with the answer. I suddenly had the idea of checking out the aircraft museums. There are only two, the Shuttleworth Museum near Bedford and the Mains Memorial Air Museum right up the road here. That's why I had to rent a house in this part of the world. The Shuttleworth only has a small field and nothing bigger than an Avro Anson 19. The Mains Memorial has a two thousand yard strip laid south-west to the prevailing wind. Besides that there is . . .'

'Just a moment . . . I'm not going to fly an antique straight out of mothballs. Unless the proper maintenance schedules . . .'

'Don't worry, Dumont. The Mains Museum is also in the film property business, which is why they have two of the only four Lancasters still in existence. One came back from Germany last week, where it has been flying aerial shots for the Hassler Film Corporation's movie about Dresden.'

'You'd never get it out of the country, Ingram. Four engines give an excellent radar return.'

In the silence, Ingram turned the base of his glass slowly, as if he was setting a dial. At last he said, 'I like your attitude. I'd *like* you to be a Devil's Advocate just so that I can prove it again to myself. I have all the details in my head.'

'All right,' said Dumont. 'If you cross the coast unscheduled you'll be picked up by the scanners and air traffic control will have you intercepted.'

'Wrong, Dumont. You are totally misinformed. First take Linesmen, the radar chain. It stops at the Isle of Wight and is only solid in the east of England. Don't take my word for it, check it with the files of the London *Times*. It is the hobby-horse of their defence correspondent, the fact that the British Government has spent three hundred million pounds on Linesmen and still has gotten no protection. All the Russians have to do is to fly round the corner. He says the Government has learnt nothing since Singapore, let alone the Six Day War.'

102

'You're wrong, you know. I've been under control of Hurn airport, which is only just along the coast.'

'Correct, Dumont. There's traffic control around all the civil and military fields. I have them marked out. There's one closer than that. There's a climb-out lane from the Royal Aircraft Establishment at Boscombe Down crossing the coast just east of Bournemouth. But Lyme Bay is clear, Dumont. Take the car and drive forty miles in either direction. You can go anywhere you like – there are no Ministry of Defence restrictions anywhere. That means there are no scanners.'

'You don't really know the range of these things . . .'

'But I do, Dumont. I also know the system is totally inefficient when it comes to monitoring off-airways traffic. Take the case of Sergeant Paul Meyer, who stole a U.S.A.F. Hercules Transport from Mildenhall Air Base only a year or two back. Meyer flew all round London Airport in one of the densest air traffic areas in the world but they never picked him up. As a matter of fact, he looped the Scillies and crossed the coast not far from here before he went into the sea off Guernsey.'

A dice pot was rattling in the other bar and an old man's voice was singing sweetly.

'How can you take a plane out of the museum without anybody knowing . . . It'll take time checking the fuel, oil levels, hydraulics . . . maybe having to top them up . . .'

'That's right,' Ingram said. 'The situation there is that the staff work a normal five-day week. But because every third Sunday is a flying day they have the Wednesday of that week off. There is no one around except the director, who lives by the main entrance.'

'Aren't they asking for trouble?'

'Why should they worry, Dumont? Who'd want to steal a Lancaster, let alone a 1918 Bristol Fighter? My plan is that our start time should be as early as possible on a Wednesday, which means you'd have arrived before they even know the plane is missing.'

'Arrived where?'

Ingram's tapered fingers kept turning the glass as if he, too, still searched for some combination.

He said, 'Go on, Dumont.'

'How do you know the director is going to be out on that day. How do you know there is enough gas there anyway? . . .'

'Don't worry, Dumont . . . Every detail has been worked out. There are no underground gas tanks at Mains but they have two trailers behind a sandbag wall with a capacity of two thousand gallons each. One of them is always full. As you know the Lancaster takes two thousand gallons plus and there is no reason to suppose the tanks are empty. In fact, the opposite is the case. As regards the director there is no problem. I can only tell you this, first, he and his wife may be out anyway . . . they get around a lot. Second, they have an only daughter married to a farmer on the edge of the Mendip Hills. If necessary we can draw them off in a number of ways . . . say, with a phone call from the Casualty Ward at Sherborne Hospital to say the daughter's had a road crash . . . There are half a dozen contingency plans, and even a back-up idea where we just go into the house and tape them up. But forget them. All you have to think about is the plane, Dumont. Tomorrow I want you to go up there and have a good look at it yourself. The *working* plane that has been on charter to the German movie is a standard B3 with Packard-built Rolls-Royce Merlin 224s. It has the usual variable pitch hydromatic airscrews. I'm sure I don't need to tell you a single thing about it.'

'No. I don't think you do.' Dumont stood up and moved around his seat. He ran a hand down the back of his head uneasily. 'Who looks after it?'

'They have real craftsmen fitters there. Every plane in the museum is fully operational. They're all in the air on flying days including the 1912 Blackburn. Besides that, I should tell you it's a very profitable set-up. They get thousands there apart from the film property side.'

'What kind of runway?'

'There's a couple of hundred yards of hard standing. Then it's grass. But it's tile-drained. There should be no trouble.'

As Dumont kept moving around Ingram stood up. 'We may as well go back now . . . Take the Land-Rover tomorrow and go on up there. Take Jamie if you think it's a good idea. He'll be riding the engineer's seat when you take off.'

'That won't be necessary.'

Ingram edged away to the hatch and put his glass on it. He said, 'Thanks, Elsie. We're just off.'

Dumont unlocked the parlour door and they went out into the frosty night.

Dumont was glad of the Land-Rover's engine noise, which

made conversation impossible, because he was remembering his own Lancaster Mark 111, which had the serial number P.E.110. Some time after the war he'd looked through an Air Ministry file of the P.E. range and out of more than three hundred, only forty-five had made it through to scrap. The rest were missing and crashed all over occupied Europe. He remembered the night that P.E.110 herself had gone into the ground in 1944. Dumont and the tail gunner had been the only crew to walk away and he remembered crouching alone in the night while the flames roared. They thought he'd gone, too, because it was two hours before he'd stopped shaking enough to walk back around the perimeter to the headquarters building.

The entry in the station log had said P.E.110, 911 Squadron. Swung on landing, 6th August, 1944.

When they went up the driveway towards the hall there was only one light burning, high in one of the attic bedrooms. Ingram switched off the engine and said, 'Looks as if everyone has turned in.'

Dumont had climbed out and was standing there when Ingram said suddenly, 'Did you have a woman today?'

Dumont was motionless, giving himself time to think. It was almost a minute before he said, 'Is that sort of detail important to you? Do you have to monitor my sex life?'

Ingram looked down calmly from the open window of the Land-Rover. He also waited a long time before he said, 'It really wasn't meant to be personal, Dumont. It's just that in some book I read a long time ago it said that men who had been under a strain or in danger, you know, cool characters like yourself, always felt like a woman afterwards. I just wondered.'

'There wasn't really any danger today. But if you want to know,' Dumont said harshly, 'danger is a great laxative. Every time I've had to stick my neck out I've felt like shitting myself.'

In the ambience of the moonlight, Ingram's face was as pale as milk. Then he said, 'I guess I'd better put this thing in the stables.'

The engine started and he followed the cobbled drive around the side of the house.

They had bought the boxer pup when they were first married.

The idea was that while Dumont was away on duty it would be company for Deirdre. They called him Rover, not traditionally like people but because he never seemed to leave his basket by the fire except to eat, and perform his natural functions in the garden. Dumont heard him now as he often had in the nights when he wasn't flying. The sound of a half-growl, half-whimper, which seemed to be protesting against some untold anxiety.

Dumont found himself already standing in the bedroom doorway. Then, fully awake, he realized it wasn't Rover any more but that the sound was coming from Max's room next door. He went in quietly. Max was lying on his back and his face was shiny with sweat, a replica of the varnished portraits in the gallery. But there was no peace in Max's face, and as he groaned again Dumont leant down and clasped the arm across his chest.

Max's other damp hand came to hold his wrist and Max's eyes opened. 'I was having an *Alpdrücken* . . . a bad dream, Dumont.' His voice was calm. 'I'm sorry if I've woken you.'

His grip relaxed and Dumont took his hand away. 'I didn't like the schnorkel. I hated it, in spite of the protection it gave. Because you know I can't live without seeing the sky every day. I promised myself never again when the war was over. But now I have to schnorkel again.'

'Don't tell me we're going in through the sewer?'

'No, it's worse than that. Let's not talk about it.' Max raised himself up. 'Get some whisky . . . Let's have a drink.' Then he added abruptly, 'No, don't let's have a drink. Go back to bed, Dumont. I'll be all right now.'

He didn't go on and Dumont moved away. When he was at the door Max said, 'We had a saying in the *Kriegsmarine* "When a ship is at the bottom of the sea no one knows what heroes the crew have been." When I was young I helped to pay for the mistakes of my elders. Now I'm old, Dumont, and if that young bugger makes a mistake I'll have to pay for that, too. Forget what I'm saying . . . It's only this bloody schnorkel . . .'

'Don't worry, Max . . . afterwards I have to fly a thirty-year-old bomber out of a hayfield. But I'm sure it'll be a piece of cake.'

'A bomber? Is that the way we go?'

106

'In one sense or another that is the way we go.'

The next morning before he went downstairs to join Jameson, he put dark glasses and a camera into his side pockets, along with a small diary. He was crossing the hall when Ingram called him through the open door of the living-room.

When he went in Ingram was alone. He said quietly, 'Take a good look this morning, Dumont, because I don't want you to visit again.'

Dumont nodded.

'And don't worry if the runway looks a little hairy. They cut it Mondays. The museum have a contract with a gang mower in Bridport.'

Dumont said dryly, 'What is the maiden name of the mother of the man who does the mowing?'

'Don't kid me, Dumont. It's a detail that could always be important.'

There was an end of season air about the museum when they reached it. They had trouble finding someone to pay the entrance money to. When they got inside the giant hangars there was only a handful of people there. They wandered idly around looking at the World War I fighters. There was a Sopwith Pup and a Bristol F2b and a Fokker Triplane, all of which were still being flown on certain demonstration days. In the World War II section there was a Spitfire and a Hurricane, and beyond them an early mark of Messerschmitt 109. Dumont walked on towards the workshops. In the first bay he saw a Lancaster. One of the engines was out and hanging from a gantry crane at workshop level. They walked on but there were no more planes. Coming back, Dumont noticed the trolleyac which was probably used to start several of the planes on flying days. It was parked in a weatherproof bay just beyond the main doors.

Then he saw the second Lancaster farther out on the hard standing. The serial number painted on the side was SW282 and she looked as solid and capable as the day she'd left the factory. On the panel below the cockpit they'd painted her name, 'The Bride of Frankenstein.' Nobody else was out there when they walked across the oil-stained concrete. Dumont drifted slowly around, looking at the tyres, then the trim and the ailerons. The skin looked bright and cared for. He noticed

107

that the filler caps of the outboard fuel tanks looked as if they might have been used that day, and it was probable that she was already gassed up. There were no Brownings in the turrets and there were other operational things missing like the exhaust flame dampers. The side hatch was open in the fuselage but there was no ladder against it.

When he had completed all the visual checking he could, he walked out across the standing towards the runway. He turned twice to hold up his camera for imaginary shots. The wind-sock was half-filled with the breeze from the south-west. When he reached the grass it was firm and hard the way Ingram had described it. He walked to and fro but there was no softness anywhere, nor any moss to show where water was used to lying.

He walked out to a flank on the way back, still pretending to take pictures. There were two Shell-BP trailers behind a sandbag shelter that had been roofed with corrugated iron. There was also a dolly pump parked there with what looked like a five horse-power motor. Dumont walked down beside them. He slapped the tanks idly as he passed and only one of them had a slight boom.

As he came back on to the hard standing Jameson walked out from under the wing to join him, and together they walked on towards the exit. There was no one at the gate to see them out, and as they drove slowly up the road Dumont saw a woman at the back of the director's house pinning bath towels to a clothes line. She looked like the daily help and Dumont wondered if Ingram had checked.

Somehow he was sure he had.

The warmth of the autumn day was unexpected and Ingram had the Spanish couple carry luncheon over to a table under the Cedar of Lebanon tree. During the meal he asked if Dumont was happy.

Dumont said, 'I'm reasonably happy. There are a few points . . .'

'I'm sure we can deal with them.' And when the others got up from the table, Ingram said to Dumont, 'Stay with me and tell me about those points.'

'I've written down the registration number of the Lancaster and I'd rather like to check it with the log which has been published. They probably have a copy in the county library at Bridport. I want to be quite certain it hasn't been struck off charge and then rebuilt by some crazy engineering unit.'

'You'll find it's okay, Dumont. The log was also published in the States by Aero Publishers Incorporated, of Los Angeles. I don't recall the exact number of the Library of Congress card but it was a 1963 issue.' Ingram picked up the two white Spode jugs and poured coffee and milk into his cup. Then he held them out to Dumont, who shook his head. As he put them back on the tray they rattled slightly. Dumont might not have noticed had Ingram not looked up at him. The smile which came and went was more automatic than usual. Then he held out his tapered hands across the table. They were as smooth and white as the china.

'It wasn't really a tremble, Dumont.'

And when Dumont didn't say anything he added, 'Well, maybe it was just a small one. I'm running on boost this week because there are so many details to think of. I can't even switch off at night . . . What else is bothering you?'

'I have to put rather a lot of faith in the fitters that work there. How do I know that she'll really be serviced for a long haul and not just a flip around the airfield?'

'They're the best fitters in the country, Dumont. You've *seen* the sort of old crocks they keep in the air. But there's a different reason I know she'll be ready for a long haul and it's this: we booked it three months ago on behalf of Pan-European Advertising for use in historical prestige ads which they're making for television. Our cheque for the thirty thousand dollars' deposit has been cleared and when Marnix rang them a couple of days ago, the director said a Lancaster would be on the line and ready to go from next Thursday. That's when he told her it had just got back from Germany.'

'But if I lost an engine, say . . . or possibly two. She wouldn't fly for ever.'

'You wouldn't have to. Don't worry . . . It's a point that's already taken care of. I'll tell you at the briefing. By the way, I have a photostat copy of the relevant page from the Lancaster Production Log so you don't need to go to Bridport. I'll let you have it.'

When he stood up Dumont remained sitting. He looked at Ingram's untouched coffee. Dumont said, 'You haven't finished your coffee.'

Ingram stared down at the cup. 'It's probably cold. I don't want it now.'

They went back into the hallway, where a huge Cuban mahogany staircase rose to a mezzanine landing before dividing and returning upwards to an equally large hallway above, which ran out to the front of the house again. Ingram opened the door of the small salon and they went in. At the other end by the window Doggo, Jamie, Max and Marnix Hoffman were standing around the sofa. At the sound of the door closing they turned and moved outwards and Dumont saw the sofa was the ornate one that he'd last seen in the gallery.

He said, 'How did you get hold of it?'

'It's not the same one, Dumont. Harrods supply them to the Ministry of Works for furnishing museums and art galleries and even some of the public rooms in the Houses of Parliament. I bought it a while back . . . this particular model is called Versailles.'

As they came up to it Dumont was looking at Marnix, but her eyes were on Ingram. Ingram said, 'Of course, we've had to play around with it,' and he bent to take hold of the seat panel with both hands. He opened it up and Dumont saw the shallow coffin beneath. There was a bicycle lamp clipped to the headboard and a plastic bottle and a tube with a Roberts valve.

Ingram said, 'That's where Max does his schnorkeling.'

Max said, 'Schnorkel, schnorkel,' in a comic voice, but when Dumont looked at him he wasn't smiling.

'It's really not all that original,' Ingram was saying. 'In fact the idea is as old as Greek mythology.'

'Why Max?' Dumont asked carefully.

'Well, again, that's not really your concern, Dumont, but it so happens that Max was the Regional Inspector to Steinitz Systems in Switzerland. He is the only one who knows how to defuse the alarm when he gets inside.'

Dumont turned abruptly to look at Max, who was staring back at him. His smile had the mirthless fixity of a carnival mask.

CHAPTER THREE

Doggo and Jamie were wearing blue overalls when they came out into the stable yard where the van was waiting.

The sun hadn't yet risen above the haze and the air was chill. Against the pale sky, gulls were flying inward to the plough.

> '*Vor der Kaserne vor dem grossen Tor,*
> *Da steht eine Laterne und steht sie hoch davor*
> *Alle Leute bleiben steh'n*
> *Wenn sie bei der Laterne geh'n . . .*'

Jamie snapped, 'Belt up, Max!'

'*Wo man singt,*' recited Max sombrely, '*dort lässt euch ruhig nieder, Böse Menschen haben keine Lieder . . .*'

'Max, for Christ's sake . . .' Doggo's eyes were snapping.

Dumont went off away from the others, stamping his feet. Suddenly he had been irresistibly reminded of operations again, of the moment when they waited for the crew truck to take them round the perimeter track and the banal conversation that was only uttered to hold back thought. As he came back he said, 'You won't be singing tonight, Max.'

'*Nein* . . . I'll be pissing in a little plastic bag.'

'Never mind, Max, we'll be thinking of you,' Doggo said.

Out of the tail of his eye Dumont had seen Marnix come out into the yard. She was carrying her overnight case. She was riding with them as far as the railway station at Sherborne. A moment later he saw the slight figure of Ingram hesitating at the corner. In the morning light he looked more pale and attenuated than ever. His hands were in his pockets, as if he were afraid that they might betray him again.

Dumont went to meet him and said quietly, 'Just tell me before we go where I'm flying tomorrow.'

'I'm sorry, Dumont.'

'I've flown a hundred missions, Ingram. I'm experienced . . . There may be problems you haven't thought of.'

'There may be problems but I've certainly thought of them. We have to go step by step, Dumont. All I want you to do is to concentrate on the job in hand and not be distracted by what is going to happen next.' He walked on up to the truck where the others waited.

Marnix was already sitting in the front passenger seat with the window down. Ingram said, 'The final word I want to give you all is this, there is nothing to bother yourselves about. Every detail has been thought of and if anything turns out differently remember there is a back-up plan to take care of it. In some cases there are two back-up plans. Doggo is running this phase, the way Dumont will be running the next phase, and Doggo or Marnix knows what all the contingency plans are. Let me check the loading.'

They all moved to the back of the van and Jamie opened the doors wide. The sofa had been angled in and on either side the narrow plywood boxes were roped to the van. There were rolls of thick cellulose wadding and a suitcase in the angle space.

Ingram said, 'Okay,' and stepped back. 'With any luck you should be back here by midnight but if it takes longer don't worry.'

Ingram took his hand out of his pocket at last and held it out to Max. 'Good luck, Max . . . It all depends on you.'

'Don't worry, Ingram. Don't worry . . .'

Max climbed up across the seat and Doggo followed. Dumont went last. He was glad Ingram didn't shake hands with all of them.

Jamie closed the doors and went round to the driver's seat, and a moment later the van started lurching away over the cobbles. From his seat by the rear window Dumont saw Ingram coming after them, not as though he was trying to catch them up but more as though he was being dragged along in their wake, unable to free himself from them. He followed around the side of the house and finally dropped away as the van accelerated down the driveway.

Dumont watched until he'd disappeared, looking thin and fragile against the tall columns of the house.

When they went into the station yard and stopped Marnix looked back over her shoulder before getting out. Then a moment later the rear doors opened and she said to Dumont, 'I want you to see me on to the platform.'

Jamie called, 'There isn't time.'

Dumont had already levered himself out of the settee. He

112

walked across with her into the ticket office and they faced each other just inside the door.

She said without artifice, 'I want to see you in London, Dumont.'

'What is the bloody point of that?'

'I'll be at Keeles Hotel again. I don't know what room number, but I'm booked in so ask at the desk.'

When he didn't say anything she went on, 'The bloody point is that we may not see each other again after today.'

Although her voice was matter of fact she was giving him some kind of hope. She was inferring that she found the last day an occasion.

He said, 'We'll only have about an hour . . . if that.'

'An hour is enough . . . please, Dumont . . .' She was looking at him with serious eyes and Dumont thought it couldn't be *all* carnality. There must be some other feeling for him there.

He kissed her roughly. 'I don't promise you,' he said as he walked away.

Jamie had turned the van and parked it nearer the door. Dumont climbed into the front seat beside him and they roared out of the yard with a spurt of gravel.

When they were out on the A30 driving along towards Shaftesbury Jamie said, 'Which was the wog, Dumont? Her old man or her old woman?'

Dumont didn't answer. The sun rose slowly out of the mist and the van warmed up. In the back Max Sendelbeck started singing again.

They had lunch at a pub the other side of Salisbury and Max took an amphetamine tablet with his coffee.

When Dumont said, 'Is that necessary?' Doggo leant across the table.

'Ingram thinks it is,' he said. 'Can you imagine the situation if he fell asleep?'

Max said, 'Don't worry, Dumont.'

They reached the outskirts of London at 3.30 and Jamie turned south into Fulham after they left the Hammersmith flyover. He found his way to a quiet mews off the Wandsworth Bridge Road and pulled up. There was silence in the car after he switched the engine off.

Then Doggo said, 'Okay, Dumont . . . Open up the back.'

113

Dumont went round and opened the doors. Max and Doggo climbed out and stretched.

When Jamie came to join them Doggo said, 'Go back to the phone box in the square and ring Marnix.'

'I can do that,' Dumont said.

'No, I want Jamie to do it,' said Doggo. 'Tomorrow is your day for giving the orders.'

After Jamie had gone they all climbed into the back of the van and opened the seat. Max sat down carefully in the box with his elbows on the ledge.

Doggo took a card from his pocket. 'Check it off, Max . . .'

'We've checked it off.'

'Ingram said to check it again.'

Max closed his grey eyes patiently. Doggo began to recite, 'Torch, spare battery, glucose, piss bag, tools, pistol . . .'

Dumont said, 'Pistol?'

Max touched the side pocket of his jacket. 'The Walther's here.'

'I should make sure it doesn't go off,' said Dumont carefully. He was aware that they were both looking at him.

Then Max said, 'Don't worry about it, Dumont . . . It's only a frightener. The cosh is in my other pocket.'

Doggo said, 'Surgical tape . . .'

'About two kilometres of it. Come on, Doggo . . . Let's go, for God's sake . . .' He lay down, half settled himself, then sat up again to get a paperback from his pocket. Then he lay down again, buttoning his jacket with the paperback on his chest.

'*Seeklar*,' he said and closed his eyes.

Doggo folded over the cushioned lid and they heard the bolt go home. Doggo hit the side and after a moment the bolt was drawn again and Max pushed up the seat. Dumont caught it.

As Doggo said, 'Right,' Jamie came back.

'Everything's okay. When she phoned the gallery they said they were very glad to be getting it back this afternoon. Afterwards she spoke to the workshop and told them a decision hadn't yet been reached about the repairs. They both reacted normally.'

'Nothing from the man?'

'No, nothing at all.'

Doggo looked at his watch, then down at Max. 'Do you

114

want us to stop at a public john?'

'No, thank you.' Max settled down again. As Doggo was about to close the lid Max put a hand against it. 'If anything goes wrong . . . Don't try and get me out. You understand?'

Doggo said, 'Christ no. He made a special point of mentioning that.'

'I know,' Max said. He took his hand away.

Almost for the first time Dumont felt a touch of comradeship.

'Good luck,' Max said and smiled. '*Gott strafe England.*' The lid went down and the bolt went home.

They climbed back into the road and went around to the cab.

Dumont waited by the passenger side window while Jamie got in. He took down a cap with an enamelled Harrods badge on it from the roof net, opened the glove compartment and got out the clipboard with the delivery notes. Doggo leant across him to say, 'We'll be about half an hour if traffic is normal. Then we start the watch at seven. Make sure you're here before six-thirty.'

'I'll go back to the main road and get a cup of tea,' Dumont said.

Doggo said, 'Great,' absently and kicked the starter. He let out the clutch immediately and the van leapt away.

Dumont walked after it and watched it disappear. Then he walked on till an empty taxi-cab came by.

'Keeles Hotel,' he told the driver.

When he knocked and went into her room she was sitting by the dressing table writing something in a notebook.

She said carelessly, 'Hello, darling,' in the same casual way that Deirdre used to say it to him, as if it was normal and they both belonged to a big acceptance world beyond the bedroom.

He stood looking at her for a moment and then went to pour himself a small whisky. He said, 'I really mustn't be long.'

She reached up a hand for the glass and he gave it to her and picked up another. He went to sit on the edge of the bed. She said wearily, 'You've got till six. *I* have to stay in this place all bloody night.'

'Why?'

'Until you're all home. *A ta santé.*'

He couldn't see her face for the fall of her hair. He was suddenly aware of his longing for her, she had become inextricably mixed with his dream of peace. He put out a hand to touch her waist just below the breast.

Her hand came down to press his own. 'This is really the last time, Dumont. This is the one for the road.'

'You never know.'

'But I do know.'

She turned towards him on the stool and opened her legs. Then she pushed his hand down until he felt her pubic hair as stiff as wire. For nearly five minutes she was leant against him, then she turned back the bed and rolled on to it sighing.

Dumont undressed slowly while she watched him. She said, 'I turned the heating up.' He had complained, the last time, that his back was cold. Still watching him, she turned her head sideways on the pillow.

Dumont bent to pick up his clothes, piece by piece, from the floor and laid them on the chair. He moved the chair back against the wall beside the dresser and hesitated. As usual they were both consciously delaying the moment of contact. She turned her head the other way and drew up her knees.

It was part of a game they both enjoyed playing, a kind of erotic brinkmanship.

The bell push was high up on the post of the gallery gates, and after he'd pushed it Jamie had to wait several minutes before the smaller side door was opened.

The tall man who looked out at him had his cap peak drawn down to the level of his eyes and a short bristle moustache. He said. 'What is it, lad?'

'Harrods. We've brought a sofa back from the repair shop.'

'Right, lad. Just a moment . . .' He stepped away, and a moment later Jamie heard the long bolts of the main gates being drawn.

The gates swung back and the sergeant commissionaire waited by them. 'Off-load it at the usual place.'

Jamie hesitated and then said, 'This is my first time . . .'

'Over there. Tell your mate to back up to the ramp with the roller door.'

Doggo drove in on one lock, then backed up to the ramp with Jamie guiding him. They went around to the back and opened the doors.

The sergeant commissionaire came back down the side of the van. 'Just push it in and leave it, lads. We'll attend to it later.' He jumped on to the ramp and pushed up the lattice a little higher.

Jamie and Doggo lifted the settee over the gap and a little way into the storeroom. The sergeant went with them and as they lowered it he drew his cane along the seating.

'Very nice work, tell your foreman. Looks as good as new.' He jumped down and walked away, making for the big gates again.

Doggo closed the rear doors and got back into the cab. The sergeant was waiting stiffly by the gates. Doggo said, 'We've forgotten the delivery note. He hasn't signed.'

'Leave it! The bastard doesn't know . . .'

'It's a detail that might be important,' Doggo said coolly. 'Get him to sign it when I stop.'

He drove on to the gates and as the sergeant was waving him out he stopped.

Through the open window, Jamie said, 'Sorry, Sergeant . . . I nearly forgot,' and passed the board over.

The sergeant took it and felt in his pocket for his reading glasses and slipped them on. He read it, then leant it against the van and signed it. 'Seems in order,' he said and passed it back.

As Doggo pushed the gear lever into first the sergeant said suddenly, 'Just a moment there . . . Don't I get a copy of that?'

Jamie turned back the receipt. There was a pink copy underneath which he took out and handed over. The sergeant tucked it in his pocket then strode two paces into the road to look both ways before waving them out with his stick.

As they roared away Doggo, under stress, said, 'You *bloody* half-wit, Jamie . . . Christ . . . Ingram must have told you ten times . . .'

'It wasn't my fault. *I'm* no bloody hero! Don't forget I'm not like the rest of you.'

Dumont dressed clumsily in the half-light.

He kept his back to her deliberately but once he heard her whisper, 'Please, Dumont . . .'

He didn't turn. Eventually he said, with savagery, 'If I mean nothing to you, then why the fucking tears?'

'I'm not crying for your going, Dumont. I'm crying because

117

you're angry . . . because you don't understand.'

She was lying on her back and what tears there were came silently, as silently as her orgasms sometimes came. As though she knew he was observing her now, she turned away from him. Dumont said loudly, 'You're the one who doesn't understand! You don't understand that I'd do almost anything in the world to be able to stay with you . . . to live with you. In my whole life I've never been able to say that truthfully to anyone else!'

'Please, Dumont,' she whispered again. 'Oh, Jesus . . .' She rolled her face towards him. 'You must admit, Dumont, that I've never been to bed under false pretences. From the very first time I've tried to keep your eyes open. I have told you again and again that this . . . this sexuality is a separate part of my life. It is like a man who goes to his mistress once a week . . . he is happy to be with her and he is also happy to go home and enjoy his family. He . . .'

'*What* family? . . .' He waited with his eyes closed.

'Please, Dumont . . . . I don't want to hurt you.'

'Don't you?'

'I mean it. You are one of hundreds, Dumont . . . good men, strong and faithful, in bed and out of it. But there is only one man like Stephen Ingram. You know what an exceptional mind he has, and the danger and excitement of living with him are like a drug. I could never give him up . . . *never* . . .'

'Then why behave like an alley cat?'

Her head rolled away from him again, her body stiffened. He could barely hear her when she whispered, 'I never wanted to explain it to you, Dumont . . . not the details of it. But when we are in bed I am only married to his hand.'

'His *hand*?' Dumont laughed briefly and then stopped, blinking.

For a moment or two he was stunned. Then feeling came back and he thought why was it that one was always surprised by the rational. He said quietly, 'Poor Ingram . . .'

'There's no need to feel sorry for him, Dumont; his libido isn't affected, only his prostate. And besides, he's over-compensated in other ways you must admit.'

He started to go for his jacket, which was on a peg behind the bathroom door, and stopped again. The shock of her revelation still hadn't quite passed.

Then she said sadly, 'Now I've explained you don't need

to be angry any more, Dumont.' And when he didn't answer, she added, 'It explains other things as well, don't you think? Such as how he came to have his fixation about heroes? Courage and virility . . .'

Dumont remembered Ingram's face, white in the ambience of the moon, when he asked if Dumont had had a woman . . . if the stress of action made him randy . . . Aloud he said, 'You really can't believe in that sort of paperback psychology.'

'It doesn't matter, does it, whether I believe in it or not. It doesn't change anything. It doesn't change the way I feel.'

And then without warning she said, 'Goodbye, Dumont . . . I want you to go now. All we are doing is hurting each other.'

He nodded mechanically and went into the bathroom for his jacket. He came back and stopped by the door. He said, 'I don't think I'll ever go into a hotel room again.'

'They have their uses, Dumont.' He looked back and caught her eyes in the mirror. He had hoped to see sadness there but all he saw was a kind of cool awareness of life. 'They're so impersonal they help to insulate the heart.'

'Not mine,' he said, and opened the door and went out.

Half-way along the corridor he stopped, realizing the childishness of it all. It was an absurd way to part. He turned and went back again.

But when he tried the door it was locked and he could hear the sound of her voice beyond. She was already talking to someone else on the phone.

Max had thought that perhaps the sofa might be left in the store for the night, but eventually he heard two men arrive.

As it was trundled out of the store he braced his body against the unsprung movement and slid a hand down the side to protect his arthritic hip. They seemed to pass through several rooms and twice one of the men said, 'Hang on a minute . . .'

Max didn't know whether there was some holdup or whether he was just out of breath. Another time the sofa swayed as they lifted it to a different level. The movement stopped eventually and a new, rather foolish, voice said, 'That's splendid. Put the chairs back in the lobby.'

Then someone sat down just above his head. A moment later the silly voice said, 'I can't say they're very comfortable but that's probably just as well.' Then he stood up and he must

119

have gone away because Max could hear the faint bray of his voice in another room.

The everyday sounds of the gallery went on. There was a continuous montage of echoing footsteps and occasional voices made harsh by the acoustics. He stayed lying on his side and was conscious of the warmth. The hands on his luminous watch pointed to ten minutes past five.

Suddenly he heard the tramp of many feet which seemed to assemble all around him. Then another, deeper voice spoke. '. . . very much a one way street, it can be said, with Expressionism right at the end of the cul-de-sac. The deviation really began with Fauvism, which led where, Gregory?'

'To the Cubists, sir,' said a boy's piping voice.

'Well, yes. But it's important to remember that Expressionism is not a style of painting. In so far as one can be dogmatic one can say it has forsaken the representational for the emotional mainly through the use of colour. Of course, this is the tendency of all Baroque. It impinges on the senses rather than the purely visual.'

The feet shuffled restlessly, then someone started to bounce lightly on the seat just where Max's head was.

'So then we can sum up like this: colour but not necessarily form, German and French as opposed to the Mediterranean schools. Other styles, Cubism, for example, take their place in history, Expressionism is an eternal tendency, a tendency to express as distinct from linear form.'

The tramp of feet receded and from the door the leader called, 'Come on, Gregory . . . You've surely seen a nude woman before . . .'

'Yes, sir.'

Max closed his eyes and thought about the coming night.

When Dumont left the elevator and crossed the lobby he was conscious of being followed. As he turned, Doggo and Jamie were behind him.

Doggo said, 'What the bloody hell are you up to?'

Dumont looked past them at the crowded lobby. 'I shouldn't make a scene here if I were you.' He turned and they walked on together.

The van was parked half a block away.

Jamie climbed into the back without being asked and Dumont got into the passenger seat. He said to Doggo, 'How did you know where I was?'

'You left a trail like a dog on heat.'

Dumont looked at his watch. 'The arrangement is that we don't start watching until six-thirty or seven.'

'Only one thing is important, Dumont, and that is that we do it *exactly* as he's worked it out. And your visit here wasn't in the schedule.'

Dumont didn't answer and after a long silence Doggo started the engine and drove off towards the Chelsea Embankment. It was almost dusk on the river and the lights of home-going traffic were strung in an endless line across Battersea Bridge. When he turned his head slightly he saw that Jamie was watching him.

When he looked round fully Jamie said, 'What was it like, Dumont?' and Dumont could see the wisdom of the gutter in his eyes. When Dumont said nothing, he went on, 'I knew a tart in Liverpool once who told me that men over forty always liked it on their backs . . . because most of them had so much gut. She said it was like riding old grey mares . . . maybe mares isn't the right word.'

For perhaps a tenth of a second Dumont felt the beginnings of rage and he wanted to slash Jameson's smiling face. Instead he looked at the road again. He said calmly, 'You really must stop trying to prove yourself, you know.'

Doggo added, 'He's right, Jamie. Nobody gives a damn whether you're a hero or not.'

They drove on in silence, crawling in the traffic stream beside the river.

CHAPTER FOUR

At five-thirty the noise began to abate and Max heard the sound of people going and voices becoming more distant. It was like the blessed peace when one sank to a depth of a hundred metres after a night's buffeting in the Atlantic.

He waited half an hour before he gently drew the bolt beside his head and eased the lid up a few centimetres. The first thing that struck him was the glare of artificial light. He kept his fingers in the crack and in between deep breaths he listened intently. There were no sounds near at hand but he could hear distant voices in the central gallery. He thought it probable that the day staff would leave at six and the night staff would take over and activate the alarm system.

If security followed the pattern of other galleries the fire patrol was bound to be frequent early in the night and he wouldn't be able to move until he knew what the intervals were. He wanted a matchbox or something to prop the lid but he had emptied his pockets of everything that rattled before he left the manor house. Instead he tied a series of half-hitches in his handkerchief and made that do instead.

The lights, he decided, were the centre lights and would be left on all night.

They parked the van almost a quarter-mile down the street behind the gallery in the nearest space they could find.

Doggo and Dumont climbed into the darkness at the back. Ingram had told them not to be visible, people waiting were always the object of attention. Every half-hour they took it in turns to walk out past the gallery to the embankment and back again.

Perhaps there was a demo in Trafalgar Square or somewhere, but for whatever reason there were no policemen on duty. Once Dumont saw a police panda car stopped by the call box when he was going down to the river. He saw nothing else, only the blue glare of television sets against drawn curtains and cats walking silently on walls. The Englishman was in his castle.

Dumont had spoken to the others about the gun again. 'I didn't know Max was going to have it.' When no one said anything he added, 'He's probably forgotten how to use it anyway . . . If he ever knew.'

'He hasn't forgotten,' Doggo said.

'How do you know?'

'Look, Dumont . . . We none of us know more than we have to know about each other which seems to me a sensible idea. All I know about you is that you're an ex-bomber pilot who was running guns . . .'

'That's quite untrue, you know . . .'

'I don't give a damn . . . I don't want to know whether it's true or untrue.'

When Dumont came back from the river the panda car had

gone. There were no lights visible at any of the gallery windows and he supposed that, anyway. they had internal shutters, which were closed at night.

He thought of Max lying in the shallow coffin, biding his time. He remembered the long drunken nights in France when Max had told him how he was too old to be a hero. It seemed to have happened a long time ago instead of just the other day.

As he walked up the dark, ill-lit street he remembered Max's anxiety. 'I've only been a hero at a thousand metres or more, Dumont. I don't know whether I could be a hero any closer. I've never seen the face of my enemy.' Then he'd turned to look at Dumont with steady melancholy. 'You are the same, Dumont. How often did you see the face of your enemy . . . Did you see the people in Hamburg?'

Dumont had only gone a few yards beyond the square when the lights of a car sprang to life just ahead of him. A car pulled out and drove away past the gallery. Dumont hurried back and they moved the van up to the empty space.

It gave them a view into the square and the doors at the back of the gallery.

Every hour on the half-hour, at 6.30 and 7.30, someone, a guard, had passed through the room. And by raising the lid of the seat, Max had been able to hear his progress through the other rooms.

He decided to make 8.30 his zero hour. Ingram had asked for it to be as early as possible while there was still normal traffic in the streets. Now, from the direction of the main hall Max heard a faint ping, which he guessed to be a time clock and then voices which ended when a door closed. Gently he raised the lid and let it rest against the back. Then he sat up. The pain in his hip still hurt him.

He put his hands on the edges of the seat and stepped quickly out to stand beside it. The lighting he saw was secondary lighting, coming from a high central bulb, and the lights in the two galleries beyond looked the same density. He spent a minute doing half squats to ease his muscles. Then he bent and took up the cosh.

Ingram had read him what was almost a monograph on coshes, explaining that soft metal was better than the granulation of siliceous rock for rendering a man unconscious without damage, so the short length of two-inch rubber hose had been filled with rolled lead sheet. He bent it lightly with his hand now and put it carefully in his belt. He pinched his breast pocket, where the chalk was and then bent for the smaller roll of tape. He peeled back the end a little before putting it in a trouser pocket. Then he drew on string-backed driving gloves and lowered the lid back again. He moved away down the room to reconnoitre.

The double doors to the main gallery were open as they were during the day and held back by floor bolts. Max looked carefully into the main gallery. He could hear desultory voices again at a distance, and a bar of brighter light showed at the bottom of one of the doors opposite which was obviously the staff room. Max withdrew his head and looked behind each half-door in turn. He decided that the one away from the wall would give greater freedom of movement, and he stood there for a moment tensely. When he looked at his watch it was 7.50.

In a whisper that was audible he said, 'In one hour it will all be over . . .'

Even as he said it he knew it was only a statement of hopeful intent, like a child's promise to be good.

Sitting in the back of the van, they took turns with the Bausch and Lomb night binoculars to watch the back entrance.

Traffic was light, only an occasional car drove through the square, but up until seven there were a lot of people hurrying home along the street from bus stops in the Wandsworth Bridge road.

The tension was affecting them all, so that at a moment when Jamie had the glasses, Dumont wasn't surprised when Doggo said suddenly, 'It doesn't matter a damn, of course, but I'd like to hear you say it . . . You don't like us, do you, Dumont?'

'I don't like you or dislike you. After all, we're not together from choice.'

'You don't like Americans then.'

Dumont said resignedly, 'Oh, dear . . .'

'Go on, admit it, Dumont. We come over here and corrupt you . . . We gum up the works with . . .'

'If you really want to know, I take the opposite view. The

Jamesian view, if you like. I believe that when you come over here *we* corrupt *you*.'

'Don't you believe it. We're all bastards before we leave home, and anyway I don't know any Jamesian view. I'm not really a reading man.'

'There's usually not much else to do when you're on automatic pilot,' Dumont said. He thought he had to apologize for his reading, that he had been guilty of intellectual snobbery.

'Police!' Jamie kept the glasses up. 'Two of them going around the block.'

Doggo said, 'Let me see . . .'

By straining his eyes Dumont could just see two helmeted figures walking around the back of the gallery wall going on towards the front again.

Doggo said, 'Walk around the square again, Dumont. My guess is it's just a routine visit.'

When the door of the staff room opened abruptly, throwing a wedge of light across the main gallery, Max was sitting on the edge of one of the central chairs of the Expressionist room.

He stood and moved silently back towards the door and then, quite near him, in the main gallery, a voice spoke.

'How now, Lavinia? Marcus, what means this?
Some book there is that she desires to see:
Which is it, girl, of these? Open them, boy.
But thou art deeper read, and better skilled;
Come, and take choice of all my library,
And so beguile thy sorrow, till the heavens
Reveal the damned contriver of this deed.
Why lifts she up her arms in sequence thus?'

The voice began to move away carried by slow footsteps and Max with his eye to the crack suddenly saw a young guard come into view and stop almost in the centre of the main gallery. He was bare-headed and carried a quarto-size volume in his hands. After a moment he was walking on again.

'Soft! so busily she turns the leaves!
Help her!
What would she find? Lavinia, shall I read?
This is the tragic tale of Philomel,
And treats of Tereus' treason and his rape;
And rape, I fear, was root of thy annoy.'

A chair scraped suddenly at a distance. 'Taylor!' Someone was calling in a tired, patient voice.

The boy said, 'Yes, Sergeant?'

'Would you mind closing the door? Or even going away and rehearsing somewhere else? God knows we have enough room in this place.'

'Sorry, Sergeant.' Taylor walked down the light path.

'And don't forget it's your round in five minutes.'

Taylor closed the door gently. He came back again, turning pages to and fro. Max tensed himself and closed his eyes, waiting.

When Taylor began speaking again it was in a lowered voice.

'Lavinia, wert thou thus surprised, sweet girl,
Ravished and wronged, as Philomel was,
Forced in the ruthless, vast, and gloomy woods?
See, see!
Ay, such a place there is, where we did hunt, –
O, had we never, never hunted there!
Patterned by that poet here describes,
By nature made for murders and for rapes.'

The voice seemed to be rising, and when Max looked through the crack he could see Taylor coming nearer to the door but walking backwards with an outflung arm. About five paces away he stopped and although his voice was subdued somehow it took on tones of greater passion.

'Give signs, sweet girl, for here are none but friends,
What Roman lord it was durst do the deed:
Or slunk not Saturnine, as Tarquin erst,
That left the camp to sin in Lucrece' bed?
'Tis sure enough, an you knew how,
But if you hurt these bear-whelps, then beware:
The dam will wake and if she wind ye once,
She's with the lion deeply still in league,
And lulls him whilst she playeth on her back,
And when he sleeps will she do what she list.'

Taylor began to back again and stopped when he was nearly in the open doorway. He spoke more quickly, almost gabbling.

'You are a young huntsman, Marcus, let alone;
And, come, I will go get a leaf of brass,
And with a gad of steel will write these words,

And lay it by: the angry northern wind
Will blow these sands like Sybil's leaves abroad,
And where's our lesson then? Boy, what say you?'
Max had drawn the hose length from his belt and was holding it against his chest. He wasn't prepared for the ending of the speech and the sudden silence. He waited for Taylor, balancing on the balls of his feet.

But there were footsteps again, and when he looked Taylor had taken two paces to the side and was putting the script on a seat there. He backed towards Max again, bowing deeply to some imaginary audience in the main gallery.

Max waited.

There was no other sound from inside or out. Taylor still didn't appear and suddenly he began reciting couplets without the book.

'Now is my epilogue, there is no more,
As players from their weary masks withdraw,
You to your hearths, and hearts, now take the sight
Of marvellous history made more marvellous tonight.'
On the last line, Taylor stepped back and rose from the bow. Max wasn't prepared for him to appear so suddenly face to face. For a moment they stared wildly at each other and Max registered a narrow spotty face with clear green eyes.

The boy's mouth had started to open as the cosh thudded on the side of his head.

'Los!' As Max said it the release of his pent-up breath was like the explosion of compressed air from a torpedo tube.

The boy didn't fall backwards but just seemed to shrivel up at his feet. The only sound that came from him was as if he had swallowed loudly, the taut sound of a bass string being plucked.

As Max tucked the cosh away into his belt again he noticed that his hand was shaking and it felt cold against his stomach. He went halfway back to the sofa before he remembered the tape already in his pocket. He came back peeling a strip and cutting it. Then he bent to strap it around the boy's head so that it covered his mouth.

The boy snorted several times while he was doing it and mucus poured out over the plaster. There was no mark yet on his face where the blow had fallen. Max turned him on his back and bound his wrists round and round with a long

strip. Then he pushed the boy's trousers up from his skinny
calves and bound him with tape from ankle to knee. Finally
he took off the boy's shoes and pulled him away behind the
door.

He told himself that he had to keep going now, but all the
time at the back of his mind there was the dilemma of the
closed door. It had seemed at the time, when Taylor had
closed it, to be an advantage, something that would lessen the
sounds if anything had gone wrong. But now he didn't know
what lay behind the door, whether the sergeant could possibly
be in a position to challenge him when he went in and set off
the alarm.

He went silently out into the main gallery and crossed to
the door of the staff room.

If he were to wait, would the sergeant come out? Or would
he wait, with his suspicions growing minute by minute? Max
looked at his watch. It was 8.25. On the two previous patrols
he had heard the ping of the time clock within a minute of the
half-hour. He had five minutes to make up his mind.

He put his ear close to a panel of the door but there was
no sound. The keyhole, when he bent to it, was blind. He
straightened again, and something wet dropped on his hand.

At first he thought it was water coming from somewhere,
then he realized it was sweat. When he touched his face it was
slimy. He wiped it quickly away with his sleeve and looked
at his watch again.

It was just after 8.27.

He took the hose from his waistband. He remembered
always from the war that the attacker had surprise and con-
sequently the advantage. He mustn't wait for the sergeant to
come to him, he must go in there himself.

Having made up his mind he reached for the handle and
turned it almost casually as if he were the boy going back.
He half opened it and stepped into the room.

The sergeant was seated at a table in front of him. He was
side-on in a wheelback chair with arms, and he had a chintz
cushion at his back. He was reading an evening paper and his
head was twisted in a way that allowed him to focus through
his reading spectacles.

Max, standing there, thought he was too defenceless, as if
God were mocking him by giving him a victim already gagged
and bound. Without turning his head the old man said sharply,

128

'Well . . . close the bloody door . . .'

Max put a foot behind him and pushed the door until it latched.

'You're as bad as my old woman, the way you leave doors open. I can tell you that while she's been in hospital the house has been ten times warmer.'

Max was still motionless. God was taunting him again. Stupidly he wanted the old man to look round so that he would be compelled to hit him. The longer he waited the more the sergeant revealed his vulnerability. Then he saw the old man's stockinged foot beyond the paper. He had taken off his boot and the malformation of his big toe joint showed through the heavy ribbed sock.

As he raised the cosh the old man turned his head at last.

He said, 'Now then . . .' He spoke with indignation rather than panic and threw up a hand.

In the instant before striking, it reminded Max of a bird's claw. It was speckled and thin enough to show the veins. The arm crumpled with the blow and he struck again quickly at the balding head. It landed on the sergeant's cheek and jaw and oddly his spectacles still remained in place. He seemed to roll out of the chair with the blow and landed on his hands and knees.

He stayed there like an old dog as blood gushed in a sudden spurt from his nose. Then as Max moved quickly around the table the old man gathered himself and padded around swiftly the opposite way on all fours. For a moment it was like an absurd party game until Max struck at him again and this time the blow seemed to hit the old man on the head and shoulder together.

He stopped and the shoulder hunched painfully. 'Now please,' he began to say, before Max hit him again.

He collapsed at last. As Max bent over him with the tape he saw the spectacles with one lens shattered and the sergeant's eyes unfocused. It was his absolute calm that had shaken Max, the ordinary way he had spoken.

He struggled with the tape, which became slippery with blood, as he bound the old man's head. Then when he came to the legs, God gave him the final humiliating shock. One of them was missing and Max's hand was chilled by the perforated alloy frame. He bound both legs together quickly, then stood up.

L.H. – E

He turned the sergeant on his back and went quickly through his pockets. The Steinitz key wallet was in a side pocket of his trousers and secured by a chain to his belt. Max unclipped it from the belt and dropped it into his own pocket.

At that moment he remembered the time clock. He saw it at once behind the door and he was astonished to see that it was only just one minute past the half-hour. He studied it carefully before pulling the lever action.

Looking down at the curled body again Max remembered Ingram saying: 'Lock them in different places, never leave bound men together.'

There was a tall cupboard with plywood doors in a recess formed by the chimney piece, but when he unlocked the doors it was filled with stationery and files. He swept a shelf clear and then pushed up the shelf itself. It came easily out of the metal slots and in two minutes he had the cupboard cleared.

He lifted the sergeant from behind, not wanting to see his face again, and manhandled him, half standing, into the cupboard. He remembered the leg again as metal rang on metal and when he pressed the door slowly closed it was like closing an underhatch against a gale. He turned the key and was still for a moment making sure the cracks around the door were big enough for air.

When he went out he started to look through every doorway off the main gallery. In one of them he found a corridor and, off the corridor, a door giving into a broom closet with a lavatory beyond.

There was no window, just an extractor fan and an air duct. It was operated by the light switch. The lavatory had no lock on the outside but there was a key in the door from the corridor. Max reversed the key and went back to the main gallery. When he bent to pick up Taylor, the boy groaned faintly but his eyes didn't open. Max dragged him, heels trailing and dropped him on the floor of the broom closet. He locked the door.

Through another door from the main gallery, which was marked PRIVATE, he found the administrative offices. He walked through the typists' rooms into an executive suite and in one of the rooms there he found the safe which housed the Steinitz control. It was behind a wall chart. It took longer to find what was called the boob switch but he found it in the end by levering out the skirting board beneath the chart. The safety switch was on the under side of a knee-hole desk. After he'd flicked it up he opened the safe without difficulty, using both keys in the wallet. It was the standard installation of a few years ago.

Max opened the three gate switches one by one.

When he went out by one of the rear doors into the open courtyard he drew air deeply into his lungs. There was a murmur of traffic from somewhere to the north but the square appeared to be silent. He went down towards the main gates. He looked at his watch. It was just before five to nine.

At some time near the hour one of the others would be passing outside. The thought had barely left him when he heard the distant whistling. He knew it was Dumont passing because he was whistling *Deutschland über Alles*. When he was opposite the other side of the door Max said clearly, 'I'm ready, Dumont.'

He heard the clicking as Dumont drew his fingernail along the outside planking. There was no need now for a chalk mark on the gate as they had planned.

Max waited, feeling cold suddenly and staring up at the sky where the cloud pall was almost scarlet with refracted light. The old man's face came into his mind again, alert and unafraid. His response had confused and upset him.

Somehow it would have been easier if the old man had been afraid of him.

Dumont quickened his pace as he went along to the van and they must have noticed because Jamie had climbed down from the back and entered the cab before he got there.

As he climbed into the passenger seat Doggo said, 'No problem?'

'He didn't say so.' The engine caught and they pulled out and drove away. Doggo told Jamie to drive once round the square first but there was no policeman there, only an old lady standing by the verge with a defecating dog on a lead. She bowed her head as they passed as though it was she herself who had been caught performing her function there. As they came up to the yard doors the second time, they were opened quickly and they drove straight in and stopped.

Dumont left the cab and saw Max closing the doors. Doggo was already staring up at the façade of houses that surrounded them. Then he told Jamie to park in the shadow close to the wall, and take the packing inside.

'No problem, Max?'

'No problem.' Max looked smaller in the half-light. 'Just an old man and a boy . . . that's all.'

Doggo passed out a tool bag to Max and they followed him round the yard and into a storeroom. From the storeroom a passage led straight to the main gallery.

As they came into the light Doggo looked at Max. 'Are they asleep?'

'One is in a cupboard in the office, one in a storeroom. Do you want to see?'

Doggo shook his head and walked on towards the Impressionist room. When they got there he pointed to the Gauguin which was nearest the door, and said, 'Show us, Max.'

Max opened the canvas tool bag and got out the bolt cutters. He slipped the blade handle under the edge of the frame and eased it out from the wall. Then he reversed the cutters and snapped through the mirror plate in one movement. When he bent the frame off the wall there were two wires exposed at the edge of the canvas. Max cut them with pliers.

'Electrodes,' he said. 'Part of the system.'

As he was cutting the other mirror plate and lifting the picture down, Doggo said, 'Take over, Dumont . . . the way he showed you.'

Dumont nodded.

Doggo started to turn away when suddenly the whistle blast started.

Max was running first and when Dumont and Doggo reached the main hall he had already crossed it and was tearing open the door of the staff room. To the left there was a crash as Jamie dropped the crate he was holding. He was turning for the storeroom when Doggo shouted, 'Jamie!'

Jamie looked back at once, white-faced, and then raced on.

Doggo said, 'Stop him!' and they almost collided as Doggo went after Max, who was opening another door beyond in the staff room.

The whistle screamed on as Dumont crashed through the storeroom passage. He reached out in time to catch the door as Jamie slammed it. As he ripped it open again and went through, Jamie was ready for him.

Dumont took the first bone-crushing blow on his shoulder but managed to block the second. Then as their bodies locked and strained he knew he was going to be beaten. Jameson was younger and stronger and fitter and he broke Dumont's hold with contemptuous ease and drew back the edge of his hand again.

Then the whistle slowly died away.

In the silence they stood facing each other, their heaving breath making one huge cloud in the night air. Dumont wanted to curse but the burst of action had exhausted him. Doggo called something from the storeroom but Dumont couldn't hear the words.

Then Jameson moved past him, hitting him lightly on the shoulder, and went back inside. Dumont stayed there crouching on one knee, still gasping for breath.

After what seemed a very long time, Doggo said, behind him, 'Would you believe it! A fucking kettle! The guard had left it in their wash-up place with the gas on low . . .'

When Dumont got back Max was on his knees easing the Seurat canvas from the inner frame. There were chalk crosses on the floor marking the other paintings to be taken.

As Dumont picked up the cutters, Max said, 'I told you . . . I'm too old for this, Dumont.'

'There are compensations . . . one can't run away as fast.' Dumont eased the mirror plate on a Cézanne, which was thickly painted in a monochrome of green.

'The English and their bloody tea. Why can't they drink wine like the rest of us?'

The cutters crunched through the mirror plate and Dumont eased it back until he could cut the wires of the contact switch. As he moved on to the next one he saw Jamie rolling out fibreglass wadding in the main gallery.

Then Doggo came back from the other direction. He said, 'Both the guards are okay, and I found an upstairs window where I could see down into the front. There's no cop there at the moment.' He went into the main hall, where Jamie was already sliding the first canvas into its narrow case.

Dumont and Max worked in silence until Max said, 'One of them . . . the young one, was rehearsing for a play. He kept walking up and down . . . I think it was Shakespeare. I'm sure it was Shakespeare.'

133

Dumont took the last frame from the wall and lowered it gently to the floor. Max bent to it and said, 'Take the others through.'

Dumont was surprised when he picked up the canvases to find they only weighed a few ounces. He walked into the main gallery with them as Jamie and Doggo were coming back from the van carrying the last two cases. He laid them down and Jamie started to cut a length of wadding.

Jamie said, 'It's like making sandwiches.'

Doggo laughed. 'Why are we whispering?' He bent to help Jamie as Dumont walked back to the Impressionist room.

Max was cutting a screw, or a nail, using a small bow-shaped hack saw. Dumont walked on through an archway and into another room. Long etiolated portraits by Whistler stretched up into the dimness, where their faces were hardly visible. He went through a dog-leg of arches, where there was a bronze cast of Moore's 'Death in Battle,' and found himself in the Expressionist room again. He walked along to the sofa and raised the lid.

The paperback and the torch still lay there, and the plastic bag, unused. Dumont pushed them into his pocket and closed the seat. When he walked on out into the main hall Max was there again packing the last case.

He gave Max the paperback and said, 'I've emptied the sofa.'

Doggo straightened. 'Okay. When we go out into the yard, don't forget to listen. You'll go first, Dumont . . . and remember it's better if no one's passing. Now we'll just have one last check. Max can have a look at the boy in the loo. Jamie, rope the last crate in. I'll look at the sergeant.'

Dumont picked up the tool bag and waited. Jamie carried the last case away and Doggo was coming back from the office when the phone began to ring behind him.

He stopped dead. After a moment Max came from the corridor. They stared at each other in turn.

Doggo called to Dumont, 'What do you think?'

'It may be a wrong number.' Dumont hesitated. 'But if it isn't, they'll expect to be answered.'

'Right,' said Doggo. '*You* answer it . . . we don't want any strange accents.'

Dumont followed him into the staff room and was about to pick up the receiver from the desk when Doggo stopped his hand. 'Just say the name of the gallery.'

'Of course.'

Dumont picked it up and said, 'Turner Gallery?'

There was a long pause and he was about to repeat it when there was a click and the line went dead.

Doggo was moving swiftly. 'Let's go . . .'

PART FOUR

CHAPTER ONE

When they sprinted into the yard Dumont went straight for the gates.

He unshot the bolts and opened them wide and walked into the road. Lights were coming towards him. Behind he heard the engine of the van start up and the slam of doors, then it rolled out across the pavement with dipped lights. A taxi passed with irritating slowness and as Dumont went towards the back of the van Doggo opened the door of the cab.

He said, 'Close the gates, Dumont . . . just in case we're wrong.'

Dumont hurried on and slammed the gates shut and bolted them. Then he let himself out of the small door and ran for the back of the van. Max reached out to pull him in.

Then Doggo said, 'Go left, Jamie . . . past the police box.'

Jamie reversed slightly, then pulled away towards the river. The road was deserted. Then, as they left the square, a policeman burst from the box and started running for the side of the gallery.

Jamie put his foot down momentarily until Doggo snapped 'Slow down!' The van checked and they bumped on slowly out to the embankment. Through the rear window Dumont saw the policeman take the corner with an arm outflung to keep his balance.

When he looked at Max, Max stared back at him with troubled eyes. 'I still don't understand, Dumont.'

'That's who was on the bloody telephone.'

'Oh *that* I understand, but *why*?' Max blinked his deep-set eyes slowly.

Then Doggo said, 'We'll stop at the first call box. Keep your eyes open.' They were coming to the junction at Wandsworth Bridge Road when a police car came bursting out of a street just ahead of them in a wide screaming turn. Its blue light was flicking and its siren rose to a shriek as it hurtled by, missing them by inches.

Doggo said quietly, 'Don't hurry. Keep it at a steady thirty.' And a moment later, 'Turn left over the bridge. There was a call box by the underground where we stopped before.'

They were crossing the bridge when another police car came by in the centre lane with its lights glaring. They circled the roundabout at the end of the bridge and parked near the station.

Dumont said quickly, 'Wouldn't it be more intelligent to get as far away as possible?'

'The order was that in the event of any change or anything unusual, we were to ring the man.' Then Doggo added, 'Relax, Dumont, it may never happen.' The next moment he was crossing the road and Dumont, looking down at his laced hands, wished he hadn't spoken.

Out loud he said, 'He's right, of course. Flexibility is what most planning lacks.'

'Do you know something, Dumont? You're right about the police call but what troubled me was that while I waited tonight the phone never rang once.'

'Perhaps you couldn't hear it from your coffin.'

'Oh, I would have heard it. I could hear the bell on the time clock. But now I think I understand. When the system was switched off an alarm light came on automatically in the police box and the first patrol to visit it naturally called the gallery and checked.'

'This would be typical Steinitz thinking,' Max went on. 'The first system had time locks but they were taken out some years ago. A night guard at the Niedersachsiche Landesgalerie in Hanover had a mild heart attack and, because they couldn't by-pass the alarm, the whole security system had to be alerted.' He rubbed his head deeply in the way he had. 'No, that would be it. A light in the police box . . . that's probably why the box was put there anyway.'

They hadn't heard Doggo's steps above the traffic so they all jumped slightly as the door opened suddenly. He climbed in again and as Jamie pressed the starter he said, 'Wait!'

Jamie switched off.

Doggo twisted round and said, 'You're leaving us, Max . . . You take an underground train from here to Paddington and get the 11.15. Get a sleeper if you can but make sure the guard calls you for Yeovil. You'll be met . . .'

'I have to go?'

'You have to go. *Now*, Max.'

Max opened the door and climbed down. Standing in the

road he stared up at them. 'I haven't got my coat . . .'

Jamie said, 'It's here,' and pointed to the clothing behind the front seat.

Dumont pulled out Max's coat and gave it to him and he shrugged it on. He stood there for a moment looking creased and miserable. Then Doggo said, 'Close the bloody door, Max.'

'*Glück,* Dumont,' Max said. He closed the doors and set off, picking his way through the traffic.

Doggo said, 'Okay, we go back over the river the way we came.'

Jamie hesitated. 'Back again?'

'Yes. We've got to switch transport just to be sure.'

'Where?'

'Make for Slough in Buckinghamshire. Believe it or not, we're going to pick up a horse.'

The stables were beyond Slough on the road to Stoke Poges and there was a large wooden sign at the entrance to a driveway of yellow gravel.

It still wasn't ten o'clock. After the van had dropped him, Dumont walked up it alone. It occurred to him then as it occurred to him several times afterwards that, in spite of themselves, they had come to have a kind of confidence in Ingram. Certainly nothing else could explain why he should be here, going to pick up a horse in the middle of the night. It was part of Ingram's planning skill that he could rationalize such a situation.

There was a low complex of buildings lying behind a brick wall ahead of him and a house to the left of it. As he came up to the house he could see the curtains were open on the picture windows of the living-room and a man was standing with his back to the fire, leafing through a magazine. As Dumont turned up the path, he bent to pick up a whisky glass and drain it.

When Dumont pulled the old-fashioned tug, a rocker bell clanged deep in the house. Then the door opened. Colonel Dalgety looked bigger standing in the doorway and he was wearing a deep-skirted hacking jacket that nearly reached his knees.

'You've come for Rosie, I suppose. We'd nearly given you up.'

Dumont said, as he'd been told, 'Yes, I'm sorry. I couldn't

138

get here any sooner.'

'Well, keep straight on for the stables, my chappie is there.'

'Thank you. I'm sorry I disturbed you.'

Colonel Dalgety didn't answer but merely stepped back and started to close the door. Dumont turned but he was only half-way back to the drive when he heard the door open again behind him.

The colonel called, 'You can tell Mr Ingram it wasn't really necessary to move her at night. She's broken to traffic . . . It wouldn't have bothered her at all.'

'I'll tell him.'

Colonel Dalgety made a noise in his throat that could have been 'Goodnight,' and the door slammed again.

Dumont walked out to the driveway and under the arch. A Land-Rover and a box trailer waited in the cobbled yard. A small man dropped from the cab as he came up.

His face was pinched and unnaturally white in the moonlight. He said, 'I loaded her up when I heard you arrive, sir. Come and look at her . . .'

They walked to the horse box at the rear and all around them in the darkened stalls other horses fretted quietly.

'Always hate to lose one of my girls.' The dwarf's face was softened. Dumont put up a hand and the mare butted it lightly. Her breath was hot against his skin.

'It's an ordinary sort of tailboard ramp, sir, and the usual ball hook. Don't forget to unplug the light socket before you unhitch.'

'Right.'

As they walked back to the Land-Rover the stableman said, 'She doesn't mind the traffic, sir, but it's better moving her at night. I've left a nosebag in the back in case you have a break-down.'

'Thanks very much.' For a moment Dumont wondered if, in the feudal world that seemed to cling to horses, he should give the man a pound, but the prematurely old face looking up at him was not expectant.

Dumont pressed the starter and switched through the lights before dipping them. 'Goodbye.'

As he pulled slowly out of the yard he heard the man call, 'Good luck, sir,' and a moment later, 'Goodbye, Rosie.'

Dumont kept in low gear along the drive and as he passed the house he saw the colonel back at the fireplace again.

He didn't look up at the sound of the Land-Rover.

Dumont turned right towards Slough. The trailer bumped slightly on the hook and he let out the clutch very slowly in gear changes to avoid snatching. He'd been driving for ten minutes when lights flashed on and off ahead of him. As he slowed, he saw Doggo suddenly appear in the headlights.

A moment later the side door opened and Doggo climbed in. 'There's a lane on the right about a quarter of a mile ahead. It loops back to the main road farther on.'

Dumont slowed to a crawl when he saw the finger post, and turned off.

Doggo said, 'Go on for a bit. It gets wider.'

After another quarter of a mile, Dumont pulled up gently, and when he climbed down the van was already drawn up behind them with its lights dimmed.

When the ramp was down, Dumont led the mare out by its halter. It picked its way delicately behind him as he and Doggo walked up and down in the half-light. Jamie had begun hammering at something in the box.

'He's lining the bottom half of the sides with crates. It won't take him long.'

'Why didn't we just press on down?'

'Ingram hadn't reckoned on the alarm being given so soon. He thinks it possible there'll be stop and search blocks on all the main roads within an hour. Since the immigrant smuggling they have these emergency plans for sealing up areas quickly.'

The mare jerked on the rope and whinnied softly as a pipistrelle bat fluttered low over their heads. Dumont said, 'Steady, girl,' and turned to stroke her.

'Ingram says you're not to queue at road blocks but drive straight up to the barrier.'

'Me?'

'He thinks it better for you to go it alone. Jamie and I are to stick with the van. *If* there's a road block you tell them you've got a nervous horse who isn't used to traffic and you're afraid she's going to kick the back out of the box. Ingram says it's unlikely they'll look in the box but even if they do there'll be nothing significant to see when Jamie is finished. And on no account are you to hurry, whether there are road blocks or not. Have you got it, Dumont?'

Dumont nodded.

The torch was now flickering to and fro between the van

140

and the trailer. 'Do you want a pill?'

Dumont shook his head. In the woods to the south he heard the screech of a barn owl in flight. This was followed by a crescendo of hammering from the horse box. Dumont said, 'Do you think it'll work?'

'I don't see why not. Do you know he had three other contingency plans for getting us out of London? I hate to think what it all cost.'

'What I can't understand is why everything seems so bloody ordinary. I feel I ought to be het up at the idea of driving four or five million pounds' worth of stolen goods through police road blocks, but it doesn't seem to matter a damn.'

'Maybe it's because you're a hero, Dumont.' Doggo wasn't smiling. 'Maybe that's how Ingram has it worked out.'

'I don't think so.' The horse's breath clouded the air between them as they counter-marched.

When Jamie had finished he walked along the lane to fetch them.

Dumont ordered them away while he backed the mare in. She showed him the white of her eye once but didn't check. When she was settled the other two came to raise the ramp and bolt it. Then Dumont collected the road map from the van and Doggo explained to him how to get to the A30 at Bagshot.

After that it was the A30 all the way to Yeovil.

Some instinct made them all shake hands when they parted, and Doggo came to the window as Dumont started up.

'You bear left twice in about a hundred yards and you're back on the road to Slough, and the man said my last words were to be "Drive slowly." The smallest accident could wreck the whole deal.'

Dumont nodded. Then he let out the clutch and bumped back on to the tarmac. The headlights lit a long lane lined with may and blackthorn. He followed it continuously until he came up to the main road again. He turned south for Slough and felt a familiar comfort in the dimly lit cab. It was in a sense an extension of his life on a flight deck.

After a while he began to sing tunelessly.

He travelled at a steady forty miles an hour and it was just short of midnight when he met the A30. Traffic was light, mostly container lorries on the run to Southampton and a few late cars. He kept to the inside lane and let it flow by. Although he had been half-prepared for it the first check point took him by surprise.

Police warning flashers began suddenly as he pulled over a rise and the left-hand lane was solid with tail lights for nearly half a mile. Dumont changed down without hesitation and drove slowly along the outside lane. In the moments before he came up to the barrier he recognized that his behaviour had been instinctual, that he was totally committed to Ingram's authority. He recognized, too, that it was typical of Ingram's thinking to solve a problem with an attacking solution. It wasn't enough just to find a way through the barrier, it had to be done with *élan,* something which retained initiative.

A red light was swinging in front of him about a hundred yards ahead. Confidence was the order of the day, Dumont thought, make the bastards help. As he slowed to a halt in front of the light a patrolman appeared suddenly at the window.

'Where the hell do you think you're going?'

'I wonder if you can help me.' Dumont spoke quietly. 'I've got rather a valuable breeding mare in the box. She's highly strung and not broken to traffic and I'm afraid she might kick the thing to pieces.'

'Right. Hang ón there a minute.' The patrolman went off towards a group of officers standing around a squad car. Farther on, in the layby, Dumont saw police teams unloading lorries on to the verges.

After a moment the patrolman came back and went by the window without stopping. In the rear view mirror Dumont watched him walk to the back of the horse box. He put up a hand as if to unbolt the ramp and Dumont heard the rough voice, curiously softened.

'There's my pretty girl . . .'

He must have only been stroking her muzzle because the next moment he was walking back and the canvas flap of the Land-Rover was lifted. A powerful torch travelled over the spare wheel and the four gallon can of diesel and then went out.

Footsteps came up to the window again. 'Right, sir . . . follow me . . .'

'Just a moment.'

As the policeman turned, Dumont said, 'What's happened
. . . what are you looking for?'

'Stolen goods. Just a routine check.' He walked on again
and Dumont followed slowly with dipped lights.

After a hundred yards they came to a barrier of plastic
bollards and a second patrolman came to lift them away. The
first patrolman waved his torch in a quickening circle and
Dumont accelerated away into the safety of the night again.

The road to Southampton split off soon afterwards and the
traffic became desultory. It seemed to get cooler after midnight and he pulled into a layby on the other side of Salisbury.
He found a recirculating fan heater under the dashboard and
switched it on. Then he went back to check on the mare. She
blew softly into his hand as he touched her muzzle.

There was a second check point on the other side of Wilton
but no one was waiting. As he drove up slowly a policeman
stepped into the road and the brief examination was repeated.
He drove on. When he looked at his watch it was twenty past
one. Dumont estimated he would be home by 3.30.

Warmed by the heater he started to sing tunelessly again.

He first noticed the dimmed lights when he was driving
through the darkened streets of Yeovil. He kept close to the
kerb but they slowed also, and stayed behind him. When he
came out of the town he stayed on the inner lane and then
turned south on to the Dorchester road. There was no sign
of the lights behind him.

He speeded up again but as he did so he saw them suddenly
on the outside of a bend. They leapt to full power, glaring in
the rear view mirror. Then a horn started to sound in short
blasts. Dumont slowed right down and kept close to the verge
and the lights came by alongside and drew slowly in front of
him. With relief he recognized the van.

They were out of it before he pulled on the handbrake and
running back into the headlights. When he dropped from the
cab they grabbed him and for a moment they thumped each
other and laughed hysterically.

'What happened, Dumont? Did they look at all?'

'Not really. It was a piece of cake, old boy.'

Jamie said, 'They're taking everyone apart. They looked
underneath at the Basingstoke barrier. Everyone had to drive
over a mobile ramp.'

'Anyway, you made it, you old bastard, Dumont.'

'The biggest fright I had was just now when you buggers came up behind me.'

Then they all went back to the box to pat the mare. 'Good old Rosie . . .'

'Actually one of the policemen called her a pretty girl . . .'

'Did he *actually*?' said Doggo. 'Did he really say that, Dumont?'

'Oh, belt up!'

'But we've made it! Let's go and tell the man.'

In the momentary silence, Doggo said, 'Right. Let's get on.'

'Where's Max?'

Ingram said, 'I told him to lie down.'

The Spanish couple had been sent to Brighton for two nights and would only return to clear up, so they'd cooked their own steaks in the kitchen and were eating them there.

Ingram was standing beside the coffee percolator. In the strip light his skin looked like paper.

'Max didn't sleep on the train,' he said. 'He can grab an extra half-hour now as there's no problem at the field.' He walked slowly around the table to refill Dumont's cup with coffee.

Jamie said, 'What about the warden . . . or whoever he is?'

'He's gone.'

Ingram walked back to the cooker and put down the percolator on the asbestos mat. 'It's time we had some luck . . . When I rang yesterday to ask about the test flight I'd arranged on Thursday he said the plane was all gassed up and ready. He said he'd checked personally with the head fitter because he was going to spend his day off at his son-in-law's farm in Somerset. That means there's a night-watchman there now and he'll be relieved at eight o'clock by the day watch. We'll either sweet talk him about being a day early, or hit him over the head and strap him up. I haven't decided yet. Meanwhile, you rest till I call you at around seven. Except Dumont, that is . . .'

The easel was empty when Dumont followed him into the small salon but there were charts and papers all over the tables still.

Ingram said, 'Sit down,' and Dumont chose a button-back chair and sat on the edge of it. He looked at the empty easel as he had looked before at shrouded operation maps, with muted curiosity. What would be, would be.

Then Ingram was facing him with his white hands pressed together and pointing downwards. 'This is important . . . this next part. And it all hangs on you, Dumont.'

Dumont waited.

'Are you tired, Dumont?'

'I would have been less tired if I hadn't had to drive that Land-Rover.'

'It was a contingency plan, Dumont. We were unlucky with the phone check.'

'Well, Doggo could have driven it . . . It was *his* show, anyway . . .'

'You haven't thought about it, Dumont. A driver with an American accent would have been something different and memorable. And Jamie wasn't the type because he isn't a hero. He would have given up under the smallest set-back. Any policeman could have talked him down, kicked him back to the end of the queue. It had to be someone used to command. Authority is essential when dealing with the police. It had to be *you*.'

His hands parted at last and he picked up a newspaper column from the edge of the table. 'This was the weather picture in *The Times* this morning. A high over the Azores and another over the North Sea. No immediate changes. If there are any fronts coming off the Atlantic they'll be weak.'

'Where are we going, Ingram?'

Ingram walked down to the easel and picked up a board. There was a sheet of chinagraph over the map which caught the light so there was a moment or two before Dumont saw exactly where it was.

He said, 'Africa!'

'North Africa, Dumont. Morocco, in fact. The strip is in the foothills of the Atlas Mountains. It was a staging post for the U.S. Army Air Force during the Mediterranean campaigns in World War II.'

'That's twenty-five years ago.'

'One runway's been cleared. It's in great condition. Colonel Zouak has personally supervised it.'

'Zouak!'

Ingram walked to a chair on the other side of the room and sat down. Dumont waited.

Then Dumont said again, 'Zouak.'

CHAPTER TWO

'That's right. Life goes round in circles, Dumont . . . Surely you knew that.

'It's about sixteen hundred miles, which gives you over a thirty per cent fuel margin. You fly, say about a hundred feet, so that you won't show on any radar trace, even by accident. You keep about a hundred miles off the Portuguese and Moroccan coasts all the way, which means you're clear of the main international air routes which run down to Dakar and the Azores. There's a good probability you could go all the way unobserved but even in the event you don't no one is going to worry. Because even if you're seen you have the same profile as the weather planes as I told you before.

'The safety factor is also taken care of. You can lose one engine and still make it, and in the unheard of event that you lose two you've only got to take a ninety degree turn and fly a hundred miles to the nearest coast. Your landfall when you get down here, to the coast of Morocco, is Cape Rhir.

'You cross north of it on a bearing of 148° and at twenty thousand feet, until you meet the Sous river, just east of Taroudant. From there you start letting down on a bearing of 81° right into here behind Marrakesh. Your penetration route is almost unpopulated, there's no radar hazard and every detail is marked on the topographical map. There's also no weather hazard . . . like any other desert it's almost a permanent high pressure area. Your cruising speed is around two hundred, which means your E.T.A. there is 1700 hours. Again, you have a good margin of daylight. From Taroudant to touch down, Zouak has arranged markers and bearings and he's flown the route twice himself to check it out. Zouak has fifteen hundred metres of runway clear and he'll fire flares when you're overhead.

'I suggest you study the charts and the flight plan and if

you have any queries you raise them with me at seven o'clock. The way I plan it is this. The relief watchman comes at 0730, and we arrive at 0800. You have one hour to check everything out and take-off at 0900.'

'What happens when we get there?'

'Zouak is in charge of the last phase. You have nothing to worry about. You'll be living in comfort until I arrange pay day.'

Dumont stood up. He said, 'I rather liked Zouak.'

During the war when he was nearing the end of his third tour of operations he had found it difficult to leave his bed.

After the orderly's call his body would lie there unmoved while his mind was telling him he must get dressed. For whatever reason the mental block always operated at that one precise moment, the moment of leaving the bed. This morning he woke after only an hour's sleep to the sound of voices in the stable yard below. For a moment he was conscious of the same feeling again, as if the overdraft of fear was still there and time hadn't cancelled a penny of it. It only lasted a second, then he had rolled from the bed and was going to the bathroom.

This really *was* the last one, the one that would pay for all the others, past and future. As he showered, he thought of the vineyard in the Perigord Noir, where he would bury all the black dogs of middle age. The only flying he would see would be the jet streams at thirty thousand feet going up to Paris or down to Africa.

He moved the curtains slightly with his finger. The sky was blue except for drifting cirrus here and there. After he'd washed, he pulled on a roll-necked sweater and packed his belongings neatly into the duffel bag. He went down to the kitchen. Max was eating bacon and eggs and Marnix Hoffman was standing by the stove.

When their eyes met she gave him a tired smile. 'Would you like the same, Dumont?'

'Yes, please. You look tired.'

'I couldn't sleep on the train. It was stopping and starting all the way down . . . They were putting out mail bags.'

Max said, 'There's nothing in the papers . . . They were printed too early for the provinces. But Ingram said it was on the radio this morning.'

When Dumont sat down beside him Max added, 'I couldn'
sleep, Dumont. I don't know whether it was my conscience or
that bloody pill I took.'

They didn't look at each other when Marnix brought him
his bacon and eggs.

'I kept seeing the old man running about on his hands and
knees. I remembered my father. After he'd slit the throat of
a pig he would drive it fifty metres to the scalding vat, and
the pig would stagger all the way, responding to the stick
even though its brain must have stopped. That is what I kept
remembering . . .'

There was still a ground mist when they went out to the
cobbled yard and Dumont turned his blunt face into the wind.
It was faint and from the south-west still. The van was there
with its doors open and the picture crates had been loaded
back into it.

The food was packed in two bushel skips and Dumont
dropped his duffel bag beside them. He kept the clipboard
with the flight plan under his arm. The other three waited for
him to come up to where they were standing beside the bonnet.

'I checked the shipping forecast at 0700, Dumont. Portland,
Plymouth, Finisterre, it's clear all the way.'

Doggo said, 'How's your navigation, Dumont?'

'It's okay.' Dumont ran a hand across his head and looked
at his watch. 'Shall we go?'

'In a second . . . We're waiting for Marnix.' As Dumont
turned his head Ingram added, 'She's driving you. Someone
has to bring the van back.'

Dumont said evenly, 'Then we can load up anyway.' As he
moved back to the van Jamie followed him and he saw Max
and Marnix come down the steps from the house. He and
Jamie loaded the food skips and he said, 'Have you ever been
a flight engineer, Jamie?'

'I don't think so.'

'Well, I may have need of one today.'

'What do I do?'

'Nothing much. Just watch a few dials and flick switches
when I tell you.'

Max came and put his sea bag by the skips. He said, 'What
happens if they try and shoot us down, Dumont? Are there
any guns on this plane?'

'No one will shoot at us. Not while we're carrying five

148

million pounds' worth of insurance.' He looked at his watch and it was twenty-five to eight.

He felt something of an anticlimax when he said, 'Well, let's get cracking, shall we?'

As the others clambered into the back he went to the passenger seat up front. He wound the window down as Ingram came up. Ingram brought his pale face down to look in at him. Dumont noticed that the skin under his eyes was almost transparent.

Ingram said, 'We don't know how long matters will take but until I've made the final watertight arrangements you must trust Zouak. Do everything he says.'

Ingram waited with his pale hand on the door looking at Dumont. 'You remember everything to say to Tizzard . . . the day watchman?'

'Yes, I think so.'

'Remember, your attitude is the most important thing. It's always important to be on top of people like Tizzard.' He waited again.

Doggo said, 'What happens if we don't get off the ground?'

'There's a contingency plan for anything that goes wrong. Dumont has been briefed.'

Then Max's deep voice said, 'What if we crash? Is there a plan for that?'

'All right, let's go,' Dumont said irritably, and he began to wind up the window. The engine caught and Ingram turned away and started walking towards the house without a backward glance.

At a bend in the drive when Dumont looked back again he had disappeared. They turned on to the road and Marnix speeded up. It was all very ordinary, Dumont thought, without drums and trumpets. He hoped the take-off would be just as ordinary.

Then Max started to sing.

> 'Ich hatt einen Kameraden,
> Einen besser'n find'st du nicht,
> Die Trommel schlug zum Streite . . .'

'Shut up, Max.'

As they passed the director's house there was no sign of life.

They drew up at the gate to the airfield. There was a chain and padlock around it. Marnix Hoffman looked at him.

Dumont said, 'Give them a hoot . . . A good long one.'

He wrenched open the door of the van and got down. As the horn blared, he started to climb the gate, which was wet with dew.

He stayed on the top bar shouting, 'Tizzard . . . Tizzard, where are you?'

He waited. Somewhere in the distance a dog was jumping noisily against a chain. 'Tizzard!'

A small man came hurriedly from a side door of the main hangar, stopping to look at him for a moment, before coming on. He was younger than Dumont had expected, and spectacled, but he didn't look alarmed. When he was about ten yards away, Dumont said abruptly, 'Get this bloody gate open, will you, Tizzard.'

'Right, sir.' He brought the key from his pocket attached to a large wooden tag. In a mumbling voice he said, 'I didn't know anyone was coming. It's Wednesday.'

Dumont said, 'We're test-flying the Lancaster in an hour . . . Didn't Squadron-Leader Walter tell you that?'

'No, sir. He's away . . .'

'Oh, that's right. He said he'd be in Somerset.'

The gate was opened and as the van drove in Dumont waved it down. He said, 'All right . . . Go ahead and load up. And wheel out the trolleyac, you might have to disconnect it if it's on charge.'

The van drove on and he said to the boy, 'I shouldn't bother to lock the gate. The van will be going back in about five minutes.' They walked together and the early sun was just strong enough to mark their shadows on the hard standing. When they reached the door Tizzard had come from, Dumont went ahead automatically. Tizzard closed the door and their footsteps became a jumble of echoes in the hangar.

Tizzard said, 'I was just making a cup of tea.'

Dumont looked in at a kind of butler's pantry. 'All right, I'll join you in a moment. I'll just have a look at Douglas's desk to see if he's left a message for me.'

Dumont went on to the executive offices and opened the door which had Walter's name on it. He closed it behind him. When he got to the window and looked down at the field, the van was already drawn up alongside the Lancaster and Max and Jamie were unloading a crate. Then near at hand he heard a clanking sound at the side of the building.

He opened the window and leant out to see Doggo on an aluminium ladder only five yards away. He said, 'Hello, Doggo . . . I'm just going to have a cup of tea.'

'Oh, Christ . . . How typical!'

Dumont closed the window and went back to the desk. When he picked up the phone the line was already dead and he heard a rattle as Doggo went down the ladder. He went back into the corridor and out to the main hangar again.

He took the cup of tea in his gloved hand and added more milk from the bottle to cool it. Tizzard said, 'Well, you've got nice weather for your flight, sir.'

'Do you go up often, Tizzard?'

'Sometimes. The squadron-leader gives me a flip now and then.'

'Well, give him my best wishes if you see him tonight. I must get cracking now.'

'I'll come and watch you, sir.'

'Oh, I've all the checks to do first. Time enough when you hear the motors start.'

When he went out to the pad the van was just pulling away, and they were still loading through the side hatch in the fuselage. Marnix drove towards him and he thought for a moment she wasn't going to stop, but she braked just beyond him.

He walked back to the driver's window. He said, 'Close the gate when you go through. Tizzard is having his tea.'

'Yes, sir.'

He let his breath go.

Marnix said in a matter of fact voice, 'You're not sad, are you, Dumont?'

'No, I'm not sad. Who knows . . . I may even see you again.'

'I don't think so.'

'Everyone tells me life goes round in circles. I never thought I'd fly a Lanc again.'

'But you don't believe that?'

'Not really. I'm a flat earth man.'

She leant slightly on the accelerator and the tempo of the engine speeded up. She said, 'Remember me to the colonel.'

'I suppose he was in on it from the beginning. It seems ages ago now.'

'We wintered at Agadir last year, Mr Ingram and I. That's when it was all arranged.' Again she touched the accelerator.

'I'll watch from the lane when you go. And happy landings, Dumont.'

Before he could answer she had driven on and the van was pulling up beyond the gate. She waved to him again as she left the cab to walk back to close it, then a moment later it was dwindling away past the director's house towards the road. Dumont turned and walked towards the plane. Halfway there he turned off and went down to where a hedge bordered the director's orchard.

He found an elder amongst the dogwood and broke off a young branch about three feet long. As he walked back to the plane he peeled it cleanly. He took the ladder from the side hatch and set it in the wing root and climbed up. He walked along the wing, opening the fuel caps and plunged the stick in to check the levels. The first two were full but the far outer was only three-quarters. He climbed down and moved to the other wing. Again the far outer was light but since they were small tanks he estimated he was only about fifty gallons short of his two thousand two hundred gallon capacity.

As he walked back along the wing, Doggo dropped from the crew hatch. He stared up at Dumont. 'How is it, Dumont . . . what's holding us back?'

'I shan't be long.' Dumont rattled down the ladder and tossed the stick away. He ducked under the wing to look at the tyres and the retraction gear. It was obvious that the Bride of Frankenstein had been looked after with loving care. He completed the external check with Doggo trailing after him. The trolleyac was under the wing and Dumont opened the hatch under the fuselage and plugged it in.

Once Doggo said, 'You're a thorough bastard, aren't you, Dumont?' But Dumont didn't answer. He went up the ladder at last and picked his way forward.

The crates had been stowed flat against the sides and he pulled on the ropes in the half-light before going into the cockpit.

He sat in the familiar seat and put his hands on the half wheel. Jameson and Max were forward and below in the bomb aimer's position and he could hear the murmur of their voices through the hatch to the right of him. He pushed on the stick slightly and looked down at the bank of throttles. A moment later his hand was grouping them. The familiarity

152

of touch was almost more than the familiarity of sight and for a moment he nearly regressed to the point where he was waiting again for the start-up flare to arch up through the mist. He thought: 'I mustn't think about it now,' and his hands moved towards the switches to begin the pre-flight check.

Later, he moved over to the engineer's panel on the starboard side. The oil and fuel gauges were there and the booster pump switches. Number 2 and 3 tanks selected, he muttered to himself, and he turned the master cocks and booster pumps on and shut off the cross feed. Then he went back to his own seat on the dais and set the ground/air switch to flight and checked the D.R. compass. The long list echoed automatically in his mind like responses in a half-empty nave. Altimeter . . . Instruments all serviceable . . . rad shutters open . . . brake pressures okay.

Then he made the final run down to ignition. Throttles, pitch, cowl flaps, fuel, ignition, contact!

The inners started at a touch of the button, cleared themselves with the familiar cough and then ran smoothly. Number four did the same, and as he pushed the throttle forward the racketing sound and the clouds of oily smoke were as familiar as the sense of touch had been. Because they were Merlins he remembered that they would swing to port on take-off. The Hercules had swung to starboard.

There was a hang-up on the port outer but it caught at the fourth attempt, and while Dumont waited for them all to warm up he sent Doggo down to disconnect the trolleyac and looking down from the cockpit window he saw Doggo and Max run it back to the bay. As he poked around the cabin he noticed the radio for the first time. It was an old V.H.F. set with one crystal controlled frequency probably set on the Mains Museum's own channel, but it didn't matter because they wouldn't be needing it anyway. He sat down again, concentrating on the gauges. After a time when he looked round he found they were all standing at his shoulder.

Max said, 'How long?'

He shook his head. 'Not long.' He pulled the throttles back a bit and said, 'Strap yourself in that seat, Jamie.' Then he stood up and pushed the other two back into the fuselage.

'Doggo, you can pull up the gang-plank and close the hatch. Make sure it's locked tight.'

'Right.'

'After that, strap yourself in here beside the navigator's table for take-off. Max, you sit opposite.'

Max said, 'Are we really going, Dumont?'

'Yes, I suppose we are,' Dumont laughed.

Then Doggo laughed, and went on laughing. It seemed to have the effect of a trigger because Dumont found he was going on laughing, too, and he felt Max's hand on his shoulder. He looked round and saw Max shaking with laughter and with his eyes tight closed.

Then as Doggo reeled helplessly away Jamie said, 'What's going on? . . . What's so funny?'

'Nothing!' shouted Max. 'Nothing at all.'

'You're crazy!' Jamie was grinning in spite of himself.

Nearly a minute passed before their laughter started to die away. Then Doggo said, between sobs, 'What . . . What goes on?'

'*I* don't know,' Dumont said. 'You started it.'

'But I only asked if we were really going!'

Dumont went through to the cockpit again and sat down. As he slipped on his harness he noticed that all the temperature gauges were showing normal. He did the other final checks, from the D.R. compass and Pitot heater through all the controls to the flaps which were set to take-off.

On his right Jamie called, 'What do I do?'

Dumont showed him the A.S.I. and rev counter. 'Don't call it,' he said. 'Just tell me if the rev counters drop below two thousand six hundred.'

After he'd run each engine up to full power and checked the magnetos he let the brakes off and taxied her slowly to the edge of the apron. From half-way down the field the wind-sock was pointing straight at him. Then near at hand on the edge of the field he saw Tizzard wave and he waved back. He gave the controls a final check and then looked sideways at Jamie.

'All okay?' Jamie twisted to look back at the others. After a moment he grinned at Dumont. 'Okay.'

Dumont pushed the throttles forward, his thumb advancing the port outer to stop the swing. He held her against the brakes until she was straining. Then he let her go and they were rolling right down the centre of the field. He registered auto-

154

matically the nine inches of boost on the clock and ninety knots on the A.S.I. Only seconds later as they flashed by the wind-sock his eye dropped again and they were doing just over the hundred knots and the speed was building faster than he'd expected.

The distant hedge was still a quarter of a mile away when she passed the hundred and twenty and he eased her off. Suddenly they were climbing into bright sunlight.

He looked through a side panel and had an unexpected isometric view of the manor house from about a thousand feet. It was deserted. There was no sign of Ingram or the van. He reached for the flight plan and checked the first bearing on the compass. It was 183°, almost due south, to carry them out across Weymouth Bay to the centre of the channel.

A moment later they were crossing the coastline at fifteen hundred feet and he brought the throttles back gradually to cruising speed. He wrote the speed and the time on the edge of the chart. The sea below was undisturbed. The wind wasn't a factor. Start Point was still to starboard when he completed his post take-off check, and he put her down slowly to a thousand feet again.

In spite of what Ingram had said, he wasn't going to fly any lower until he was sure she had no vices. They passed the first steamer lane running north-east. Ships stretched into the haze on either side like a long untidy line of ants. He looked sideways at Jamie, who had his hand on the release slip and his eyebrows raised. When Dumont nodded he flipped it loose and stood up. He put a hand briefly on Dumont's shoulder before going back. Dumont unclipped his own shoulder straps.

He looked down at his watch again, counting up the last half-minute to the new bearing. There was no sign of the French coast through the haze, nor of the second steamer lane. Exactly on the dot he swung the Lancaster in a gentle turn and when she was steady he bent to set the gyro-compass at 228°. Without any effort she was cruising at two hundred and twenty knots and he pulled the throttles back a little farther.

Max came to the engineer's seat beside him and slipped on sun-glasses against the glare. He said, 'I know this part, Dumont. I was at Brest in 1942.' And after a while he added,

'This was the way to the happy hunting ground.'

Dumont said, 'Not for long . . . *grâce à Dieu.*'

'No . . . not for long.'

Away to starboard on the horizon there was smoke, where the steamer lane bent out westwards into the Atlantic.

Marnix Hoffman had parked in a layby about three miles from the manor.

She left the van and stood waiting in the silent morning. There were no sounds except the cracking of the engine as it cooled. Then far off she heard the first engine of the Lancaster splutter into life. She paced slowly up and down waiting as the other engines were run up. Most of the wild flowers in the hedges had died back with the frost and only yarrow survived here and there. A tractor went by, driven by a boy who looked no more than fourteen, and his head stayed turned smiling at her, until he passed out of sight round a bend in the lane.

She went back to the van again and sat in the cab waiting. After a while the distant engines surged to full power and she heard the faint acoustical change as the plane became airborne. She left the cab again and stared upwards.

The Lancaster came suddenly into view over a line of distant elms. It was coming straight towards her, climbing steadily as it passed overhead with a flat roar. The undercarriage wheels were still in the act of retracting beneath the inboard engines. Dumont would not have seen her, she realized, not from that angle, and then in a moment it was gone, a dwindling speck towards the coast. She started the van and pulled back on to the lane.

When she got back to the manor house she drove straight around to the stables and parked the van in a bay of the carthouse where it was usually kept. She walked through the rear of the house and into the big salon.

'Steve?' she called. 'Steve, where are you?'

There was no reply so she ran up the wide staircase and across the wide, pillared antechamber which gave on to the main bedroom and the upstairs terrace.

'Steve?'

Then below her she heard a door open quietly. 'I'm down here, honey.'

She went downstairs again, feeling relieved. She reached the

156

hallway and saw that the door of the small salon was open. When she went in he was standing in front of the easel.

The Gauguin was propped on it and the other paintings were stacked around the desk.

'It's really terrific!' he said. 'Don't you think so?'

CHAPTER THREE

She'd helped to carry the canvases up to his bedroom where they were to be re-packed and afterwards when they came down she had brought coffee for them both, to the small salon.

Ingram was sitting at the bigger table, moving the telephone about with an air of concentration, as if it were a jigsaw piece that wouldn't fit. She left his coffee cup beside him and went back to the other table, where she was steadily working her way through the accumulation of files. After a while she heard him get up and walk into the window bay.

Then he said abruptly, 'I want you to know, honey, that I never minded about Dumont. It was something I found easy to understand. In fact, let's say it was something I expected.'

She waited for a long time but he didn't say anything else. She cleared her throat. 'I won't be seeing him again.'

'No. You won't be seeing him again.'

She waited but he didn't explain. 'I suppose that means that Colonel Zouak will detain him again as long as it's necessary.'

Ingram didn't answer. But later, as he left the room, he said, 'Believe me . . . like every phase of the operation I've given it a lot of thought . . . It's more ingenious than you think. We really don't want *any* loose ends.'

She waited, motionless, hearing his steps go away.

She was afraid to move because of the nightmare thoughts that would be released, in the way an avalanche can be started by a whisper.

Finisterre lay somewhere in the haze away to port as Dumont made the correction that put him on the longest leg of the flight. It would take him nearly a thousand miles south-south-east to the coast of Morocco. It was 11.40 and he was four minutes ahead of his estimated time.

He was cruising at 210 knots. Also he had climbed to ten thousand feet since he considered it unnecessary and hazardous to fly at sea level now that he was clear of the Channel.

As he completed the turn he saw the long chevron of a ship's wake below. A moment later he saw a dozen more in line as a naval squadron headed back for Brest. The sun was hot in the cabin and he found his sun-glasses and slid them on. Somewhere behind he thought he heard laughter above the sound of the engines. His eyes wandered among the familiar gauges and came back to the gyro-compass. He corrected three degrees to starboard. Out loud he said, 'A piece of cake.'

It was then that the jet arrived.

It climbed up from below and zoomed ahead of him, trailing a feather of paraffin fumes and, as it angled into a turn, Dumont saw the clear silhouette of a Mystère.

The jet went on climbing away out of sight to port and towards the French coast. Dumont guessed it was test-flying from the aviation complex around Toulouse and he wondered if the pilot would be reporting the Lancaster to base. There was no reason to, and in any case he would soon be out of range.

He knew he was wrong when two more jets came climbing up in the same pass and followed their leader away into oblivion on the port side. He did not want to recognize the truth, because to recognize it would be to admit to a sense of *déjà vu*, to a feeling it had all happened before in Morocco. Nobody in his right mind would fly as close as that unless they meant it as a warning pass.

As the second planes turned away he had clearly seen the winged anchors on their tail fins and he knew they were from one of the French Navy *Escadrilles*. He held his course for a moment and then started a gentle climb.

When he turned his head to listen for the others he saw Max leaning in the door looking down at him.

Max grimaced. Then he said, 'I never did have much luck either in the Bay of Biscay, Dumont.'

Ingram had said, 'I'll be back in half an hour, honey . . . in time for lunch anyway.' But it was nearly an hour before she saw the Land-Rover coming up the drive.

She was sitting at the desk where he had left her, and she

was still checking the files for the incinerator. The car stopped on the forecourt and the door of it slammed, and just for a moment she thought of moving to another room. She knew that the thought was prompted by a feeling of guilt, and although she repressed it, she was aware of her heart beating faster.

He didn't hurry when he entered the house but walked first into the larger salon, leaving the doors open so that she could hear his footsteps as he was moving around. Then he came back to the hall and went down the steps and through the green baize door into the servants' quarters. She was still frozen with the same page in her hand as she'd been holding when the Land-Rover first appeared.

She let it fall now into the large carton that stood beside the desk. As she picked up more notes he came back along the passage. Again there seemed to be a long pause before the door opened and he stepped in. She didn't look up until he was standing beside her and she noticed he was carrying a parcel under one arm. His smile came and went, then he walked on to the other table in the window.

He said, 'Did anyone call?'

'No.'

Very slowly he put out a hand to straighten the phone and then looked back at her and in that instant she knew that by some trick or other of which she was not aware *he* knew that she had used the phone.

There was nothing she could do about the colour that came suddenly to her cheeks except avert her face slightly. He still hadn't said a word so she worked on, picking and discarding correspondence. He began very slowly stripping the brown paper from the box he was carrying.

At last she came to the clip of letters that dealt with the saddlery at Slough. She cleared her throat and said, 'There's the question of the horse box. The man from the garage who's delivering it back to Slough won't be going till tomorrow. It doesn't matter, does it?'

'No. Do we know about the horse yet?'

'The Riding Club are picking it up from the garage.'

The box on the table was now beyond her vision. He said suddenly, 'You know we'll have to open up a whole new set of files.'

'For negotiating with the British authorities?'

'No, I'm afraid I've never really had that in mind. I have a private deal arranged in Texas. We may have to hire another hero to help with the transportation problem but I haven't worked out the details yet.'

Marnix waited before she said, 'That's where they'll expect them to be sent, isn't it?'

'No, I don't think so.' There was another long silence. The ticking of the ormolu clock was the only sound in the room until Ingram walked into the window bay. 'One of the reasons I never minded about Dumont was that like all heroes he's expendable. In fact, that is one of the things about heroes . . . they have a subliminal desire to be expended. It's one of the secrets of heroism . . . that they're death seekers. So I'm really helping them towards self-fulfilment. Do you agree?'

She turned her head away from the question. He laughed suddenly and came over to put the box on her table. She saw it was a leather-bound travelling cosmetic set.

'It's for you,' he said. 'I bought it at the antique shop. Go on, open it.'

She undid the silver clasp and lifted the lid. Recessed in the leather were rows of crystal pots with embossed silver tops. 'It's beautiful . . . Why . . .'

'But only seventeen pots.'

She said, 'Does that matter?'

'Well, there should be thirty, shouldn't there?'

'I don't understand.'

'Isn't thirty pieces of silver the standard price?'

She closed the lid carefully again and waited. 'Don't you like it, honey?'

'Yes, I like it very much.'

'Well, then . . . thank me . . .'

She turned to him and put her wrist behind his head and kissed his lips. They were unresponsive. He said, 'What did you tell them?'

'Just about the plane . . . that they'd be in danger if they landed in Morocco. Nothing else.'

'The *London* police, of course.'

'Yes. I only spoke for fifteen seconds . . . they couldn't possibly have traced it.'

Ingram's smile came and went with the speed of a shutter.

'I love you, Steve.' She seemed hardly to have the breath to say it. 'I love you, but I didn't want him to die. Not without doing anything. Don't you understand? It can't hurt us.'

After a long time when he still hadn't moved, she added, 'I just wanted to save his life. We'll be gone before anything else can happen . . .'

'Of course, honey . . . We'll be gone . . .'

She'd hoped that he might kiss her as spontaneously as she had kissed him a few moments before. Instead he said, 'I'm glad you called them.' He spread his hands on the blotter as though it were a keyboard. She felt a premonition of dread. 'That's why I left you alone, honey. I'm glad I was right about you . . . About your warm and loving nature.'

She didn't want to look at him but because of the tension she couldn't seem to look away. He said, 'They'll pick up the plane pretty soon, of course, and that's what we want. You see, it's important that somebody's watching when the plane goes into the water. That way the heat will be off all round. They'll *know* the pictures are at the bottom of the sea with the men who stole them.'

When she spoke she seemed to hear her own voice like the voice of a stranger. 'But why should they crash?'

Perhaps, in fact, the question had never been uttered and she had only heard it in her mind. Because he went on speaking as if he hadn't heard it either.

'The heat will be right off,' he said. 'In a couple of minutes' time they won't be looking for anyone else, any more.'

One of the *Aéronavale* fighters came alongside to port and the pilot waved the palm of his hand slowly and insistently towards England. Then he touched his Martian helmet briefly before peeling away. He vanished within seconds, diving back towards France.

'It's possible we're in their training area,' Dumont said to Max.

It was at this moment, when he was again about to tell himself that it was a piece of cake, that Max's body suddenly came spinning across him. At the same time the Lancaster was pitching to the right and Dumont was picked up and flung to the left snatching at his waist harness. His head crashed against the side panel and splinters of glass swirled around him like a rain shower.

Afterwards he never knew whether he'd lost consciousness or not, only that the wind was hitting him with a blinding coldness and the plane was still banked to the right in a power dive. Automatically he rolled the wings level and hauled on the stick but Max's body was lying in such a way as to block it and to hold the throttles forward.

There was blood coming from somewhere, he noticed, as he got a hand to Max's collar.

He dragged and pushed Max sideways until he fell half-way through the bomb aimer's hatch. Then he snatched back the throttles and heaved on the wheel with all his strength. Pieces of glass were still being torn from the frame and clattering away down the inside of the fuselage. The scream of the engines was slowly overcome by the screaming wind. He could feel the flesh pulled back from his face and just once he was conscious of the deep blue peace of the sea ahead of him.

After an age the wheel came towards him. He couldn't tell how far because his hands were no longer capable of feeling. He braced his feet to give strength to his locked body but there was hardly any movement in the wheel. It seemed to come a little aft of centre but no farther. Then again he must have lost consciousness because he came to with his hands pressing his chest in a replica of the pre-natal position.

He had slipped forward on the wheel, which still had only about a third of its normal movement. The sea had lightened into sky, and he was vaguely aware, though he couldn't really see, that Max's body had gone.

He rolled to the right just in time to save the stall. His frozen limbs began to move automatically. He eased the throttles forward again and heard the engines pick up. Then he levelled the nose on the horizon. He was low enough to see the chop of the sea and when he looked at the altimeter it read three thousand. He wondered briefly how low he had been in the dive and if any of the others were alive.

If they'd been hit by rockets then perhaps they were in a training area in the middle of some exercise. Then he noticed that, even with the nose levelled, he still had to hold her and his hand moved automatically to the trim wheels. They spun uselessly with no effect on the stick pressure, and he knew they were out. He had to bend his head away then because his eyes were laced with intense pain from the cold wind. He knew he would have to try the ailerons next.

He went to starboard first and she yawed badly and when he tried to correct to port there was only a limited response.

He knew then that some of the control surfaces were damaged, and certainly the rudders.

They would be like the legendary bird known to all airmen that flew in ever-decreasing circles until it disappeared up its own anus. He noticed the sea much nearer and he tried to hold her steady at a little over two thousand feet while he thought about putting down.

It might be safer to do it now because if anything else were to give they'd go in out of control without a chance. Then a hand touched his shoulder. He felt an intense pain in his back when he turned his head. Doggo was there, crouched on his knees. His hair was streamed back in the wind and where his mouth should have been there was a mass of red. Dumont bent slowly sideways as far out of the slipstream as he could get and Doggo stayed crouched against the throttle bank. Doggo's front teeth were still there, only his lips seemed to be split into shreds.

But his eyes, Dumont suddenly noticed, were full of laughter. Dumont shouted, 'Jamie?'

'He's bad! And the bomb's taken out the entrance hatch . . . and one of the turrets.'

'Bomb?'

'In one of the crates, Dumont.' Doggo held his pulpy mouth for a moment as if it were hurting him to shout. 'Don't you get it? He really meant us to be the last heroes!' He hit Dumont as if the joke was excruciating. And again Dumont felt the sickening pain and knew that his neck or his shoulder must be hurt.

He had the illusion that he was being turned to stone but he knew it was only the intense cold freezing him into his new position. The only life of which he was conscious was a steady drum beat somewhere inside him that must have been his heart. He raised himself slowly and painfully to check his air speed and altitude. As he crouched again he saw that Max had crawled up from the hatch beside Doggo.

Max's eyes were as calm and grey and deep as ever but his face was set in weary resignation. It was almost as if he had been disappointed, an actor who had grown tired of rehearsing for death and who had been asked to do it just once more. Max began to pull at Doggo's ankle and when Doggo looked round he pointed back into the fuselage. As Doggo nodded and began to ease his body away, Dumont bent slowly. He was conscious of the solid thumping of his heart again.

'Protection!' he shouted and moved a stiff, frozen claw across his body.

Doggo put up a thumb and started pushing himself away along the floor.

When Dumont looked at the compass they were flying almost due east, straight towards France. He knew he couldn't correct to port, that even another touch on the rudder might have unforeseen results, so he turned her very gently to starboard and kept turning through an angle of nearly two hundred and fifty degrees. When he stopped the reading steadied at around 020°. He ducked his head again so that it was almost below the level of the stick. He began to work out the correct reciprocal in his head but immediately he was visited by a terrible rage.

They must get back!

Nothing in the world mattered except killing Ingram because Ingram had betrayed them all. Even piracy had an ethic and it didn't even appear paradoxical to Dumont that Ingram should have failed to live up to it. One did not betray one's own side.

'*Ordure! Crapule salaud!*' he kept saying over and over to himself. 'Dirty, dirty bastard!' And he knew with a terrible certainty that, if he could keep the Lancaster in the air, they would surely find Ingram, wherever he was, and kill him.

He felt a hand on his shoulder, and as he roused himself, Max backed in front of him cutting off the air blast. He had an oxygen mask with a single plastic eye-piece and with the tube hanging free. Max spread the harness with his hand and eased it gently over Dumont's face. His skin felt nerveless, he couldn't feel the touch of the mask and his eyes were suddenly full of water. As he blinked it away, Max was bending to his ear.

'Keep slow, Dumont. Keep slow!'

And when Dumont nodded blindly, he added, 'Skins gone, but most main spars are okay.' Dumont nodded again.

'One tail fin twisted.'

Dumont nodded. That was why the rudders were out. The hatch would have hit the tail unit on the way back and that would also account for the damage to the trim. Then Max was taking the P.V.C. dinghy cover from Doggo. The wind flattened it against the back of the cockpit but Max dragged it off, rolling it, little by little. His sea knife was in his hand and he cut a slit in the P.V.C. and eased it over Dumont's head like a poncho, then he started getting medical dressings from his pockets and laying them in around the edge of the mask. Dumont saw his own hands for the first time as Max crouched to bind them. The wind had already opened great apple-cracks on the joints of his fingers.

When he had finished Max went back for a minute and returned with a brandy flask. He lifted Dumont's mask and Dumont took the bottle and swallowed two or three mouthfuls with difficulty. Where it spilled it seemed to scorch the skin of his face.

Then Max shouted in his ear. 'France?'

Dumont wagged his head.

'England?'

Dumont nodded.

Max leant past him to take the chart from its slot and go off with it. Dumont, staring down through the mask at the gyro, saw that he had drifted five degrees off course. Luckily it was to port and he carefully started making the correction. He craned his neck to search through the shattered side panels but there was not a sign of the Mystères. He thought they might have already been heading back for Brest when the bomb went off. Ingram must have emptied the crates and set the bomb when they were all resting. If they had been flying at fifty feet, the altitude for which Ingram had briefed him, they would have plunged straight in. Even now he couldn't understand what magic had kept the elevator control intact.

He eased her up and down a little to check it again. Then Max came back with the chart and backed to the wind, holding it for Dumont to see. He'd drawn a thick line from a point just north-west of Finisterre to reach the Lizard peninsula in Cornwall. The bearing written alongside it was 042°. Dumont nodded his head vigorously to show he understood.

Then Max turned the chart over and on the back he had printed in thick script, 'JAMIE HAS LOST ONE EYE AND SOME FINGERS. WE NOW REPAIR DAMAGED SPAR.' Dumont nodded again, though he thought Max had said the main spars were okay.

When Max went he checked his air speed again, then his altitude and the turn and bank indicator. He was still frozen, without feeling in a single part of his body, but he could see.

There was a deep-laden tanker about three miles ahead to starboard and his mind registered automatically the drift of her diesel smoke to the north. At least they had a little tail wind to help them along.

It was about forty minutes after they'd left the tanker when the sun was suddenly blotted out.

When he looked up an air-sea rescue Shackleton seemed to be sitting only fifty feet above and behind them. She remained fixed there, as if in formation and Dumont saw two crewmen standing in the side hatch. One of them was watching through binoculars and he must have seen the movement of Dumont's head because he put up a hand. After he'd waved he left his hand up, waiting for Dumont's acknowledgement.

Dumont raised a stiff arm and felt the wind snatch at it. The crewman brought his hand down and started talking into his inter-com, and after a moment the big ship drifted behind him and then pulled up alongside, exposing another open hatch. The crewman with binoculars was already crouched in it, examining the side of the Lancaster in detail. Then the other man appeared behind him with an Aldis lamp. He started blinking out a message.

Dumont couldn't remember much of the code and certainly couldn't have read it at the speed the operator was sending, but he recognized the row of dits that ended the message. At the same time he felt a touch on his arm.

When he turned his head he saw that Max and Doggo were both crouched beside him.

Doggo pulled the packing away from Dumont's ear, 'V.H.F. . . .' he shouted. 'He's asking, do we have V.H.F.?'

Dumont shook his head.

The man with the binoculars must have seen because a moment later the lamp was winking again. He could only half watch it now because he had to concentrate on keeping the plane steady.

Then Doggo shouted in his ear: 'He says we're in a restricted area and there's an air/naval exercise in progress. We're to maintain our present heading.'

Dumont put up a hand to acknowledge and the lamp started winking again. This time it was to ask his destination and intention and after checking the gyro-compass Dumont pointed straight ahead in the direction of the English coast.

The lamp kept flickering. Another crewman had come to

stand in the open hatch. The air/naval exercise accounted for the Shackleton being on patrol in the first place. It was the only contingency that Ingram hadn't thought of, a contingency that might save their lives.

'He says the tail unit's badly damaged!' Doggo yelled. 'Do you have full control?'

Dumont put up a thumb and waved it blindly. He put it up again when they asked about his fuel and endurance. The Lancaster was wandering off to the east a little and soon he'd have to fly a slow circle to starboard to get back on course. The Shackleton had dropped back a little where he couldn't see it but Doggo was still reading signals with his face shielded.

Then Doggo was shouting. 'He says St Mawgan is the nearest master field and they have full emergency services ready. Course bearing 045°. Got it?'

Dumont nodded. When he looked down he was on 050°. He decided first to try correcting with a little left rudder. Gently, he told himself. But as he put on bank the unco-ordinated trim caused the big plane to begin slipping away. He realized his mistake even as it began to happen but when he tried to correct it only aggravated the bank angle.

The circle was getting faster and tighter and he heard one of the others shouting behind him. Under the P.V.C. cloak he moved as slowly and clumsily as an astronaut in space. After he'd snatched the throttles back he struggled desperately to level the wings and bring the nose back up. Somewhere behind he heard a sudden crack and something went crashing away down the fuselage. The angle steepened. There was white-flecked sea filling the window frame. It wasn't more than a thousand feet away.

'Nothing to lose,' he said calmly into the mask and gathered himself physically and mentally for the effort of pulling her out. His muscles ached as they convulsed with all the strength he had left. Nothing happened, and in the gyrating frame ahead he could see the creaming on the edges of the Prussian blue waves.

She'd go straight on down, he decided, with the sidescreen and the hatch out. He waited for it, without any particular feeling.

CHAPTER FOUR

Then something else crashed in the fuselage and the wheel eased.

At the same time the rudder effectiveness improved. The windscreen ceased to gyrate. Without the speed the nose came up slowly but just for an instant they seemed to be in a trough with ridges of blue water on either side of them.

He punched the throttles forward again and they began to howl out of it. He was conscious of the cold and realized he'd torn off the mask at some time during the descent.

The others were gone, he saw briefly, and he knew they'd had enough sense to get to the other side of the bulkhead before impact. The Lancaster was climbing again and the speed was nearly back to 180. He was easing her gently back on course when Doggo came. He stood above Dumont gripping the canopy frame, grinning down at Dumont in a way that was fixed and asinine.

Dumont smiled back and he knew he was smiling in the same way but he could do nothing about it. It was a smile that he knew by heart, a piece of behaviourism that had nothing to do with happiness nor for that matter with relief. The crocodile smile one might have called it, because its ritualism was as meaningless as crocodile tears.

Then Doggo was shouting, 'We've lost some more skin!'

He helped Dumont to pack the mask back on. Then he was pointing away out through the starboard window.

Turning his head Dumont saw the Shackleton again, beside him and above. As he slowly swung back to his right bearing, the Shackleton turned with him.

Then the Aldis lamp started winking again from the open hatch.

Some time after one there was tapping at the door and when she went to open it, Ingram was waiting with a huge silver buffet tray. It was loaded with coffee and sandwiches.

'*I* would have done it,' she said.

'There was nothing to do. I stopped off at a delicatessen

after I'd bought your present at the antique shop.'

He put it on the larger table and poured the coffee himself. 'I thought we'd make it a working lunch so you can get everything tidied away by three o'clock, say. I've started a bonfire in the garden at the back of the stables.'

'Where are we going?'

'Not far.'

'But why?'

'Just a part of the contingency game, honey. Never take an unnecessary risk.' He started to walk up and down with a sandwich.

'What about the house?'

'The house is okay. Manuel and his wife are coming back tomorrow.' Then with a rush he said, 'It's just a *precaution*. We'll probably come back tomorrow, too. And, anyway, we deserve a little relaxation, don't we? We'll stay at some nice little inn with a blazing fire.' He turned to smile at her. 'And we'll listen to the six o'clock news bulletin. We'll take most things with us just in case there's been any foul-up. They're good, these sandwiches . . . they're really good. I nearly bought a pot of coleslaw as well but I remembered you didn't like it.'

Marnix looked away and felt cold. She didn't know why. It was as if the magnetic field that had attracted her for three years had suddenly failed. As if he'd switched it off.

Later, when she was going to and fro to the bonfire, she glanced up at the house on her way across the cobbled yard. Ingram was standing close against the arched window of the staircase landing looking down at her. She realized that from that window he could watch her all the way to the orchard where the bonfire was and back again.

He waved and she smiled mechanically, but walking on she had the feeling of being cut off from something again. For some reason she suddenly remembered reading about one of the judges at the time of the French Revolution. It was said that when he condemned people to death, the faint shape of the guillotine could be seen in his eyes, as if the words produced the stigmata.

As she looked up at Ingram now she wondered, without fear, in what way he had decided to kill her.

Later still, when she had gone up to her room to pack, she saw him again looking up at her from the staircase well. She leant over the hand-rail to say, 'Shall I take all our personal things? Mightn't we be coming back at all?'

Without moving he said, 'Pack everything.'

She walked on into the bedroom, leaving him still looking up. It was as if she had made an appeal which had been dismissed, as if the sentence of death had been confirmed.

The ASR Shackleton was somewhere out to port and Dumont could just see the nervous flicker of the Aldis lamp out of the corner of his eye.

He knew what they were signalling long before Doggo translated it and he swore gently into his oxygen mask. Max was crouched by the bomb aimer's hatch with his legs hanging through and a handkerchief tied over his face. Dumont knew intuitively that Max had guessed what the signaller was saying, too. Then Doggo was mouthing into his ear again.

'Dumont! He says we're way off course!' And when Dumont didn't move, he shouted, 'Can you hear me? He says we're way off course!'

Dumont still didn't answer and Doggo then said, 'Just a moment . . . Maybe they've made a mistake. They're signalling again.'

Doggo straightened and shielded his face while he tried to read it.

They had told Dumont a little while ago that Jamie was in great pain. He had refused the morphine in the aid pack, because if they had to ditch he wanted to be fully conscious. Dumont knew that by doing what he was now about to do he was committing all of them to his idea.

Doggo lifted his ear pad suddenly and screamed: 'Do you still have full control, Dumont? That's what they're asking now. We're way off course!'

Dumont turned his head away from the instruments to stare at Doggo and after a moment Doggo's bloody face grinned back at him. 'Oh, Christ . . . why didn't I get it before!' Doggo hit his shoulder as Dumont looked back at the panel again. 'You old *bastard*, Dumont,' Doggo shouted. 'I'll tell them to go home . . .' But before he could wave Dumont had checked him roughly with an outflung deadened arm. They wanted the Shackleton with them until they crossed the coast.

The Lizard was already behind and away to starboard, the Eddystone Lighthouse was visible with the sea foaming at its base. Dumont estimated that they were only about thirty minutes from touchdown. The Shackleton had given up signalling and was just keeping station. He was glad they were there because there was still the threat of instant disaster. If they lost any more control they'd have had it. As the vibration of the air frame had kept on increasing, Dumont had been gradually easing the throttles back until now the Lancaster was almost hanging in the air at 130 knots which only gave him a margin of 20 knots over the stalling speed. He decided to select five degrees of flap. When Start Point appeared ahead he knew there were only fifty miles to go. He'd fly straight across Lyme Bay and try and pick up leading marks between Lyme Regis and Portland Bill.

He had been too occupied to notice much on the way out except that Bridport had lain a few miles off on the starboard side. He waved his stiff arm again, trying to catch Doggo's attention, and when Doggo crawled over he pointed to the mask. As it came away the lash of wind made him grunt, and he had to keep his left eye closed against the piercing cold.

He leaned sideways out of his seat and let his head rest on Doggo's shoulder. 'Tie Jamie down!' he shouted. And when Doggo nodded he said, 'You and Max sit against the bulkhead!'

Doggo shouted, 'Now?' and Dumont nodded.

When they'd gone he knew he'd have to do something about the altitude. They had been losing height ever since he'd put on flap and now they were nearly down to a thousand feet. He pushed the throttles forward a little until the plane was shaking like a roller coaster. He watched the air speed indicator creep up to 140 knots then he began easing back the stick. Far ahead of him he could see a Brixham trawler wallowing in the bay. It must have been going home because it was followed by a great cloud of herring gulls.

The Shackleton had banked away from him and was keeping station about a thousand feet above. The signaller had given up and gone away but the crewman with binoculars was still crouched in the open hatchway. Dumont looked ahead again, shielding his windward eye with a bandaged hand. The trawler was out of sight in a trough.

Then without warning the flock of gulls soared upwards and veered towards him like a rain squall.

For a few seconds the windscreen was almost obscured by

them and he could hear the thud of their bodies striking the fuselage. The birdstrike that counted came a moment later and the Lancaster was almost torn apart by the violence of the vibration. Clinging desperately to the wheel, Dumont saw the revs going wild on number four and knew the propeller had been damaged.

He snatched back the throttle, then grouped the remaining three and slammed them through as far as they would go. Then his hand travelled on in one clean movement to hit the feathering button. But they were going down, and slightly to port he had a quick vision of stunned faces around the wheelhouse of the trawler. They were staring in at him from just about the same level.

Dumont held her off the waves with one hand while the other felt around to find where the quick release catch of his harness was. Between the trawler and the ASR plane, which carried a raft, he thought they had a chance. The white caps streamed beneath him only seconds away. But when he looked down at the A.S.I. he saw the speed was slowly increasing and was almost back to 140 knots.

Ahead through the haze he saw the grey cliffs of Dorset. As the air speed rose gradually, he eased the stick back a little and with a shock he realized that they were climbing. Very, very gently he eased the stick back. Ahead of him he saw the Shackleton pulling out of a shallow dive and climbing away to the north.

Dumont estimated he was still a hundred feet beneath the cliff level and with a mile to go. He decided to make a wide climbing turn to starboard just to be certain. As he came slowly around he saw the trawler rocking in the bay with the men still clustered around the wheelhouse. The streamers from her rigging were hanging straight down, which meant he could land from any direction.

As he came out of the turn he was clear of the cliffs and Bridport was to the west where he expected it to be. He sailed over the cliffs with a hundred feet to spare and he set a course of 032°, which was a reciprocal of the course he'd flown out on.

Dumont knew he had now reached the moment of decision.

If the gear went down he'd fly straight in to the strip at Mains Memorial. There was nowhere else to go because even with brakes he needed a mile of runway to put the Lancaster

172

down. But if the undercarriage didn't go down then he'd have to crash land. And if he was going to crash land anyway then he'd put her down in front of the manor house right on target. Also, it would be softer going there.

He lowered the hand that was shielding his face and grasped the wheel with it, then his other hand moved to switch on the hydraulics. One glaring eye watched the pressure gauge. The needle seemed to flicker for a moment and then settled back to zero. Wherever the leak was it had probably started with the explosion.

Dumont muttered, 'Wheels up, Mother Brown,' and banked away to the right. He peered ahead into the cutting wind, searching for the manor. One hand was easing the throttles back. He crossed a line of pylons he remembered, and then he saw the lane that led to the village.

Dumont banked to starboard. Any moment he expected to see the thatched roofs of the village. When they came up he was still a little south of course and he banked again. It cost him fifty feet in altitude and he had to lift the plane over a sudden windbreak of poplars.

Then he was over the village at zero feet and he had a brief vision of people running. He looked quickly at the air speed indicator, which showed a hundred and fifteen. The manor house came suddenly into view. It lay in the fold of two hills like a target in a gun sight.

Dumont flew through the shallow valley and estimated he had only seconds to go and that the run-up to the long terrace was less than half a mile. Water flashed beneath them, lashed by the slipstream and Dumont closed the throttles and pushed her down.

The sloping ground rose up at them swiftly and they struck with a shattering crunch. As he hit the magneto switches she bounced once before settling in an angled run that streamed mud up as high as the cockpit. She was going straight for the terrace with the starboard wing advanced. The propellers had folded and the scream of stressed metal was deafening. They flashed by the ruined temple of French worthies and the long terrace steps were only two hundred yards away.

Dumont thought he saw something flash at an upstairs window but his forward vision was almost blotted out. Then something impeded the port wing causing the starboard wing to lift. It started slicing through a row of Portland stone

balusters as if they were matchsticks, but Dumont was alread
bracing his legs and wrapping his arms around his head.

He felt a prolonged dinning against the fuselage before th
nose dug in and he was flung against the harness. He hun;
there half-conscious, his hands groping vaguely for the release

Somewhere near at hand there was a soft whoosh as :
ruptured tank went up. Clear-voiced he said to himself, 'Well
I shan't be fucking cold any more.'

He was aware of his resignation but still held captive by it
Then something struck him on the shoulder and he turned to
see Max there. There was blood on Max's face but his eyes
were blazing and he slapped at Dumont, flinging him back into
the seat again.

'Wake up, Dumont! Come on!'

Dumont saw the blade of Max's knife flash and the nex
moment it was slashing the harness straps. Then Dumont fel
himself pushed forward against the panel and jerked upright
Max pivoted with him and they were lurching out of the
cockpit together.

He wasn't prepared for the glare of light when they fell
headlong into the fuselage section. Most of the outer skir
seemed to be missing right back to and beyond the mid uppe
turret, and the ground visible through the spars was on fire
for a hundred yards behind the starboard wing. The hea
scorched his lungs, suffocating him. Then he felt himself lifted
and dragged and the next moment he was rolling on the turf

He staggered to his feet and Max held him again. 'Dumont
. . . Are you all right?'

Dumont turned his head slowly and saw the outline of the
house through the drifting smoke. 'All right,' he said mechanically. 'Just take my bandages off, Max . . .'

'They've gone already . . .'

Dumont looked down and saw his hands like cracked claws.
There was no feeling in them. With Max watching him he
brushed his face and neck but felt nothing there either. He
said, 'Come on . . .'

They set off together to skirt the tail plane and the flames,
and as they came round the other side Dumont saw Doggo
with Jamie sitting on the grass beside him. Jamie's hand was
wrapped in a bloody bandage and strapped into his belt. He
was naked to the waist and beneath the yellow burn dressings
Dumont could see where the blast had flayed his skin. There

174

was also a dressing plastered over one eye socket.

Jamie came to his feet without help but leant lightly against Dumont. Their shadows, dancing in the light of the flames, looked like the damned supporting each other on the edge of hell fire.

'I'm okay, Dumont . . . Don't think you can leave me behind.' One naked eye, without brow or lashes, blazed at Dumont.

He said, 'Don't worry . . . it'll take all of us.'

Jamie pushed himself off Dumont with an effort and pivoted to face the house. 'Then what are we waiting for! Let's fucking go!'

Dumont looked at Doggo and Max. Doggo had the flare pistol stuck in his belt and his shirt bulged with shells at the waist. Then instinctively they all turned and started moving up to the house. Dumont vaguely remembered the flash from an upstairs window. He said, 'We'd better not bunch up . . .'

They spread out as they tramped on, four diminutive figures, dwarfed by the tall columns of the house ahead. Behind them the starboard wing settled in a shower of sparks which flared upwards into the sky behind them. It was the sort of Wagnerian climax, Dumont thought dryly, that was suitable for heroes. They reached the steps of the terrace together and went on steadily up past the eroded Greek figures.

As they reached the top, Ingram stepped out of the portico ahead of them.

A machine pistol was dangling from his hand.

CHAPTER FIVE

Ingram said quickly, 'Don't come any closer . . .' and his smile came and went as usual, as though nothing was wrong.

They all stopped except Max, who went on a couple of paces but he, too, stopped when Ingram flipped the machine pistol up so they could all see it. It had a metal frame stock.

Max said loudly, for them all to hear, 'If it's a Schmeisser he can't stop us all.'

'Correct,' said Ingram quietly. 'Nor could a Sten. It's right you should know that it's one of the new Armalite automatics made under licence by the Howa Machinery Company of Japan. It's gas-operated and has the same characteristics as the 5.56 rifle, with one other advantage. It has a firing rate of four-seventy shots a minute. I've calculated I can take you all in one and a quarter seconds at this range, so don't come any nearer or I might have to prove it. I've practised with this thing.

'Something else you know about me is that I have contingency plans for every foul-up and I have one for this. If you rush me or try anything else we may all end up dead, so just think about it for a moment. What we have here is a really big problem of communication but I want each one of you to try and handle it. Just stop there and *think*. Think of the options and then let's talk about it.'

There was a sudden roar above them as the Shackleton swept over the house in a low pass. Jamie was the only one to look up. Dumont guessed they'd lost him on the run-in and only picked up the smoke of the crash. The sound of its engines faded and still nobody spoke. Dumont knew there couldn't be a deal, knew that he couldn't accept any solution other than killing Ingram.

Ingram backed against the panelled door and stood beside it ready to step through. 'Think!' he said again. 'For Christ's sake . . .'

Then Doggo said in a quiet conversational voice, 'When the shooting starts the important thing is to divide. Max and I will go right . . . Dumont and Jamie to the left. Go straight for cover.'

If Ingram heard, he gave no sign. He said, 'Think,' again and waited. Against the dark oak of the door he looked almost transparent.

Then they were brilliantly lit in a sudden glare as a tank blew in the plane behind them. As they flinched in the blast Doggo was shouting, 'Go! Go!'

Almost as he'd said it, he crashed through the glass of the french window into the small salon. Dumont dashed to the left and dived over the balustrade into soft earth. He heard the Armalite automatic firing as he ran. It seemed to make no more noise than someone riffling a pack of cards.

When he rose in a crouch to look for Jamie he was hit in the face by a spray of masonry kicked up by another burst

He ducked away, groaning out loud in spite of himself. He came up again between two balusters farther along and saw Jamie's legs. He was rolled on his back with his head towards Ingram. He was making a terrible noise, like a train whistle in the night which went on and on.

Then a door slammed and Doggo shouted, 'Here, Dumont! Here!'

Dumont flung a hand up to the balustrade in an effort to vault but there was no strength in his arm. He rolled over it instead and stumbled on to a knee beside Jamie. There was no blood, just neat black holes saddle-stitched across his chest.

Then Doggo was screaming his name again, 'Dumont, here! *Dumont!*'

He noticed the front door was shut as he ran on automatically, but he tripped after a few paces and as he went down he turned the fall into a complete roll-over. He hurtled on through the window where Max caught him and held him up.

Then Doggo took him from Max and slammed him against the wall. He hit him once with a stinging back-hander, 'You dope!' His brown eyes were snapping.

For the first time since he'd left the plane Dumont felt fully conscious. He said, 'All right . . . I'm all right.' Then he added, 'Stupid of me.'

'We can't give him any chances. You were making a sweet target out there. Open the doors, Max . . . open them wide and open the ones in the other room first. Walk close to the wall . . .'

Max said, 'Don't worry,' and went down to open the double doors into the dining-room. They could still hear Jamie's breath whistling in his lungs. Then Doggo broke the flare pistol open.

As he dropped in a cartridge, Dumont said, 'Are we going to split up?'

'You were great back there in the ship, Dumont, but now it's my turn. This is something I know about. If we split up he'll take us one by one. He's got cover . . . this isn't like an aerial battle. What we have to do is go together, help each other forward.' He slammed the breech shut as Max came back.

Max had opened the double doors from the small salon to the dining-room beyond, and the double doors from there back into the hallway. As he came up to the doors beside them, that also opened into the hallway, Doggo said, 'Grab something to throw.'

Dumont picked up the easel and went on to the glass cabinet. He knocked the panels out of one door and began to stuff paper-weights into his pockets. Max came to join him.

When they went back Doggo had hold of one handle of the double doors. He said to Max, 'Take the other one.'

They waited for a moment facing each other and then Doggo said, 'Okay . . . open up!'

They opened each half together but there was only silence from the hall and the staircase beyond. Pressed to the wall, Doggo said clearly, 'You made a mistake back there, Ingram! You should have cut *me* down . . . or Dumont.'

After a moment Ingram called quietly, 'You're wrong, Granger. What I did was to take out the only unknown factor. I know what capability the rest of you have.' It was a computer's answer.

'Now we know where he is,' Doggo whispered. 'He's gone up.' Then he called again, 'Ingram? Ingram?'

Ingram must have registered that he'd given something away because this time he didn't answer.

'Ingram, let's talk about a deal?'

There was only a crackling sound as some part of the air-craft collapsed.

'He'll be on the far side of the gallery looking down this way,' Doggo said. 'When we get going keep looking for dead ground and ways to outflank him. Throw something whenever there's an opportunity . . . hound him! I can't use this thing unless I'm certain of a lethal shot. If we fill the place with smoke he may get away. To begin with I want you both to run together . . . straight through this door. Dumont, you go dead ahead against the stairs, and Max to the other side, under the overhang of the gallery. Start your run in the middle of the room so you go through the door on the burst. When you get there we'll know which side of the gallery he's on and one of you will have to tease him while I get out. Right . . . Let's go!' Doggo walked down to the far door in the dining-room, picking the seat cushion from a button chair as he went.

Dumont waited with Max about five yards from the open doors of the little salon. It seemed incredibly foolhardy to

178

run through a gap where Ingram surely must be waiting for them to appear. Doggo looked back at them with his brows raised. Dumont tensed himself, ready for the dive. He looked at Max, who was crouched, as if on a marker.

When he looked back and nodded, Doggo called softly, 'Go!' and tossed the cushion through into the hallway. The gun fired immediately and Dumont was half a shoulder ahead of Max as they burst into the hall together. He hurtled straight for the darkness of the stair well, hit the wall and dropped. Ingram was too late switching from the other door but he must have seen them go because he let go with several long bursts, trying to hose out the corners around the stairs. Hot shell cases and splinters of wood dropped all around Dumont but he wasn't hit.

He lay there breathless, listening to his heart thudding, and knowing that Ingram was on the west side and that now he, Dumont, would have to draw him first. He twisted to look back and saw Doggo just inside the door of the small salon.

Doggo grinned and whispered, 'Your turn, boy. Ready when you are.'

Dumont got a paper-weight from his pocket and pushed himself up the panel. He moved sideways to where the deepest shelter was and tensed himself again. There wouldn't be time to look, just up and throw. He was doing it while the thought was still half-formulated. Even as the weight left his hand and went smashing into the gallery above, Dumont saw that Ingram must have moved. Then Doggo was crashing by, swinging on the post and scampering up the first flight of stairs for the shelter of the entresol columns.

A short burst of fire picked him up when he was nearly at the top and he seemed to fall out of sight with it.

There was total silence, then something hit the stairs and came bouncing down with a lazy clatter. It slid across the parquet and stopped half-way to the front door. It was an empty magazine from the machine pistol.

There was no other sound until Max called softly, 'Granger?'

Still there was silence.

Then from under the gallery Max called softly again, 'Are you all right, Doggo?'

The silence went on and Dumont could hear the tick of the ormolu clock from the little salon.

Then Doggo said tersely, 'I'm okay!'

Dumont heard him moving around behind the pillars. Then he spoke again. 'The heel of my shoe is shot off. That's all. And he nicked my leg, but it isn't serious.' Then, raising his voice, Doggo said, 'For a five point five millimetre that thing doesn't have much stopping power, Ingram, and there's something else I should tell you . . . I have the flare pistol from the Lancaster here. I only have to hit you once and you'll be burnt in half.' He paused. 'I just want you to know how it's going to be when we get up there.' The echo of his words died away and the silence settled again.

Dumont guessed that telling Ingram about the pistol was a deliberate move on Doggo's part, to keep Ingram well back. If Ingram had been firing at Doggo on the first flight then he must have already moved back to the central lobby somewhere on the south side from where the main bedrooms and corridors went off. Dumont decided to take a quick look.

He went slightly deeper into the well and then jumped lightly on his toes. As far back as he could see in that fleeting moment, the gallery was empty, but beneath it he saw with a shock, Max was now somehow hanging. He had a grip on the moulding below the ledge which carried the railing. Dumont didn't know how he'd got there except that he must have climbed up on something. When he looked cautiously again Max had turned his head and was looking towards him. The sea knife was between his teeth and his eyes smiled.

Dumont wondered if Doggo had seen him as well. He crept silently to the bottom stair and looked around the newel post up the first flight.

Doggo was already looking back around the pillar and he pointed urgently in Max's direction. When Dumont nodded Doggo gave him the flat of his hand indicating that he was to stay where he was.

Dumont nodded again and then moved back to where he could see Max more easily. Max had put his hands higher, around the bottom of two of the uprights and was slowly raising his head to look. Dumont held his breath while Max stared first down the corridors on either side and then across into the square gallery towards the main bedrooms and the upstairs terrace. He spent almost a full minute inspecting it before raising himself farther up.

Very slowly he put an arm between the uprights and got

180

an elbow hold. Then he kicked lightly sideways and got a toe hold as well. He waited again, searching ahead, before climbing on silently up. He was astride the rail at the point of balance when Ingram shot him down.

There was only a short burst and Max seemed to be frozen there for several seconds while the knife dropped away with a clatter into the hallway below.

Then he half fell back to his original position, hanging from the ledge. An artery near his waist must have been cut because blood spurted suddenly like wine from a punctured barrel. The burst must also have cut his belt because his trousers dropped suddenly as far as his knees and Dumont could see one of his testes hanging loose from the scrotum against a bloody leg.

Max's body turned for a moment, like a huge, grey mobile and his deep-set eyes crossed Dumont's without recognition.

Then as he fell away Doggo said sharply, 'Move, Dumont!'

Dumont, dazed, rushed the first flight like a rabbit. When he stumbled behind the pillars there was no one there. Doggo had gone. Dumont looked around the right-hand pillar and saw him lying on the second flight of stairs to the right and just below the first floor level. He was to one side, close against the posts, and he was looking over the top.

Dumont waited until he withdrew slightly and turned. Then Doggo pointed again, straight ahead towards the hallway to the front where the burst had come from. He waved Dumont to take the flight which led up the other side. Dumont went across to the second pillar in two silent jumps and then looked cautiously round it up towards where Ingram was. He could see the tops of the huge windows which gave on to the first floor terrace and nearer at hand the ornate voluted tops of the central pillars. He could see only as deep as the first bedroom door. After waiting for a minute he crawled carefully half-way up the second flight and flattened below the level of the top stair.

Looking sideways, he could now see Doggo opposite him. Doggo had the flare pistol held in front of him and Dumont saw it was cocked. Then Doggo turned his head and smiled.

He flicked the barrel of the flare pistol upwards several times, indicating that the next run was with Dumont. Dumont nodded calmly but his heart had lurched suddenly. He moved over to the side rail nearer the centre, then raised himself slowly up another step. The curtain of his vision was lowered farther so that he could see half-way down the fluted pillars and two of the three doors on either side. Also he could now see the centre pieces of the huge windows and he noticed they were all open on to the terrace.

It was possible that Ingram was lying up on the terrace. That would give him maximum depth from the top of the stairs in which to stop a rush. If he were there, then Dumont saw that the next logical step was to run for the entrance of the corridor on the left. He eased himself back and looked across at Doggo, pointing towards the end of the corridor.

Doggo nodded.

Dumont rolled over one and a half times to meet the uprights on the other side. Then he eased himself slightly up again. He had a different angle view this time and he searched it in detail, measuring every shadow thrown by the light from the windows. From these he was almost certain that Ingram wasn't behind any of the centre pillars.

He drew his legs up under him, mustering the will to act. Do it quickly, he thought, don't think about it too long. He looked across at Doggo again and when Doggo smiled at him he grinned back miserably.

Then he sprang away and in two bounds was flattened against the wall of the corridor.

He stayed there tensely, a paper-weight gripped in his hand, but the long silence continued, only now he could hear the steady dripping of a tap. The door of the bathroom was open. After half a minute he relaxed. He couldn't see Doggo from where he was so he moved quietly away down the corridor and crossed over to the other side of it.

Doggo was watching for him with his heels drawn up into a crouch. He pointed ahead to the middle of the lobby where the first centre pillar was. Then he smiled again as if the whole thing was a game.

Dumont was just moving back to the corner, when out of the stillness a key turned in a lock and a door opened.

Then he heard her footsteps and her breathless voice saying, 'Dumont, what's happened? . . . Are you all right?'

He held his breath and she added with sudden consternation, 'It's all so *pointless.*'

Then her steps accelerated and she walked to the head of

the stairs and, turning her head, saw him standing there in the corridor.

She smiled wearily and said quietly, 'Dumont . . .'

Then as she took the first pace towards him, Ingram shot her from somewhere out on the terrace.

The machine pistol must have been set to single shot because there was just the one sharp sound and she sank where she stood. Dumont had taken one pace until something held him there and he realized that it wasn't Marnix screaming, but Doggo.

'No, Dumont, no!' he was yelling. 'It's a trap! Stay there! Stay! Stay! Stay! For the love of God!'

Her body was moving but he clenched his eyes tight shut. He was barely alive for a time, his body locked against consciousness. He knew he was shaking because the paper-weight was thudding against the wall.

He whispered, '*Sacré Mère* . . .' in real agony and he wanted to storm around the corner, then to have his hands on Ingram's body . . . The spasm didn't really pass, it just ebbed a little and he opened his eyes again.

She was curled with her head and her legs thrust back. The bullet must have lodged somewhere along her central nervous system because both her legs were jerking back together, like the legs of a rabbit caught in a snare. He had to close his eyes and turn his head away.

Mercifully he couldn't see her face. As the scuffling sound went on he said, 'Christ Christ Christ . . .' over and over.

Doggo must have heard because he said harshly, 'Don't *move*! He's waiting for you, Dumont!'

After a long time Dumont whispered, 'Don't worry, I'm all right.' And after a little longer, 'I'm really all right.' But there were tears dripping from his cheeks. He turned into the wall suddenly hitting it with a savage fist.

He looked back at her and the convulsions had moved her a little farther from the stairs. Her legs were still kicking backwards faintly as if death was now at her heels and she was struggling to keep it away.

He shouted suddenly, 'I'm sorry, Doggo! I'm going . . .' and leapt out. As he moved he heard the gun firing and a burst of fire whining off the banisters.

But he hadn't gone towards her at all.

He'd spun around the corner and dived for the half-open door of the bathroom. As he crashed through it, Ingram saw him and switched targets and while Dumont lay there on the floor gasping, he sprayed the rest of the magazine into the room after him.

The whistle and scream of ricochets dissolved in a crashing crescendo as the basin and lavatory pan just seemed to blow apart. Dumont curled himself by the laundry basket behind the door. Somewhere a tap was splashing noisily.

'I'm all right,' he told himself and hoped it was true. Another part of his mind was registering that Ingram was on the balcony to the right behind a huge manger full of plants, and that from there he'd been covering Marnix's body but he hadn't been able to cover the corner where Dumont had come from.

Ingram knew where *he* was now though and he would be waiting with his sights on the door. Unless he, too, had moved.

It was a hot tap that was running and steam had begun to rise steadily at the far end. Dumont shifted around until he was clear of the door, which was a mass of splintered holes. Then he took the lid off the laundry basket and gingerly pushed it out to rest on the handle of the door.

Nothing happened. Very slowly he opened the door wider. The first thing he saw was Doggo again, only five paces away, pressed against a pillar and staring back at him.

Doggo smiled and Dumont knew he must have moved there while Ingram was spraying the bathroom door. For the first time Dumont noticed that his right shoe was missing and there was a bloodstained handkerchief around his ankle. He pointed out towards the right where Ingram was and Doggo nodded and put the barrel of the flare pistol briefly to his lips.

Then he raised it above his head and started tracing letters on the pillar. 'F-O-L-L-O-W M-E' Dumont read. He nodded again to show Doggo he'd understood. Then he moved around carefully to get his legs ready for the spring. He thought, we can't possibly make it, but he knew at the same time they had to go. It was like seeing a target marker right in the heart of a flak storm and knowing you had to dive straight through the middle.

He hoped that she was dead now and that she hadn't been conscious. It was his *own* last really conscious thought because was then that Ingram decided to come and get them.

he Armalite rattled suddenly and a spray of fine plaster flew f the column around Doggo's head, then Doggo moved with e burst farther around.

The firing stopped and Dumont saw cartridge cases rolling cross the floor on the opposite side of the gallery, which told m Ingram was moving down that way.

Doggo looked back at him with a wolfish grin and then lled softly, 'After me, Dumont . . . You poor old bastard.' e waited for Dumont to smile back, then without further arning he leapt sideways, feet astride, pistol raised and firing. Even as his feet touched the ground and he catapulted for-ard, Dumont was springing after him.

Ingram was already firing from the middle of the balcony d Dumont realized he'd thrown the empty cases to his left mislead them. The second imprint on his retina was of the noke flare hitting the balustrade to Ingram's right and sailing way into the sky.

Then, still moving forward himself, he realized sickly that oggo was running on the gun.

'Follow . . .' Doggo's scream was choked suddenly but umont realized what the play was and he'd already taken ff after him in a crash tackle.

He hit Doggo in the middle of the back and he could feel e kick of the bullets zipping into Doggo's body but his npetus took them both on until suddenly they were falling d Dumont saw Ingram's outflung arm beneath them still olding the machine pistol. They hit the angle of the floor nd the balustrade with a sickening crunch and he opened his yes and saw Ingram already rolling away. As he staggered p over Doggo's body he registered that the magazine had een knocked from the gun and that Ingram was already ivoting to side-swipe him with the barrel.

There was no time to raise an arm, nor did he try and the low bounced off his head and shoulder as if they were made f steel. Dumont wasn't conscious of it striking, only that in e half-second that it took he had seen Ingram's smile come nd go as if taking a last snapshot of the world.

Because Dumont's toe was already hitting his knee-cap and s he went back Dumont's hands were clawing for his ankles.

He got a grip on one and swept it shoulder high, then h
jerked Ingram's whole body into the air. The gun went clatte
ing away over the edge as Dumont turned blindly on his hee
swinging Ingram's body upwards in a great arc.

He was half aware of his own atavistic screaming, ha
aware of his reversion to the primeval forest, and as Ingram
head struck the plaster beside the window, time and tim
again, spraying the wall with bright pink blood, his scream
reached a crescendo.

Then he'd let Ingram go and the body sailed out across th
terrace below.

It seemed to fall as slowly as a handkerchief and it struc
the edge of the steps and lay there crumpled. The sound die
in Dumont's throat and he looked down at Ingram's moccasi
shoe still in his hands. After a moment he tossed it after th
body.

Beyond the smoke flare a fat Westland Helicopter was settling
It had TRAFFIC CONTROL painted in white on its sid
panels, and it had barely touched the ground when uniforme
police came tumbling from it and running up towards th
plane. Beyond again in the driveway, a boy on a tractor wa
followed by running people. Dumont turned away and walke
slowly back to the stairs.

As he passed an oriel looking-glass above an empire tabl
he turned his head and saw the stony face of a strange
streaked with froth. He walked on, wiping his mouth with
sleeve.

Her body was still at last and he closed his eyes as h
walked by it. Downstairs there was a burst of sound and h
heard running feet. He was only vaguely conscious of peopl
around him and he shook off a hand which touched his arm
There was a vagueness about everything as if he had bee
suddenly curtained off from life, as if everything else wa
happening beyond a barrier of cheesecloth.

The voices trying to speak to him had a strangled sound
'Shock,' someone kept saying. 'Shock.'

He walked out across the terrace and down to the grass. H
stopped there and crouched down. Even the sense of *déjà vu*
was faint. He couldn't remember which orbit it was long ag
when he had knelt in the grass beside another burnt-out plan
with all his companions dead.

Two men jogged by with a stretcher and a moment later someone took his hands gently and turned them over.

Then a thumb pinched back one of his eyelids and the doctor's voice was suddenly clear. 'I'm going to give you an injection . . .'

Dumont heard his own voice say, 'I'd rather not bother.'

'I'm afraid you have no choice,' the doctor said.

'No choice . . .' The words went crashing on inside his head. 'No choice.'

Then he felt the prick of the needle and afterwards the soft appeasement of cottonwool, and what he came to think of later as a kind of peace.

From somewhere beyond the periphery of his consciousness the doctor was saying to someone, 'The rest are all dead, I'm afraid. Except the girl . . . There's a faint chance . . .'

EPILOGUE

It was four o'clock in the afternoon when Edward Quenne[l]
decided to go and see Dumont for the last time.

He opened the narrow, stone-mullioned window of hi[s]
office, which looked down on Lincoln's Inn Fields where th[e]
soft grey rain of the morning had given way to weak sunligh[t]
He turned away with relief and moved to the mantelpiec[e]
where the envelope was. He dropped it into a side pocket, th[e]
one where he kept his snuff box, and went out.

In the cloakroom he washed his hands before putting on[,]
so to speak, the armour of a professional man. His three[-]
quarter-length coat had a velveteen collar and he appraise[d]
it in the looking-glass as he picked up his bowler hat an[d]
umbrella. As he wound his way down the stone caracol stair[-]
case he began to hum softly a passage from one of the Bran[-]
denburg concertos. His musical taste revolved round th[e]
seventeenth century and polyphonic music. Sometimes h[e]
thought fancifully that its contrapuntal fussiness resemble[d]
the processes of law. He came out into the lobby and crosse[d]
to the dark reception booth.

'I shan't be back today,' he told Wilberforce, the duty clerk[.]
As he walked on he heard the faint clack, as Wilberforc[e]
lowered the mahogany flap over his name on the attendanc[e]
board.

He stepped out into the square raising his umbrella, con[-]
scious as he always was of the permanent thunder of arteria[l]
traffic from Holborn and Kingsway. When he had first entere[d]
the practice, he could still remember bird song in the square[,]
and when the wind was in a certain quarter the long melan[-]
choly hoot of barges on the river. And once, long ago before
the war, he had heard the sweet bells of St Mary's in the
Strand.

He walked through to Kingsway and waited, with hi[s]
umbrella raised, for a cab.

As it jerked its way around Aldwych and along the Strand
he wondered whether Dumont would be awake and sober. A
short way down the Strand the cab turned off towards the

Embankment and a moment later it drove through the moulded *porte-cochère* of the Orpheus Hotel. Edward Quennell did not associate Dumont with the Orpheus Hotel and, indeed, Dumont had only gone there because it was near the Royal Courts of Justice, where his appeal had been heard. He had, of course, registered under another name in order to avoid the reporters who were still hounding him.

Edward Quennell did not announce himself at the desk but crossed the lobby and entered an elevator which was already waiting. He left at the fifth floor and followed the carpeted corridor through numerous turnings until he came to Dumont's room. When he knocked no one answered. He waited a full half-minute before knocking again. He was just about to leave, when the door opened abruptly.

Dumont faced him clad only in trousers. 'I'm sorry . . . I was in the bath,' he said. 'Please come in.' He closed the door behind Edward Quennell and went away through another door into the bedroom. 'I shan't be a moment,' he called.

Edward Quennell laid his umbrella and hat on a side table and trailed over to the window. There was an ice bucket in the centre of the room with beer cans piled in it and there was already a row of empty cans on the sideboard.

Dumont came back, still buttoning his shirt, and sat down in one of the armchairs. He said, 'Do sit down, Mr Quennell. Would you like a beer?'

'No, thank you.'

'I can send down for whisky or anything else . . .'

'No, if you don't mind. It's rather early.' He stayed by the window watching Dumont as he snapped open the tab of another can of beer. He swallowed twice from the can and set it down beside his chair. His calm, buttressed face looked up steadily at Edward Quennell, and again Quennell was impressed with his battered integrity. Counsel for the Defence claimed that it was Dumont's face which had won the verdict and he had described it as looking like the last bastion of truth. Dumont's stare brought him discomfort now and he turned away towards the window.

He said, 'There are some minor details . . . If you happen to go away I shall want to know how to get in touch with you. There is the question of counsel's fee and there will, of course, be other charges.'

'I'm going to France tonight for a week or two in the

Périgord but after that I don't know what I'm doing, I'
afraid. I can give you the address of the bank in Switzerlan
It will take a while but you can be sure of reaching me in th
end.'

Edward Quennell opened his notebook against the wall a
carefully wrote down the address which Dumont dictate
Afterwards he said, 'I think counsel did us very well, thoug
there was a lot of public sympathy on your side, and of cours
you have already spent some time in custody.' One of h
hands wandering about in his pockets felt the hard edge o
the envelope. 'Oh, I nearly forgot . . . There is something else

Dumont picked up the beer can and stared at it carefull
afraid to look anywhere else. He was aware of his heart-be?
as he always was in moments of stress. And, thinking o
another visit in another country, he said quietly, 'Are yo
going to say that you have brought a woman to see me? I
that what you've come to say?'

Edward Quennell also took a long time to answer. Perhap
the question had surprised him. 'No,' he said at last.

Dumont remembered a line of poetry. 'The deepest wound
are those from unknown blows.' He reached down for hi
beer can and drank half of it off. He was giving himself tim
to recover from the moment of hope.

Then Edward Quennell added, 'If you are referring to Mr
Hoffman, I should tell you that, although her sentence wa
remitted, the Home Office have obtained an order for he
deportation, and she was put on a plane this morning.'

'I see.'

'However, she left a letter for you. Cooper sent it round t
my chambers.'

For the first time Dumont noticed the letter which Quenne
was holding. He said casually, 'Oh, thanks.' He stood up an
put it upright on the sideboard between two of the empty
cans.

Edward Quennell started moving towards the door. 'Whe
you come back will you be staying in England?'

'I doubt it. If there's any money left when I've settled every
thing I may try and buy a few acres of vines near Sarlat.
don't know . . .' His voice tailed away and they waited awk
wardly. Colonel Zouak would have had the *mot juste*, h
thought fleetingly, but in the cold dryness of English lega
practice there was no room for the aphorisms of Mohammec

190

r his prophet.

'There were a lot of photographs of Mrs Hoffman in the early evening papers . . . she looked very attractive, as if the ordeal had actually enhanced her. But I mustn't delay you . . . it takes some time to get to London Airport these days.' He put a hand down and opened the door.

Dumont said, 'You know how grateful I am to you.'

After they'd shaken hands Edward Quennell, smiling, delivered another unknown blow. 'It's nothing, it's my *raison d'être* after all.'

Dumont stood at the window drinking another can of beer. The long strings of altocumulus were stretching away into the sunset and there was a slight mist coming off the River Thames. He saw Edward Quennell leave the hotel entrance and cross the courtyard towards the gateway. He carried his umbrella on his shoulder, like a rifle, and his walk had a kind of military rhythm about it. Someone, one of the juniors, had told him that Quennell had once been a hero, too.

Still carrying the can of beer, Dumont went into the bedroom and finished dressing. He was ignoring the letter, which probably contained yet another unknown blow. He packed his things into the new duffel bag and went back to the sitting-room. He rang the reception desk from the wall phone and told them he was leaving and to make up his bill. Then he put down his empty beer can and picked up the letter at last.

'*Mon Roc*,' she wrote, 'I am going to the villa Julian, which because of some contingency plan was bought in my name. The lawyer says that it is properly mine. I don't know yet whether you are free but whatever happens I will always be waiting there for you.

Marnix.'

As he walked along the Strand there was a 747 moving slowly across the lenticular sky in the landing circuit for Heathrow. He saw it only for a moment with the sun glinting on its wings, then it dropped away into the haze.

At Victoria Station he bought a ticket for Nice, and when he asked if it was necessary to reserve a berth on the night ferry the booking clerk said, 'Not really, sir. There's bags of room . . . everybody flies nowadays.'

Waiting in the short queue for the Blue Train he started thinking of her again. He always imagined her body fully

191

clothed and never naked, perhaps because they had spent s
little time together out of bed. It was a curious inversion c
the erotic thoughts that most men had of their loves.

'I'm going because I want to go.' In his anxiety he uttere
the thought aloud.

The man beside him said, 'And that's a bloody good reaso
mate!'

Faint laughter followed him as he went through the barrie
at last.